IT'S A WONDERFUL
WONDERFUL
DOG

SUMMERTIME

MERIVELLE HOUSE INC.

Library of Congress Control Number: 2025912223

ISBN 978-1-965265-03-1 (hardcover)

ISBN 978-1-965265-04-8 (paperback)

ISBN 978-1-965265-05-5 (ebook)

Cover art by Damonza

Also by Keri Salas

It's a Wonderful Dog - A Christmas Tail

Book One

It's a Wonderful Dog - Easter Eggs

Book Two

It's a Wonderful Dog - Thanks & Giving

Book Four

Arriving Autumn 2025

It's a Wonderful Dog

A Healing Journal

Arriving 2026

IT'S A WONDERFUL DOG

SUMMERTIME

KERI SALAS

To Thyra
Always remembered

The earth has music
for those who listen.

-George Santayana
Born Jorge Agustín Nicolás Ruiz de Santayana y Borrás

Chapter One

School was in session at Butterfly Academy. In a field of wildflowers, dog mats had been laid out for the puppies in attendance. However, the little dogs of every kind toppled off their spaces, too engaged with the colorful butterflies, bees and birds swirling about them. Nipping at one another in play, the pups somersaulted into one another's area, scattering the balls and Frisbees they were learning about to prepare for playtime on Earth.

The angel Gheeta, known for her love of small things with wings and music, sighed as she looked out at the puppy mayhem. "Puppy souls, please listen. You'll soon go to Earth. Many of you still have much to learn." She pointed at a large chalkboard that had words written on it.

Potty outside. Also known as "Do Your Business" or "Showtime".
Don't beg for food. Avoid chicken bones and chocolate.
Never chase vehicles.
Careful what you chew—wait for permission.

"If you can't sit still with butterfly distractions here in Heaven, you're going to have some issues on Earth."

Almost every puppy's head snapped in worry.

The angel continued speaking, a kind look on her face. "But I have full trust in every one of you sweet wiggle bottoms."

The whole classroom filled with gleeful yips.

An English Bulldog puppy held up their paw. "How will we know when it's our turn to go?"

The angel smiled. "Remember what we learned?"

All the puppies barked excitedly as they thought of their own journeys to Earth soon.

"*Sit!*"

At the angel's instruction, all puppy behinds were instantly on their mats, solemn looks of regret on their faces as they waited.

"Butterfly Academy works in harmony with the Rainbow Bridge. When a dog crosses over from Earth, it's almost always time for a puppy soul to begin their own journey with a human family."

A Vizsla puppy with long legs and floppy ears pointed to the front entrance of the school grounds. "That's why sometimes souls who are already in Heaven come to pick one of us Butterfly puppies. To send to a human they love on Earth."

Gheeta nodded in pride. "Good listening! Treats for everyone!" Dog biscuits fell from the sky as the puppies giggled.

At the back of the canine crowd, one Aussie puppy faced the opposite direction.

"Betty's still scared to go to Earth," the Vizsla puppy said. "She's a real scaredy cat." He chomped his biscuit and thought. "More of a scaredy dog."

The little dog spoke rapidly, her anxiousness clear. "Can I hear more about Bear Bailey? The Great Pyrenees who makes life more wonderful for everyone he meets? He's changed a whole town with his love and loyalty. Even that old coyote, Riven Chapowits, is doing things that would surprise people. Mary's living her best life with Theodore. Cybil's booth at Bear Bailey's Co-op and Grocery is a magnificent success. Lupe is close to citizenship, so she and her children are almost safe—" She fell to the ground, out of breath but calmer. "I *love* stories."

"You need to sit and listen to your lessons right now, Betty. With all your friends."

Puppies were chewing on the edges of their mat, a few chasing butterflies around the open classroom as they waited for Gheeta to resume teaching.

"What if I sneak over to the Golden Meadow and listen to Angel Lea tell more Bear Bailey stories? I feel I would learn more that way."

"What if I read you some nursery rhymes here?"

"I need a more of a *story*. One that has a lot of ups and downs."

"You say that's exactly why you don't want to go to Earth. Too much drama."

"I can read about drama, but that doesn't mean I need to live it. I'm never going to Earth."

"What should I tell that kind gentleman that chose you to send to his daughter? She could really use a friend like you."

"Can't you show him another Butterfly puppy?"

"He's come nearly every day for an entire year, specifically for you. We can't keep telling him that you're still learning. You've already graduated from the Cocoon, Caterpillar and Butterfly classes. It's time for you to have courage and fly."

Betty shook her head as she looked down. "Have you seen Earth these days? Sadness, fear, anger, fighting—not to mention all the coyotes on Earth."

"There are no coyotes where the gentleman wants you to go to help his daughter. She lives in a big city."

"But coyotes can be real *or* imagined." Betty swayed in place, appearing to be near fainting. "Dark Dens can be in your mind as much as a burrow under the ground."

Already bright with sun, the area around Butterfly Academy grew even more luminous with the appearance of Josephine and Lea, the angels from the Rainbow Bridge.

The miniature Aussie jumped in surprise. Watching the glimmers around Josephine, her mouth fell open.

"How do you know about Bear Bailey here at Butterfly Academy?" Lea asked with an amused expression.

"Everyone knows Bear Bailey. He's famous in Heaven."

Josephine lifted an eyebrow.

Falling on her back with her feet in the air, Betty spoke in a contrite tone. "When I'm supposed to be napping, I go over to the edge of Butterfly Academy and listen to stories floating over on the breeze from the Golden Meadow."

Gheeta looked at both angels. "Betty's very curious and gets distracted. But she's also very kind to her fellow puppies. She loves to assist however she can."

The sparkling light around Josephine shimmered. "With that kind of devotion, why aren't you already down on Earth? You could be a real help to a human who needs you."

Betty shivered as the center fur on her back stood up on end. "Earth is such a tragic place. I wouldn't even know where I would want to go."

"A heavenly soul keeps coming back," Gheeta explained. "He's sure Betty is a match for his daughter. But Betty won't go."

"Souls always know best when they try to send a puppy from Butterfly Academy," Lea said.

"Do you see how many dogs are down there without homes, abused and mistreated? No, thank you."

Lea stroked Betty's ears. "Some stories that come over the Rainbow Bridge are harrowing."

"Harrowing—an adjective. Extremely distressing or painful," Betty said, nodding. "Exactly what I'm scared of."

"The dogs who are mistreated on Earth get very special attention once they cross the Rainbow Bridge," Lea said, glancing back to where the two angels had come from moments before. "Angels come from all over Heaven to shower those dogs with great love for all their courage."

Betty growled, her eyes wide in fear.

Lea looked at the distressed dog. "It makes little sense to your puppy soul. But those dogs understand what they're trying to accomplish on Earth. They agreed to it before they went. A soul contract, of sorts. And while it's heartbreaking, most humans love their dogs and would do anything to make their life special."

"I don't know," Betty said, backing up from where the angels stood. "I think I'd rather sleep up here among you angels than wake up to a life on Earth with humans."

Josephine dangled her fingers in front of Betty, prisms of light dancing again in front of the dog. "What if Bear Bailey hadn't gone to Merivelle? Mary and Theodore wouldn't be together. Riven would be a miserable old man with no friends. And Cybil wouldn't be on Earth showing so many people the joy of finding new hobbies and purpose later in life."

"What about the Posada family?" Betty whispered, though she already knew the answer.

"A snake would have bitten Pablito. He would have lost his leg, or much worse. His mom and sister would have had a much different life without the joy he brings them."

"Bear stepped in and that snake didn't have a chance," Betty said admiringly. "The whole town changed because of that wonderful Great Pyrenees. You don't even hear of coyotes out at Sagebrush Farms anymore. Everything is finally safe and sound."

The strains of an orchestra tuning up filled the space as an oboe played.

"Do you hear that?" Betty asked, a bleak look on her face. "It's so melancholy. Like impending doom."

A breeze swept through Butterfly Academy as the sound of woodwind instruments filled the air. "Listen to the clarinets, flutes and trumpets with the oboe. It's a break in the sadness. The sound of hope and good things to come," Josephine said.

Betty opened her eyes.

"And now—trumpets, trombones and other brass horns."

The Aussie giggled. "The trombone is funny, isn't it? And don't get me started on a flugelhorn."

The symphonic sounds of violins, violas, cellos and double basses filled the air. Gossamer strings of spider webs glistened in the sun as they floated over the school, giving it the outline of a bandshell. The sweeping swell of notes lulled Betty into deep thought as she yawned, fighting sleep.

Josephine looked at the other two angels. "Perhaps Betty could spend some time with us in the Golden Meadow. A few stories to make her path forward more inviting."

Chapter Two

"Can you tell me another story?"

"You don't feel the tiniest bit tired, Betty?" Lea couldn't remember when she'd told a single dog so many stories.

"Tell me again when Bear peed on the pant leg of Riven. He was such a mean man. Almost ruining Christmas in Merivelle."

"But the more important part of the story was that Bear helped change the man. His kindness softened his owner, Mary Bailey, and she became a better person. Allowing her to form a group of like-minded people to come together and form Bear Bailey's Co-op and Grocery. The entire community united. Which made Riven Chapowits want to join in. His present-day behavior is much different."

"He said he wanted to hurt Bear to get at Mary. I don't trust that guy," Betty said, her eyes narrowed as she gave a menacing growl.

"Bear's stories are to teach you the miracle of a wonderful dog. His presence changes everyone he comes in contact with."

Betty panted in excitement. "I think I could go to Earth if I knew Bear was there to help me see things in a better way. I wouldn't be so anxious."

"You said you were too scared to go to Earth. We thought that maybe we'll find you a flock to guide around the Golden Meadow. A busy dog is a happy dog."

Betty twirled three times, her tail-less, fluffy bottom wiggling in glee. "Nope—I've changed my mind. Send me to Merivelle, Angel Lea!" She yipped in joy. "I really think I'm ready."

A whoosh of breeze and radiant color appeared. Betty's eyes widened as Josephine appeared. Never experiencing life as a human, Josephine had always overseen the Rainbow Bridge. A different demeanor than Lea, she was still kind and loving, but her all-knowingness coupled with enormous power made her a formidable presence. No dog had ever put a paw out of line in her presence.

"That was a quick change of heart," Josephine said. "You want to go Earth now?"

"Bear Bailey gives me a lot of courage," Betty said, her bottom shaking in place. "I want to hear *him* tell me about how he handles coyotes."

"You've only been here a few days," Josephine said. "Perhaps you need a bit more time before you decide."

Lea nodded in agreement. "No need to get you in over your head before you've had time to consider things fully."

"I'm pretty sure—"

"We'll let you know when it's time," Josephine said. "A few more stories. You're still a puppy."

The angels walked away as Betty laid down, crossing her paws, whispering to herself. "Well, now that they don't want me to go—I really want to go."

Chapter Three

The summer months at Bear Bailey's had always been busy. With each passing day of sun and heat, produce was more plentiful. Winter root vegetables and spring strawberries made way for tomatoes the size of softballs. Cucumbers curled in whimsical shapes and enormous watermelons readied for the Fourth of July festivities less than a month away. In the wake of the original vendors' successes at Bear Bailey's, more stalls opened within the co-op to showcase local citizen's talents.

When Bear Bailey's outgrew its indoor square footage during summer, Mary's best idea had been to use the store's front sidewalk for more space. A solution that had come to her seeing Katie's honeymoon pictures of southern France's seaside food markets. And while the western Kansas wind made the striped umbrellas and colorful awnings tricky, the effect was still charming to anyone passing by on Main Street. Bear Bailey's Co-op had formed a solid city core encompassing a decades-old diner—The Hen's Nest, a thriving yoga studio and the Prairtisserie, a French bakery that had found national recognition for their creations. In between, there were other small businesses such as the new coffee roaster, as rustic as the bakery was elegant, but still delightful in every way.

"Last meal on our own, big guy," Theodore Bailey said, driving down Main Street with Bear in the backseat. "Mary's coming home today."

At the word *Mary*, the Great Pyrenees panted heavily, searching back and forth between both sides of the street as Theodore adjusted the radio volume.

"Look at what you and your mom have done, Bear," Theodore said, continuing at a leisurely pace. "People from all over the world are here in our small town." Coming to a stop at a traffic light, he looked over to the corner store with a banner hanging from the front entrance—*Mare Coffee Roasters*.

A man dressed in a white shirt with tapestry trim at the collar and sleeves waved as he opened the front door of the shop.

Rolling down his car window, Theodore shouted. "Tamru! I can smell those roasted beans from here!"

Bear sniffed the air as he closed his eyes and grinned. Coffee. One of Mary's favorite smells. He barked in recognition of the man who brought him a Wishbone dog treat every time he delivered bags of coffee for Mary to sell at the co-op.

"Ethiopian coffee!" Tamru shouted back, tapping his fist to his heart. "The best in the world, my friend!"

As the light changed, Theodore eyed the approaching traffic in the rear-view mirror. "Tell Saba and the kids hello!"

The tall and slender man extended his hand. "Bring Riven and come play *lamlameta*!"

"Another time we will! Mary's coming home today!" Theodore waved before continuing on.

Barking out the window, Bear held his paw in the air and gave a small *woof* to Tamru.

Turning to look at the dog, Theodore smiled as he drove.

"It's funny how things work out. I guess if Mary isn't going to travel the world, the world will come to Mary."

Bear closed his eyes and tilted his nose in the air, searching for the scent of his beloved owner on the gentle summer breeze.

"I mean, we're here in the middle of Kansas and have food from all over the world. Rich, Ethiopian roasted coffee and board games, French pastries, Vietnamese *pho,* amazing curries from Taiwan. And don't even get me started on the Mexican food around here." Theodore rubbed his stomach. "I'm surprised I fit in my pants these days."

Bear put his head over the front seat, shifting his eyes between Theodore's stomach and face.

"Okay, okay. We'll take a walk after breakfast at The Hen's Nest." Theodore pulled into a spot in front of the diner and put the truck in park.

Turning at the sound of an engine, Riven Chapowits waved in recognition as Bear jumped from the backseat, waiting eagerly for Theodore to open the door before he then charged to the old man's side.

"Gentle, Bear! Gentle!" Theodore shouted, grabbing for the dog's leash before he shut the door and joined the pair.

Standing on his back legs and letting his front paws rest on Riven's shoulders, Bear panted in happiness as the old man stroked his back. Hard to believe the pair had once eyed each other as enemies—to anyone passing by, they looked like life-long, beloved companions.

"We're good, aren't we, Bear?" Riven asked, though he braced his body onto the brick wall near the entry to The Hen's Nest. He pulled out a plastic bag full of bacon, extending a tidbit. Bear took it gingerly in his mouth and ate, salivating drool on the sidewalk.

A woman came to the glass entry door of The Hen's Nest and smiled at the trio, pushing the chrome crossbar open. "I hate to tell my favorite customers, but there must be a thirty-minute wait before a table opens up. I have people standing at the counter as it is. You should have called ahead of time, Riven. You know that I'd always save you a table."

The bell atop the glass entrance door rang as a man near Riven's age exited. "Great grub, Frannie," he said, holding a toothpick between his forefinger and thumb.

"How you are doing, Charlie?" Riven extended his hand. "Good to see you."

Pointedly ignoring Riven's gesture, the man looked at Theodore. "Everything good out at the Webb place?"

Bear sat up on his back end and placed one of his paws into Riven's empty, outstretched hand, leaning into him.

Theodore patted the dog's head in appreciation. "I've lived here almost a decade. I'm still not used to when people call it by Mary's parents' last name. Small-town memories sure run long."

"And not always incredibly kind," Frannie said, raising an eyebrow.

"It'll always be the Webb place to me." Charlie tipped his hat, avoiding eye contact with Riven. "Good to see you, Frannie, Theodore and Mary's dog."

Riven watched the man get into his truck as Bear growled. "That's all right, Bear. I probably deserved it and even more."

Theodore and Frannie's eyes met as both their faces softened at Riven's reaction.

"Let me treat you to a good breakfast, old man. Even if you need to sit in the kitchen office. I'll always find room for you."

Turning his attention back to the pair, Riven said, "I can wait in line like everyone else."

"But you're the one that gave me a loan decades ago to keep this place open when no one else would listen."

"Paid in full and always on time. No need to mention it,"

Riven said, his voice kind. Attempting to change the subject, he motioned to Bear. "When are you going to have some sidewalk seating, Frannie? So Bear doesn't have to wait outside?"

The Great Pyrenees looked up. His eyes were almost cartoonish-ly wide, reflecting his desire to follow the scent of breakfast food inside the diner.

"My old walk-in refrigerator was on its last leg a couple of months ago. As soon as that's paid off, Merivelle's canines and their owners will be first on my list."

"You'd think dog-friendly seating would bring in more customers in the warmer months," Theodore said.

"And there you have the conundrum of most small businesses," Frannie replied, sighing. "Spending what you don't have, hoping to make more money."

"I didn't mean to pressure," Theodore said. "I only thought you told me the online article about Cybil brought a lot of out-of-town people to The Hen's Nest?"

"*Act Three—Everyone's Favorite Aunt*," Frannie said, nodding. "For a bit of time, we had a real upswing in traffic. Now we're back to our regular clientele, give or take a few travelers every few days. Even so, I'm still thankful for the steady business."

Despite her words, Bear sensed the woman's anxiousness. He looked up at her, giving her an empathetic nudge with his snout.

"I better get back to it." Frannie gently tapped Riven with the menus she was holding. "I'll see *you* later." She opened the door and went back into the diner, the bell on the door ringing at her departure. The two men looked at one another, neither blinking for several moments.

"*I'll see you later?*"

"Don't start. I mean it."

"But that's what friends do, *you old dog*," Theodore said, elbowing Riven in ribs. "I'm proud of you."

"For what?"

"Putting yourself out there. Heart semi-open and all."

"Let's see what the Prairtisserie has this morning. I prefer a hearty breakfast, but a pastry from there and then a walk over for Tamru's coffee works in a pinch too."

"Don't change the subject." Theodore clicked the remote in his pocket, locking his truck. "How long has that been going on?"

"We're old friends. Who enjoy each other's company. That's all."

Leaning down to clip a leash to Bear's collar, Theodore stood up again and trotted a few steps to keep up with Riven, who had already begun making his way down the city block. "This could be the real start of something for you."

Riven stopped mid-stride to face the younger man. "Your love of telenovelas does not need to come in to play with this situation."

"Well, now you sound like your daughter."

The lines in Riven's forehead softened.

"You and Katie and your deep and abiding distaste for Latino soap operas."

"To be clear—not only Latino. *Any* soap operas. I've had enough drama to last a lifetime."

"Fair enough. But don't leave out that it's the happily ever after aspect that makes Latino soap operas different. It's messy and crazy, but then you definitely get what you wanted for the characters. Their own bit of individual heaven. How is that wrong?"

Riven reached for Bear's leash, nodding at the sidewalk. "Your shoe."

Theodore looked down at his sneakers, handing the lead

over as he bent to tie his laces. "It's okay for you to have your own happily ever after. Like everyone else. You do not need to self-impose a life of loneliness to make up for all the years you were a jerk in Merivelle."

"You think I do that?"

"Yes, I do. You hole up in your giant house and then only come to town to work as a devoted employee at Bear Bailey's when we all know that you don't need the money."

"How do you know? I sold the last of my businesses a few years ago. Lost some money, followed by a national downturn," Riven said, his voice solemn.

"You're a terrible actor," Theodore said, standing up. "Mary's told me you haven't cashed one check since you asked for a job a couple of years ago, despite her mentioning it to you many times."

"Mary needs every cent she can get in that store. You should know that better than anyone."

The two men started walking again. Bear trotted happily between them.

"The co-op makes her feel close to her mom," Theodore said. "Bear helped her tremendously, but I don't know that she's completely over the loss of Margaret. So much left unsaid between them."

"It's lonely without parents. A person does about anything to feel them when they're gone." A sudden gust of wind blew down Main Street as it encircled the human and canine trio for a few moments, swirling debris at their feet.

The pair walked in silence for the length of a city block, Bear sniffing the sidewalk in curiosity.

"Mary said she has good news that she wants to tell us as soon as she gets home. She thinks everyone will be over the moon."

Riven snapped out of his thoughts. "Can't wait to hear. You

15

must be so proud to have her as your wife. You're a lucky man, Theodore Bailey."

"Man, don't make me choke up here. I'm barely hanging on as it is."

"Do not start crying on Main Street," Riven said, his voice taking on a stern tone as he looked around. "I was complimenting Mary, you knucklehead. Get a grip on yourself."

Bear looked between the pair and barked happily at the buzz of friendship between the two men, despite the words coming out of the older man's mouth.

Walking past storefronts, both men were silent until a woman tapped on the front window of a yoga studio as people inside were rolling out mats in preparation of class. Riven waved and pantomimed a phone to his ear, signaling his intent to call her later.

"Still doing yoga with Alicia?"

"You can't tell by my limber body?"

"I'm unsure if you're joking."

The old man chuckled. "I owe a debt of gratitude to Alicia and her continued patience working on my balance." He stared at the younger man's mid-section.

"What?" Theodore stopped mid-stride.

Bear tilted his head in a knowing manner.

"Remember how you once told me that friends are honest?"

Theodore groaned.

"You could stand a few yoga lessons yourself."

Bear looked up at Theodore before sitting on Riven's feet.

"He does that when he strongly agrees with someone."

"I remember Mary telling me," Riven replied, ruffling Bear's mane as they started walking again. "She's a smart woman. I always want to stay on her good side."

As if a lightning bolt had shot through his body, Theodore

froze in place. "Mary's home at noon. I promised her I'd check on Cybil."

Chapter Four

Walking through her house, house slippers shuffling on the wooden floors like a record player needle finding the end of a vinyl track, Cybil Barnes moved through her home as if she were seeing it for the first time. Mid-morning summer light poured through the colorful stained-glass window above the second-floor landing. Each step in the staircase below had colorful light on it, causing the old woman to look up in wonder.

"Through the house give glimmering light," she whispered.

The rooms of the old house were spacious, filled with exquisite pieces of furniture curated in a manner that, despite the different design eras, melded together in a warm and inviting way. Large pieces of art adorned the walls, a few paintings leaning elegantly against the baseboards. A breeze blew throughout the home, fluttering curtains like silent bells and swaying houseplants in a peaceful manner. Picking a book up off the coffee table, Cybil sat on the sofa beside it, becoming lost in the text as she read.

The doorbell rang.

Fully engrossed in the book, Cybil shook her head as if the bell were merely a passing, pesky fly. She sank back into the worn cushions and continued reading.

Several barks took up the task the doorbell had not accomplished.

Cybil startled before her face visibly relaxed when she recognized the figures through the front windows. She groaned in exertion as she leaned forward, plucking a dried stem from the vase on the table in front of her and placing it as a bookmark before making her way to open the front door.

"Coffee for you, my friend!" Theodore said, holding a *Mare Coffee Roasters* white paper cup.

"Come in! Come in!" Cybil stepped back, a look of sincere welcome on her face. "Have a seat!"

"Careful—it's rather hot." Theodore extended the drink to her. "We can't stay. Lupe needs help at the co-op." He motioned over his shoulder. "And this guy always wants to be there."

"Bear or Riven?"

"Now that you mention it—both."

Glancing at Cybil's pajamas and robe, Riven tilted his head. "Absolutely no pressure. But I thought Saturdays were your best days."

"Yes, of course. I'll be in first thing tomorrow. I only need a day."

"*Today* is Saturday," Riven said, taking a step toward her.

"Are you sure?"

Theodore eyes lit in happiness. "Positive. Mary will be home—" He looked at his watch again. "—in two hours."

Riven looked around the room. "I thought you told me you were expecting visitors to your booth today."

A bona fide social media sensation, rarely a week went by when Cybil did not have people come into the co-op in search

19

of her. All were delighted to tell her their own stories of teachers who had made positive impacts in their own lives. The *Act Three—Everyone's Favorite Aunt* online and print feature had brought her an even wider audience of out-of-town guests.

"Not to seem ungrateful. I love to welcome visitors like family." She sighed as her shoulders dropped momentarily. "But today, I'm tired. Thought I could rest and maybe get a call if someone comes in." She glanced at the stairwell, still twinkling with light.

Riven eyed the table before turning around.

"Something wrong?" Cybil asked.

"You have money scattered all around the room. It's none of my business. But shouldn't you put it somewhere safe?"

"Honey was good with money. I get overwhelmed with it."

"Do you need us to take you to the bank?"

"I'll put it away, if it makes you nervous." Cybil took a few steps to where Riven's eyes had rested. Reaching for some of the cash sitting on the table, she shuffled it into a neat pile before going over to a shelf on the wall. She opened a book and placed the money inside before returning it to the shelf.

Theodore's eyes nearly bulged out their sockets. He looked up and down the wall of books. "This is your banking system?"

"It's fine. I'd really rather talk about anything else."

Bear sniffed at the hem of Cybil's robe and panted. His nose tilted upward as he walked over to Theodore and placed a paw on the man's thigh.

"He's trying to tell you something," Riven said.

Cybil chuckled. "I'm out of treats, my friend. But I'll pop by the Prairtisserie and get one of their peanut butter snacks to make it up to you."

Riven shook his head. "That's not it. Something is bothering him."

Bear ran to the kitchen area, all three humans following.

The smell of something sweet burning filled the air as a scorched pan smoked.

"Good heavens!" Cybil went to the stove and grabbed the copper pan by the handle, burning her palm. "My strawberry jam got out of control."

Riven reached for a nearby kitchen towel, using it to lift the pan off the gas burner as he turned off the stove knob. Theodore opened a nearby door, allowing smoke to exit the room. Bear panted in relief.

"I get so distracted in summer," Cybil said, shaking her head.

"Well, good thing we brought coffee and Bear's nose," Theodore said. "All's well that ends well."

"Still the fine's the crown; Whate'er the course, the end is the renown."

Riven's face was solemn as he listened to Cybil.

"Shakespeare. I was quoting the next line after Theodore's words. I may have burned the jam because I was mesmerized by the summer light in my house, but I have not lost my mind, Riven Chapowits."

"Of course," Riven replied. "Accidents happen."

Taking the towel and pan from Riven's grasp, Cybil placed it in the sink. She ran water from the faucet into the burned mess as she recited to him.

> *But with the word the time will bring on*
>   *summer,*
> *When briers shall have leaves as well as thorns,*
> *And be as sweet as sharp. We must away;*
> *Our wagon is prepared, and time revives us:*
> *All's well that ends well; still the fine's the*
>   *crown.*
> *Whate'er the course, the end is the renown.*

21

"Well, there you have it," Theodore said. "Cybil—lost in thought, but clear in mind—burnt her breakfast. Happens to the best of us."

Bear went to Cybil, licking her palm gently.

"Do you have any aluminum foil?" Riven asked.

"Over there in the drawer," Cybil answered.

"You need to rest. I'll man your booth. Give your regards to any visitors hoping to get a picture with you." Riven pulled the drawer open, grabbing a roll of foil and pulling off a small sheet of it. "Put the shiny side face down on your hand."

"What does that do?" Theodore asked.

"Pulls the heat out from the burn. Gives it a nice, cool feel. An old hobo trick," he said, wrapping the foil around Cybil's hand gently. "Put some salve on it later when you're resting."

Bear went to the counter and sniffed at a discarded bowl of ingredients that sat abandoned on the counter. Both he and Riven noticed the spilled batter on the counter.

"Stop giving me that look, Riven. It's only a failed attempt at muffins. I've known the recipe by heart for years, but somehow this morning, with all the beautiful sights in the house, I couldn't quite remember."

Riven raised his eyebrows.

"I was modifying an old recipe. Trying to add in flax and chia seeds, psyllium and whatever else is supposed to help people our age. I ruined the batter. Nothing to worry about."

Theodore let out a low whistle. "Mary tries to sneak all those things into my morning smoothies. The close calls I've had between home and town a few times—you don't even want to know. We'd have had to torch my vehicle, for sure."

"Thank you for that personal information that no one asked or wanted to hear this morning," Riven said, pulling a paper towel from a roll and wiping the counter clean. "We're all aware of the random perils of country living."

Bear panted, grinning at Theodore.

"At any rate, before we learned more than we ever wanted to know about your riveting bathroom habits, Theodore, we were speaking about how Cybil's expecting visitors. And she's had no sleep."

"I can still go in," Cybil said, yawning.

"Don't forget—we also have the Midsummer event tonight," Theodore said. "You don't want to wear yourself out and miss the music you love."

"Take the day and see how you feel. We can send Pablito over with food from the co-op for you," Riven said.

Theodore remained as quiet as Bear, both watching the older pair.

Smiling in encouragement, Riven said, "It's nice to see you recognized and celebrated by people outside of Merivelle. Let's keep you rested and taken care of so you can keep up with your visitors."

"You're really a wish come true, Riven," Cybil said, sighing. "It's nice to have someone fuss over me at home. I can't tell you how lonely it gets here by myself."

Chapter Five

The summer countryside passed outside Mary's train window as she traveled across the geographic width of Kansas. Over the course of several hours, rolling green hills met the deep ocean-blue tint of the sky. Large cumulous clouds suspended above, casting shadows on the ground below. Scenes of golden wheat fields with bowing heads of grain would then shift to vast meadows of sunflowers—heliotropes that found the sun, imperceptibly turning ever so slightly with each minute of the day. Small towns randomly whooshed by—whole worlds of people with hopes and dreams, lived out on the stage of their own communities. Nearly home to Merivelle, Mary sighed as she gazed out at the scenery, noticing what had escaped her growing up in the region. Kansas had a unique beauty all its own—the quiet heartbeat of an entire country.

Listening to her husband's voice as the pair spoke on the phone, Mary felt giddy with the information she'd not yet shared with him. Months of hard work, secret errands, and trips to visit her cousin Katie in Kansas City had finally come to fruition with her last meeting. Wishing to tell her good news in person at the co-op, the train trip across the width of Kansas felt longer than she could ever remember. So close to Merivelle, it took everything in her not to blurt it out to Theodore. Instead, she'd asked a myriad of questions, trying to get him to fill her remaining travel time with stories from home that she'd missed the previous week.

Theodore stood at the main counter of the kitchen area at the co-op as he filled glasses—air pods in, with his phone in his pocket. "It's sweet how much Riven watches over everyone," he said, after recounting the jam-burning fiasco. "Who would have guessed years ago, the town bully would become Bear Bailey's grandfather-of-sorts?"

"I sometimes worry that the rest of Merivelle will never forget how he was," Mary said, frowning.

"You should have seen one of Frannie's customers at breakfast. Refused to shake Riven's hand. Bear had to lend a helping paw."

Across the store, Riven looked up in the middle of the mayhem of Cybil's booth. A travel bus making its way across the state had stopped in town, eating breakfast at The Hen's Nest before making their way to the co-op. He stood in the midst of them as they reached for Cybil's metal wind spinners and cutting boards.

Theodore held up glasses of lemonade, gesturing that he was on his way. "Anyway, Riven and I both think we need to rally around Cybil more."

A young man appeared in the doorway of the train compartment, holding a guitar case. Without a word, he nodded in question at an empty seat. Mary jumped to move her bags.

Sitting down, the young man arranged a heavy backpack on the seat next to him. He placed the guitar case at his feet as he clutched it, looking out the window.

Unaware, Theodore continued on his end of the call. "We averted a potential fire today. But what if you hadn't insisted that we check on Cybil this morning? What if she'd been upstairs sleeping?"

"She sleeps on the couch. I'd like to think she would have caught the situation on her own. But your point is well taken."

Across from her, the man looked up for a moment, a puzzled look on his face.

"Sorry to bother," Mary said, the volume of her voice much lower as she put her call on mute. "I lost my earbuds while I was away. And my phone is stuck on speaker."

He nodded his head cordially.

Theodore continued. "We've talked about it before, but Cybil may be close to the time when she needs someone living with her."

"We'll figure it out, honey. Reyna's finishing up her internship with your firm in Chicago. Pablito hasn't selected a college yet. Maybe he's planning to stay and attend Merivelle Community College. He and Cybil get along like a house on fire." She paused for a moment. "Pardon the pun."

"Love the pun, hon."

The man's eyes met Mary's as she playfully grimaced at her husband's words before continuing. "We've had so many people who came to town because of Cybil's *Act Three* article. Who knew her love of mentoring young artists would seem to bring them out of the woodwork?"

"I don't understand what that has to do with Cybil and Pablito," Theodore said.

"Pablito is an amazing artist—"

"And soccer player," Theodore added.

"Yes, both. But Cybil could really help him hone his artistic skills. Almost like an artist residency with her."

Theodore groaned. "I just spilled some lemonade."

The sound of crumpling paper followed and what Mary imagined was the sound of napkins wiping the counter. "I'll let you go, Theodore. You sound swamped."

"Lupe and Pablito are flying around here like buzzing bees," Theodore said, his hands full as he carried drinks to the waiting clientele. "Even your dog is trying to direct the mayhem."

Bear was happily weaving through the crowd wearing a vest with the co-op logo that held treats for customers. As if by magic, he had re-directed the traffic snarl blocking the front entrance as Theodore delivered the lemonade on a tray. "Honey, I'm going to jump off and help. If I don't see you at the depot in a few minutes, you'll know what happened."

"Don't meet me. I only have a small suitcase, and I can walk to the co-op. I'll look for extra help on the way," she said, a giggle in her voice.

Theodore smiled as he handed out drinks to the waiting customers. "And don't think I've forgotten about whatever your amazing news is. I want to hear the minute I see you."

Chapter Six

In a short time, the train approached the station. Mary remembered how she liked to exaggerate the swaying movement when she was a girl riding the train with her mother. She would move her body dramatically in tandem with the train's side-to-side sweeping motion as it slowed toward the station. She pictured the image of her mother standing with bags around her, waiting for the Merivelle stop, smiling down in amusement at her daughter dancing in joy. Train rides had been one of her favorite memories—no interruptions to divert her mother's attention. A rare solitude afforded to the otherwise busy Margaret and her only child.

The conductor, who had been making his way through the cars, arrived at Mary's compartment as she stood beside her seat, ready to dash to the co-op.

"Hello, Casper!"

"Ready to see Theodore?"

"I am. It's good to travel. And it's also wonderful to come home."

"The definition of a well-lived life," Casper said, nodding. "Someone should put those words in a song."

Still seated, the young man tapped on the sill as he gazed out the window, humming.

The sound caught Casper's attention. "Where did you come from? Mrs. Bailey should be the only person in the compartment."

The man searched through his belongings. "I was s-seated. In the back. M-moved to be closer to the exit. A few minutes ago," he said, speaking in a halting manner.

The train came to a full and abrupt stop, causing Mary to sway forward as she nodded. "He only arrived a few minutes ago."

Casper turned to direct passengers to the exit.

"*Thank you,*" the man mouthed, a look of extreme appreciation on his face as lifted his baggage and rose.

"He's really a pleasant gentleman," Mary whispered. "Just takes his job seriously." She pulled up the handle to her rolling suitcase and waited as a mom shuffled her kids down the aisle and down the outside steps.

Once the aisle was clear, Casper turned back. "Did you bring me a quote?"

Though she hadn't taken the train for several years, Cybil liked to play a quote-stumping game with Casper via Merivelle residents who used the transportation.

"*Neither a wise man nor a brave man lies down on the tracks of history waiting for the train of the future to run over him.*"

"That's almost too easy. Dwight Eisenhower—raised right here in Kansas."

"Cybil's going to be so disappointed. I'll tell her it stumped you a little."

"You tell that sweet woman whatever you think best," Casper grinned as he nodded. "Until next time, Mary."

"*Eight and Sand,*" she said, smiling.

The young man, seeking to disembark, turned in question.

"The train crew says it to one another. It means a safe and speedy journey," Mary replied.

"I'll have to write that one down. I like it a lot."

Clearly softened with the younger man's enthusiasm, Casper smiled. The train's horn blew, signally its imminent departure. Mary made her way to the exit before stepping down from the train as the younger man followed.

Sitting his guitar case on the ground, the man opened his backpack. "Th-thanks for helping me. I-I didn't want to fight." With the breeze, a piece of paper fluttered from behind him over to where Mary was standing.

She picked it up and handed it to him. "I think this is yours, Gavin."

"How did you know my name?"

"It's printed at the top of your ticket," she said, extending it to him. "*Gavin Ring.*"

Nodding his thanks, he reached for the ticket, folding it in half before he stuffed it inside his backpack. He looked up and smiled. "A b-beautiful station."

Mary stopped for a moment and gazed at the station she passed by without a second thought.

"Art Deco res-restoration. How did such a small town manage it?"

"We tried collecting spare change and couldn't really move the needle. Then an anonymous grant seemed to drop from the sky."

"Any idea who?"

Mary shrugged as she gripped the handle of her suitcase. "I was sure it was my cousin's husband. He comes from a great deal of wealth and wanted to help Merivelle any way he could. But his family is quite strict with how they spend their fortune. He's emphatic that he doesn't get the credit for the station."

The train churned forward again, steam rising outwards, heating the vicinity.

Engrossed in the building's architecture, Gavin stopped. "Th-think of all the people who have p-passed back and forth on journeys over the years. All their stories."

Nodding her head, Mary agreed. "We have people in and out of Merivelle all the time. Overseas business people are interested in the agricultural aspect of the area. Also, artists who are keen to capture our phenomenal sunrises and sunsets."

The town sheriff pulled up, turning on the red lights of his vehicle in greeting for a few moments.

The young man froze, gripping his guitar case almost like a shield.

"Donkey's a childhood friend." Mary said, a reassuring look on her face. "We aren't in any trouble." She paused as she tilted her head. "That I know of."

Donkey rolled down his window as Mary approached. Walking wide of the patrol car, Gavin followed. "Theodore sent me to pick you up."

"He just wants to hear my news as soon as possible."

"That big dog of yours tried to get into the car when he understood where I was going."

"Bear," Mary said, her face drooping with sappy emotion. "Let's get to him quickly." She laughed. "And *Theodore*."

Gavin continued on with his heavy backpack as they spoke, walking past the pair.

Donkey looked at Mary. "How is he also carrying a guitar case? He won't make it far in this heat."

"Do you need a ride?" Mary asked, shouting above the wind that had picked up. "

"J-just headed to the Windsor to find a room."

From inside the patrol car, a dispatcher's voice called out a non-emergency code. A few seconds later, the lights flashed atop the vehicle. "Hurry and jump in, Mary. I'll drop you on the way. You're going to have to be light on your feet as I go by the co-op."

Chapter Seven

The moment Mary walked into Bear Bailey's Co-op, her enormous Great Pyrenees bounded to the door of the store, jumping on his back legs with his front paws hooked around her shoulders. He panted in complete joy and equal relief. He'd barely slept since she'd been gone.

Kneeling to pick up the stickers and candy that had fallen out of his vest, Mary looked around for Theodore, who was listening intently to a man talk about grandchildren back home. His eyes caught his wife's attention from across the room. Relaxing his shoulders dramatically, he winked and smiled at Mary as the customer continued to speak.

From the kitchen at the back of the co-op, Lupe peeked over the high counter and cheered in delight as she ran to Mary, zigzagging through customers, embracing her with enthusiasm. She held Mary's face in her hands for a moment. "Everyone had a missing piece in their heart while you were gone."

Mary hugged her friend. "It looks like you all have done more than fine with my absence," she said. The entire co-op was buzzing in motion. The scene that Mary had imagined a decade before when she stood in front of the old, unoccupied Gibson hardware store with Bear and Theodore.

"Your dream came true," Lupe said, watching Mary's face. "Even with all the twists and turns. You and your dog made this happen."

"I couldn't have done it without you, Lupe." Shaking her head, Mary blinked back tears. "It seems like such a long time ago. And then again, like yesterday."

Nodding to the front of the store, Lupe said, "I think Riven especially feels lost without you here. He wants so much for you to be pleased."

Riven was in the middle of Cybil's stall, patiently answering questions. He looked up, his face radiant with joy. "You're in for a real treat," he said to the customers as he waved Mary over.

"I have telenovela-level news for everyone," Mary said as she and Lupe walked to the front of the store.

"Yes, I know. Your husband has been dancing around this store waiting," Lupe said. "*Tranquilízate*, Theodore."

Mary giggled. "Yes, he needs to calm way down."

Both women arriving at Cybil's booth, Mary waved to Riven and the small crowd around him.

"The amazing aromas here in the co-op are all thanks to Lupe Posada, a true culinary genius," he said, nodding to her.

"*Mucho gusto*," Lupe said. "It's a pleasure to meet you."

Touching Mary lightly on the arm, Riven said, "Please meet the founder of this store—Mary Bailey, the young girl who moved away to the big city and came back with a bigger vision for her hometown than any of us could imagine. We couldn't do without her in Merivelle."

Clearly touched by Riven's praise, Mary smiled at the visitors. "Thank you for visiting Merivelle and spending time at Bear Bailey's. We're so happy to have you here."

Still at her side, Bear barked. Everyone laughed as all attention shifted to the canine.

"And this is Bear Bailey—Mary's wonderful dog. The real star of the show," Riven said, bending down to shake Bear's extended paw. "He has some treats for you in his backpack."

The group took turns petting the delighted Great Pyrenees as they pulled out their phones to take pictures. Bear posed with each person as patiently as a seasoned celebrity.

The customers momentarily occupied, Riven looked at Mary. "I understand you have some news."

"We've all been waiting on pins and cushions," Lupe said, immediately shaking her head to correct herself. "Pins and *needles*." Less than a decade with English as her second language, Lupe was a language whiz. She'd made sure that everyone in her orbit signed up for *Word of the Day*. Only English phrases had given her hiccups, as she learned a new language. "Whatever sharp thing we've been waiting on—we can't wait to hear your news."

Overhearing the conversation, Theodore excused himself for a moment from the browsing customer, walking to the assembled group, kissing Mary on the cheek. He grabbed a small jar from the table in front of them. "Do *not* say anything before I'm here. Promise?"

Mary laughed, gently swatting the backside of her husband as he turned to go.

Returning to the customer, his words floated in the air. "*The best salsa in the entire world. From right here in Merivelle.*"

"He sure loves anything you do, Lupe," Riven said. "You'd think he was on commission. He's sold half a dozen jars today."

A customer in the *Ms. Barnes* booth held up a cutting board, signaling their desire to purchase it. Riven nodded as he returned.

"*Mamá!*"

The smell of something on the edge of burning filled the air.

"Aye, Pablito," Lupe said, turning to the kitchen. "Simple tortillas. Do not burn down the kitchen." She started walking to the back of the co-op. "Come get me if you want to talk about news."

Alone for the first moment since she'd arrived, Mary knelt to Bear, balancing herself with her suitcase on one side. "The smell of you, Bear." She touched her head to his as he panted in joy. "I love everyone here. But you're what made this place home."

Chapter Eight

"I think I'll stay away more often." Mary wrapped one arm around Theodore. The co-op was empty in the late afternoon. Nearly all the goods in every booth were gone. Even if someone had come in to shop at the end of the day, there was little inventory to choose from.

"Do *not* leave again," Theodore said, kissing her. "Bear and I can both finally relax."

"Speaking of Bear—is he mad at me?"

"Why would he be mad at you? Your dog thinks you hung the moon."

"I *was* gone all week. Now he seems smitten with anyone but me. Especially Riven. Look at him."

Bear sat next to Riven, leaning in with a paw on the man's chest.

Sheepish at the dog's attention, Riven said, "I don't know how you do it, Mary. I'm exhausted."

"You had a banner week, for sure. Cybil, in particular. She's going to need a lot more inventory to sell."

Joining the group, Lupe said, "Pablito can help Cybil. He enjoys spending time with her."

"I love their friendship," Theodore said, nodding in thanks as Lupe brought him a cookie she'd set aside in the afternoon's rush.

Mary sighed, sinking into one of the chairs at the Round Table in the center of the co-op. One by one, the others followed her lead. *Round Table* was synonymous with a discussion of important matters.

"Let's put Theodore out of his misery," Riven said. "What's your big news, Mary?"

Instantly energized, Mary sat up. "I didn't want to say anything because last time we got excited over the co-op getting grant funds—"

"All my fault," Riven said, raising his hand. The look on his face was one of deep remorse. Riven had accidentally scuttled a large, out-of-state grant, trying to impress a daughter who didn't yet know her connection to him. His actions (as well as the Rural Initiative's representative falling in love with Katie and presenting an ethical issue with dispersed funds) torpedoed the project that Katie and Mary had worked on for over two years. Lacking the expected funds, Mary had tightened the co-op's budget, refusing any offers of help from a guilt-ridden Riven while trying to brainstorm new ideas.

"Everything happens for a reason," Mary replied. "How would we have our beloved Violet had everything not gone the way it did?"

Visibly touched by the mention of his only grandchild, Riven nodded. "That's very kind of you to see it that way."

"Besides, Katie and I have been working on something that would help Merivelle for years. The biggest thing we've undertaken yet."

"Every time you start an enormous project, you keep yourself from being able to travel and—"

Mary's cheeks reddened. "I know you mean well, Theodore. But please hear me out."

Riven sat up in his chair. "No arguing. Not from you two. I can't bear it."

Giving Theodore a sideway glance, Mary continued. "To your point, *dear*. This deal is done. And you were none the wiser. By design. I didn't want you to worry about me."

Bear gave a small, encouraging *woof* to Theodore, putting a paw on the man's knee as Mary continued talking.

"Over a year ago, Katie and Percy were at a party and overheard Clay Overstreet was trying to locate a charming small town to film a music video."

"Clay Overstreet? Kansas country music star sensation, Clay Overstreet?" Theodore's eyes were wide as he sat at the edge of his chair.

"They've all become close friends. Percy even plays drums at local venues when Clay randomly drops in to surprise fans."

"How did I not know that Percy was a drummer? Another amazing talent! Thank god Katie married him."

"Settle down, Theodore," Riven said, chuckling.

"I thought you'd love the drum part," Mary said, reaching for Theodore's hand. "I could barely keep it a secret even when I'd signed Clay's NDA."

"NDA?" Lupe asked.

"*Non-disclosure agreement*," Theodore said, visibly relaxing. "Of course, you couldn't say, honey."

Mary smiled. "I met with Clay's people in Kansas City this past week, wanting to have everything wrapped up, paperwork done, and contracts signed before I told all of you."

"You didn't need me to look the papers over? I could have helped. After I signed Clay's NDA."

"Theodore, if you think you could have eaten at The Hen's Nest every day and not leaked that secret somehow—you would be wrong," Riven said, winking at Mary. "I wouldn't have told him either."

Bear sighed, seeming to nod in agreement.

"Really, honey. I didn't want you to lift a finger. You're already so busy. We were all in Kansas City, working secretly, thrilled with what we were putting together for Merivelle. Reyna has even been flying in from Chicago to help on some of our busier weekends."

"My Reyna?" Lupe asked.

"It's a quick regional flight. She's there in an hour and a half."

Lupe smiled proudly. "She wants to be an entertainment attorney."

"Which is another great thing about this entire project. It lets Reyna have some exposure to the industry before she fully decides. She's been incredibly helpful, Lupe. You'd be so proud."

Lupe glanced outside through the co-op's picture windows. "I miss my girl. But I'm thrilled she's been with you and Katie. Doing big things."

Mary leaned in, her forearms on the table. "Let's get to some of the even better news. Would you believe they're going to pay the town of Merivelle fifteen thousand dollars a day?"

Riven blinked heavily, clearly impressed.

"And they think they'll need around a week's time to film around town. They particularly love the train depot. All thanks to whatever angel sent money for that old, pigeon-infested building to be transformed."

Riven tapped his fingertips on the table and coughed. "I thought music videos were a dying thing."

"The old MTV-style music videos on television—yes."

Mary touched a palm lightly on the table. "But these would be for a YouTube channel and social media platforms. Clay wants to tell a story with his new album. Each song will be part of a narrative about an entire life cycle in a small town."

"When is this happening?" Theodore asked.

"Here me out before you say anything."

"Just let us have it," Theodore said. "It can't be that bad."

Bear put a paw on Mary's knee and whined.

"This week."

"Mary, you're kidding. Right?"

Squirming in her chair at her husband's question, Mary mumbled, "Tomorrow."

Theodore's jaw dropped as he leaned forward. Usually always supportive of anything Mary proposed, Riven's face also reflected shock.

"Clay has a small leg of make-up concert dates from his last album tour. He wants to make sure the video production team has all the film they need before he leaves."

"Isn't this all a little sudden?" Lupe asked. "We're going to be swamped with people this week as it is."

Mary nodded. "I know it seems like it, but we've been planning this for months. I feel the Midsummer crowds will dovetail nicely into some of the video scenes."

Pablito came to the table, having finished the kitchen duties from his summer job at the co-op. "Sounds like something fun for this boring town. This could make Merivelle famous."

"You think so, Pablito?"

A look of disappointment crossed the teenager's face.

Mary paused after the young boy sighed heavily. "I'm still not used to calling you *Pavi*."

"*Aye*, this guy thinking he can grow up by simply changing his name with a magic wand," Lupe said.

"Pablito sounds like a little boy. I've graduated high school.

41

I'd like the world to know me with a different name. All my friends use it already."

"Your name has meaning, Pablito," Lupe said.

Riven watched the mother and son as they spoke.

"Then *you* can call me that, Mamá. *Pavi* is for the rest of the world." He lifted an eyebrow. "Besides, I'll sign my art with the name." Pausing for a moment, his face lit with imagination. "Or it'll be easier for an announcer to pronounce at a soccer game."

"*Mijo*, be reasonable."

"Reyna even calls me Pavi now," he said, sitting down. "You'll get used to it."

Lupe shook her head, turning her attention back to the conversation at hand. "Anything else, Mary?"

"Clay's crew will need food from you, Lupe. It's why I sent off for such a large grocery order," Mary said, nodding. "Tamru is going to have a coffee bar at the locations."

"Tamru knows?"

"Honey, I can't spring a full-fledged coffee operation on Tamru. He signed an NDA and—"

"And Tamru kept it under his hat even when he saw us this morning," Riven said.

"All this to say," Mary said, smiling down at Bear. "There'll be wonderful opportunities for everyone in Merivelle."

Chapter Nine

Out on the sidewalk in front of Bear Bailey's, the group waited as Theodore armed the alarm system before stepping outside, where Mary and the Posadas chatted excitedly. The day had been hot, and the temperature still clung to the pavement, despite the cooling shadow of the store facing east, away from the setting sun.

"Riven Chapowits, are you stealing my dog?"

The old man looked up from petting Bear, a puzzled look on his face.

Bear leaned over and put a paw on Riven's chest, whining.

"No, of course not. It's only because Bear and I have been spending more time together while you've been gone."

"Be honest, Riven. Flinging bacon around like birdseed— you're a dog's dream come true," Theodore said.

"I'm only teasing Riven," Mary said, a smile on her face. "Who would have thought those two would be so close?"

"You're standing nearly in the same spot where Bear peed on your pant leg that first time, Riven." Theodore's eyes lit up with the memory.

"He got me fair and square on that one. He was sticking up for Mary."

Mary rubbed the man's arm with sincere affection. "You're a good sport, Riven."

All eyes went to Bear. Normally following human conversations with uncanny perception, his were ears were up as he focused on a man approaching where the group was standing.

Mary turned around, following her dog's gaze. Gavin was walking in front of the co-op's storefront.

"Mary Bailey." He sat his guitar case, fanning his shirt as he looked at the co-op. "Th-this is your store?"

"Did I tell you that on the train?"

"The sheriff was t-talking about the co-op. But it was also in the online ma-magazine."

"*Act Three—Everyone's Favorite Aunt*," Riven said, studying the young man as he spoke. "You only just came in with Mary on the train today?"

Nodding his head, Gavin continued haltingly. "I thought I co-could find a room. At The Windsor."

Watching the man struggling to speak, Mary jumped in. "The Windsor—it was also in the article about Cybil. I should have told you that every room in town is booked for at least a week. Merivelle's Midsummer celebration is tonight," Mary said.

"Midsummer?" Gavin asked, dropping his backpack.

"A yearly celebration to bless the crops about to be harvested. But mostly, it's really a fun night of music that kicks off a week of activities," Mary said. "Gives people the opportunity to dust off instruments and welcome the longest day of the year."

Theodore unlocked the door of their vehicle with his remote. "It's kind of taken off. People plan trips through Kansas to catch it. The co-op was swamped today."

Still staring at Gavin, Riven's face was solemn. "I feel I know you from somewhere."

"I've never been to M-Merivelle before." Beads of sweat formed over Gavin's upper lip. "I heard my-my dad talk about it."

"Does your dad live close by?"

Gavin backed up as Riven spoke, nearly toppling over his guitar case. "I don't know—"

"You don't know where your own dad lives?" Riven asked.

The young man's face was red as he stumbled over his words. "I-I don't know him. But I w-wanted to—"

Bear went and stood by Gavin, leaning into his legs as he looked up in encouragement.

Gavin's check flushed as he started again. "I'm s-sorry. When I get flustered, I stammer."

"We've only just met, Gavin. No need for you to give your full family history. Isn't that right, *Riven?*" Mary raised an eyebrow in warning.

"I was only asking a simple question. I didn't mean to offend. It's just that you seem very familiar to me."

Trying again, Gavin spoke slowly. "I'm here because I want to learn about family."

"*You* have family here in Merivelle?" Riven asked, crossing his arms.

Gavin picked up his backpack and slung it over his shoulder. "Once."

"But *you're* here now?" Riven pressed.

Gavin shook his head. "Cybil. The town auntie—"

"Is your family?" Lupe asked, putting her hand on Gavin's shoulder. "I can see the resemblance between the two of you." She studied his face and looked around him as if he were a much larger man. "Of course, you belong here in Merivelle."

Gavin looked at Lupe, his face frozen in confusion. "N-no, I—"

"You should have told me back at the train station," Mary said excitedly. "I would have taken you directly to Cybil's house."

Gavin took a few steps backwards. "Pl-please listen—"

"Absolutely not," Theodore said. "We like to think of ourselves as Cybil's family too. We'll take you before we head home. No trouble at all."

Riven frowned. "Mary just got home. I left my truck down at The Hen's Nest this morning. Come with me, Gavin. I'll drive you myself."

"Let me t-tell—"

"She lives over there," Pavi said, pointing diagonally from where they all stood. "So close. Most days, Cybil walks to work."

"I can walk. On m-my own," Gavin said, picking up his guitar case. "P-please."

"I insist," Riven said, stepping in front of Gavin. "The least I could do. To get things settled."

Mary shook her head. "What Riven's trying to say is that we're all protective of Cybil's age. Even a well-meaning surprise might take her back a bit. It's nothing personal."

"If you c-could let me ex-explain—"

Lupe placed her hand on Gavin's arm in a motherly fashion. "Almost everyone assisted me and my family when we first arrived. It's how we are in Merivelle. We love to help."

Pavi reached down and traced the scar over the top of Bear's eye from the snakebite the dog had sustained at their first meeting almost a decade before. "I can walk Gavin," he offered. "The rest of you have things to do."

Theodore went to Pavi's side. The two were the same height. Though the younger man's stature seemed almost chiseled from daily workouts and running up and down a soccer field most days. "That's much appreciated, Pavi. As always—we're a phone call away."

"Come on, Bear," Mary said, yawning. "Let's go home."

The dog had taken a few steps in the other direction with Riven.

Mary stopped mid-yawn, her face dropping in disappointment.

"He can come with me," Riven said. "I'll bring him with me tonight. You can take him from there."

"Do you need his leash?"

"I always have one in my truck," Riven said, pressing the traffic light button as he glanced up, waiting for the walk signal. "For just in case."

Bear sat on the corner, his back to the group as he waited in unison with Riven. At the sound of a click from the metal box, he walked across the street with Riven.

"Well, they're both taken care of," Mary said, shrugging. "I guess that's what you want—your kid taken up and loved by other people in your absence."

Chapter Ten

Cybil sat alone on her front porch, gazing up at the trees surrounding her home. As traffic passed by, the sound of the friction of vehicle tires on the bricked-paved street was almost hypnotic. Unseen birds, high in the boughs of the tree, tweeted with one another. Though the temperature of the afternoon was hot, Cybil rubbed her hands over the goosebumps on her arms. "*I all alone beweep my outcast state,*" she recited, whispering to herself. Something caught her eye as she rose from her chair and looked as far as she could see toward Bear Bailey's.

Crossing the street two blocks over, Pavi and Gavin continued walking from the co-op. "Cybil's in her own world these days. We won't go charging up and startle her."

"I—I don't think now is the time or place for me to m-meet Cybil."

"She loves visitors. Everyone at the co-op has been so busy. You've come at the perfect time."

"I'm not—"

"Hey—by the way," Pavi said, interrupting. "Are you Hispanic?"

Gavin furrowed his brows.

"No offense, your complexion is like mine. You nearly match my sister's. I was just wondering."

Nodding, Gavin said, "My mom was part American Indian. But she never told me what tribe. I don't even know if she knew."

"It's no big deal around here. There's people from all over the world living in Merivelle."

A passing car came to a full stop in front of the pair. "Are you playing Saturday?"

Pavi leaned into the vehicle filled with boys near his own age. "Maybe next weekend. It's a big week at the co-op."

Someone from the backseat shouted, "Pavi Picasso can't play again."

"Always at the dog store," another teenager said. "Helping his mommy."

Pavi looked at Gavin, rolling his eyes. "All this. Over soccer."

A vehicle honked from behind as Pavi hit the roof of the car, waving it on. "They're good guys. Just giving me a hard time," Pavi said, walking. He looked at Gavin, still loaded down with his backpack as he carried his guitar case. "Can I help you carry something? You look pretty overloaded."

"Really, I only n-needed a room to stay for a few nights when I walked by the co-op. No-nothing else."

Pavi nodded toward Cybil's house a few doors down. "Don't be shy. Merivelle loves new people. And you're here when Cybil needs you most. Everyone is grateful you've come. I could tell."

"That's w-what I'm trying to tell you. I—" Gavin said, hesitating. "—write words, lyrics for songs."

Surprised, Pavi stopped walking. "Anything I've heard?"

Gavin swallowed hard, taking a few breaths as he tried to speak again. "I'm trav-traveling. Trying. To be seen. Not r-really even a songwriter yet."

"That's not how it works with creative people. Cybil told me that a long time ago." Pavi continued walking. "If you're writing—you're a writer. If you sing—you're a singer. Same goes with painting, sculpting or any other creative endeavor. Don't let the label of something trip you up. You are what you do—not what you say."

"How old are you?"

"Nineteen. I graduated from high school a month ago. I had an issue with English when we first came to Merivelle. The school held me back a year."

"You're in-insightful."

"It's this town full of old people," Pavi said as they approached Cybil's house. "They'll teach you a lot, if you listen."

"Must be nice. Having p-people around. Even if you're not related."

"When I was younger, I only wanted it to be me and my mom." Pavi laughed. "But I had a pesky sister, Reyna—she's the smart one in our family. Graduated college a year early. While she interned at Tio Theo's law firm. She's a big act to follow."

"*Tio Theo?*"

"*Tio* is Spanish for uncle. It's what Reyna and I call Theodore Bailey. You met him at the co-op."

"You aren't r-related?"

"Like I said, around here it's more what you do. Theodore is the best uncle. And not a drop of blood between us."

Gavin straightened up, readjusting his backpack, listening with great attention.

"Quickly, let me tell you one more thing about your aunt."

"I'm t-trying to t-tell—"

"I spend a lot of time with her," Pavi said, interrupting. "She's sharp. Really smart with everyone. There's not a problem Cybil can't help you solve."

Another car drove by and waved out an open window as Pavi returned the gesture.

"But there are moments, she's not quite herself. Forgets simple things. But then she'll quote an entire Shakespeare sonnet. It's hard for me to make sense of it. And I don't want to tell the others right now."

"Pavi?" Cybil stood at the edge of her porch, leaning over the wall as the pair walked in front of the neighbor's house.

"One second!" Pavi shouted. "You're going to love this!" He turned toward Gavin, stopping for a moment. "I'm scared someone's going to want to put her in a nursing home."

"Some of them are ni-nice. My m-mom used to work—"

The expression on Pavi's face glowered for a moment as he shook his head. "We don't do that where I come from. The *viejos*—"

Gavin scrunched his eyebrows at the word.

"*Old people.* We don't cart them off where I'm from. Putting Cybil in a home would be like putting a butterfly in a jar."

"I n-need to tell you. I just read the m-magazine about how—"

"If Bear trusted you—I trust you. He wouldn't have let you take a step forward if there was something coyote-like about you." Arriving at the front of the sidewalk leading to Cybil's house, Pavi lowered his voice. "Help her. However you can. I don't care where you came from. Promise me?"

As they spoke, Cybil grabbed the stone baluster railing.

Turning around swiftly, Pavi jogged the few steps up to Cybil's side, giving her a hug.

"I've been so lonely here by myself," Cybil said, grasping Pavi's hand in her own. "It's a wish come true that you've come to visit."

Pavi turned to Gavin and gestured as if the stranger was a prize on a game show. "Here's your surprise!"

Shuffling uneasily, Gavin looped his thumbs under his backpack straps.

Cybil leaned forward with a thoughtful look on her face as she studied the young man. "You seem familiar. But I'm having a hard time connecting who we are to one another. Please forgive me."

Pavi grasped Cybil's hand in encouragement. "Gavin is your nephew. Remember?"

"Gavin Ring," Cybil said, letting out a sigh of relief. "Yes, Mary already phoned me that you were on your way. I told her to send you right over."

"He's a musician. See his guitar?" Pavi said, motioning to the case. "You know how you love artists of every kind, Cybil."

"*And* you're a songwriter?" Cybil asked. "How extraordinary, Gavin. What wonderful gifts you possess."

Gavin glanced down at the street.

Pavi cleared his throat, looking pleadingly at Gavin. "We're here to help you get ready for the concert."

"You young kids don't need weighed down with a slow-paced old woman. Go have fun tonight. I can sit on my porch and listen to the music from here. It's lovely on the breeze." She sat back down on her porch chair. Though she smiled good-naturedly, sadness framed her eyes.

Gavin took off his backpack, balancing it with his guitar case. "I-I would love to h-help you, Cybil," he said, a congenial expression on his face. "A concert might be inspiring. Instead of me alone, strumming on my guitar, hoping something comes to me."

Chapter Eleven

"You know we're checking on Cybil before we head home?"

The Great Pyrenees sat in the passenger seat of Riven's truck as the old man turned on the air conditioner. Once the vents blew hot air, white hair floated around the cab of the truck.

"Good grief, you have a lot of fur," Riven said, swatting the air at the offending strands. "If I could borrow some for the thinning on my own head, we'd be in business." He glanced in the rear-view mirror.

Bear made a questioning groan as he tilted his head.

"You don't think it's weird a guy shows up and suddenly Cybil has relatives?"

The phone rang in the front pocket of Riven's stiffly starched shirt.

"When people have money, they need to be more cautious. Cybil has worked hard in her senior years. Then this guy shows up out of nowhere?"

The phone continued to chime as Bear turned his head at the sound.

"This is where it might get dicey," Riven said, ignoring the call. "My past behavior being stingy with money. I'm probably not the person who should point out the very obvious, am I?"

Listening with solemn eyes, Bear panted.

Riven reached out to adjust the vents off of himself and onto the dog. "Even though I've tried to change my behavior, it doesn't mean I don't have to reap what I sowed. I realize that, Bear. I really do. But we can't let a complete stranger into Cybil's house. Even if Mary seemed fine with all of it."

With the cool air directed on to him, Bear's eyes were closed in contentment. However, at the sound of the name *Mary*—he opened them again.

"And let's talk about what happened back at the co-op. Why'd you give your favorite human the cold shoulder?"

Bear put his paw on Riven's chest and whined.

"I heard her going to great lengths to explain her trip to you before she left."

As Bear stopped panting, he looked at Riven with solemn eyes, sniffing the man's chest.

"It hurts when people you love leave, doesn't it?"

Scooting over, Bear rested his head on Riven's arm as the man grasped the steering wheel. The dog looked up at him, an expression of deep interest on his face.

"My mom died when I was a kid. It was even worse than when my dad would disappear on one of his trips. Then Julia—"

Bear groaned at the sound of the name as he always did.

"—I thought she broke my heart for good, but this child that came into my life through Julia melted me completely." He paused for a moment, giving Bear a side glance. "You know my girl, Katie."

When Bear had first arrived in Mary's life, hearing the word *Katie* caused him to groan. But when a sincere friendship between the two cousins developed, both willingly doing whatever would be best for the other, Bear panted happily whenever Katie's name came into conversation, knowing how happy Mary was in the other woman's presence.

"Just when I thought I could mend my heart, work hard and focus on my daughter—here comes a stand-in dad. And he was everything I wasn't."

Bear lifted his head in question.

"I was a poor, skinny kid with dirt under my fingernails, no matter how hard I tried to remove it at the end of a day." Riven nodded outside the air-conditioned truck. "Summer was especially grueling when I worked at the grain elevator next to the train depot."

Panting again, Bear nodded his head earnestly.

"While I was working hard to change our fortunes, out of nowhere, here comes a handsome and charming man who had nothing but time to spend with my daughter." Riven's knuckles were white from gripping the steering wheel. "But there was more to Lance. I felt it in my bones. I was amazed that no one else saw that he was a real coyote."

Hearing the word, Bear's ears stood at attention as he stared up and down the street, a low growl in his throat.

"He was living in the same house as my child. I had to do something!"

The phone rang again, this time catching Riven's attention. He looked down and pulled it out of his front shirt pocket, unfolding the phone and putting it up to his ear.

"Chaps?"

Despite his frustration, a smile transformed the old man's face as he tilted his head to Bear. "Katie!"

Bear grinned with his tongue hanging out, sitting up in the seat to give Riven space.

"Why haven't you been answering your phone? I was worried about you."

"I was just leaving the co-op."

"Maybe that flip phone isn't big enough for you to hear?"

"It has big numbers for my senior eyes and a single 9-1-1 call button for emergencies."

"Let's not think about that right now. Too much good going on. Besides, we need to get you a newer phone so you can talk with Violet."

"I talk with my granddaughter every day."

"You could *see* her on the phone wherever you are. Not just when you're in front of a computer."

"Then I'll look into it tomorrow."

"Chaps, are you still in front of The Hen's Nest?"

Riven startled in place as Bear barked.

"And why is Bear suddenly so excited?"

"Are you here in town? Did you come for Midsummer?"

"Oh, no, I'm so sorry to get your hopes up. Mary told me you had parked there and hadn't moved. I was worried when you didn't answer your phone. Violet wanted to talk to you before Percy took her on their evening walk."

Riven sunk back into his seat, a look of disappointment on his face. He covered the phone's mouthpiece with his other hand to speak to Bear. "Katie's not here. She's still in Kansas City."

"Who are you talking to? Is Frannie with you?"

"Theodore and his love for soap operas," Riven said, sighing. "Frannie's been spending some evenings with me. She's kind and hardworking. And still a very handsome woman. But if it bothers you—"

"Nobody calls women *handsome* anymore. Just say she's pretty. Because Frannie is definitely still a hottie."

"I will not call Frannie a *hottie*. But I am going to choke Theodore."

Katie laughed. "Calm down. Theodore didn't tell me a thing."

"He didn't?"

"He has a strict bro code. You and Percy should know that better than anyone." She paused. "However, he's abysmal trying to keep a secret. Remember that time at The Hen's Nest?"

"You were trapped in a booth with me and the pair of them. Finding out the town villain was actually your father." Riven shook his head. "I wish there would have been a different way for you to hear."

"It was terrible when it happened, but now it's one of my favorite stories. I promise. All's well that ends well."

"You're the second person to say that today."

"Because it's true." Katie paused for a moment. "Wait—are you ok? Your voice doesn't sound as strong as it normally does."

"It's been one long day. And still an evening ahead."

Bear leaned into Riven, resting his head on the man's shoulder and exhaling audibly.

"And I've got this giant dog all over me. Drooling everywhere." He rubbed his cheek on Bear's nose, completely betraying his seemingly exasperated words.

"Mary said that Bear gave her the cold shoulder. I think she's going to cry the entire way home. But that's what happens when you leave pets. Violet's cat, Hobo, gets very testy when we leave him. Even with the house sitter attending to him like a king."

Hearing the word *cat* through the phone at Riven's ear, Bear groaned.

Riven held the phone towards the side of his face for a

moment. "Cats are actually good, Bear." He wrinkled his nose. "Even if I am allergic."

"Are you really talking to Bear?"

"He looks concerned that you're talking about Hobo, and I wonder if he understands what happened to Henry. I don't want him confused with all the dogs and people going in and out of his life. What was the name of the corgi he loved when he and I weren't good friends in the beginning?"

"Jiff. Like the dog Franklin had when he was a boy."

"*Jiff*," Riven repeated. "He was a real character."

Bear barked happily.

"See? He knows what we're talking about. I don't want him feeling left behind in the last part of his life." He shifted the phone to his other hand and leaned into Bear. "We're both a couple of old dogs, aren't we, boy?

Katie cleared her throat. "How's Operation Chaps going this week? What noble things have you done that Merivelle doesn't know about?"

"The agreement we made when we first got to know one another was that I didn't reveal any good deeds I did. You said to be like your dog Henry—no words, only kind actions."

"I was unbalanced back then. I thought no words were the medicine I needed. You can do good and it's still okay if people sometimes know. I think you've proved yourself beyond any doubt the past three years that I've been gone. You aren't waving a banner with ulterior motives to get what you want."

"Well, now that I'm used to doing good things in secret, there's no need to change what's presently working."

"You might have to pause your anonymity."

"How's that?"

"I'm out of details to move forward with Pablito's—I mean, *Pavi*'s dad. You might have to ask Lupe for some more information."

58

"What if we still can't find him? Even with all the people I've hired?"

"Be patient. You're trying your best, Chaps. Something will pop up."

"I had to get straight with my own history before I could see the Posada family clearly. They're waiting for Pavi's dad, the same way I did growing up. The guilt I feel thinking about it."

"You had nothing to do with Pavi's dad disappearing."

"I charged his family ridiculous rent while he was gone."

"You did. *And* refused to fix the plumbing until they came up with the back rent."

"I thought that was smart business. The men that were toughest on me when I was trying to make my way taught me more than any class in school." He paused, biting his bottom lip as he thought for a few moments. "And if I'm totally honest, I added my own insecurities into the mix. Feeling left out when the co-op first opened."

"You did what you knew and now you know better," Katie said. "I think you've paid the Posadas back several times over and more." Her voice had a lilt to it. "You know, I like that you and I have this secret knowledge between us."

"You seem to know all the helpful details of the Posadas' life. I couldn't have done it without your help."

"Reyna's tuition paid in full at Merivelle Community College and then in Chicago at Theodore's alma mater. A car for Pavi—"

"You said not to spoil him. Something functional to get him to and from places."

"From my experience growing up. Too much is as bad as too little. It's a challenge with Violet. I want to spoil her rotten. But I know that's so I feel better, not having her best interests at heart."

"You're figuring it out. I respect how much thought you put

into everything you do for her." Riven squinted, making a funny noise as his tongue clicked his teeth. "I need your advice on a different subject. A young man showed up out of nowhere—"

"Just a sec," Katie said as the phone muffled on her end. She returned a few moments later. "Percy's home with Violet. Can we pause this call and talk again later? It looks like she's skinned her knee and needs some attention."

"Is she all right?" Riven sat up and leaned over the steering wheel as if Violet had fallen on the sidewalk ahead of him instead of nearly four hundred miles away.

"She's fine. Don't worry. Get a new phone and we'll talk again soon! Love you, Dad!"

Riven slowly closed his phone, placing it back into his front pocket. Bear put a paw on the man's back, a big grin on his face as Riven reached for a box of tissues on the floor. Blowing his nose, he looked at the dog. "That's the first time she's called me *Dad* instead of *Chaps*. All is suddenly right in my world."

In the parking spot next to Riven, another truck pulled up. Rolling down her passenger side window, Mary looked over. "Please don't think I'm a lunatic. But I'm checking on Bear."

Riven looked over at the Great Pyrenees, happily panting as he sat up in recognition of his owner. "She gets your point. You felt left out, and you want her to know."

Bear shook his head, putting a paw again on Riven's chest, nudging him tenderly.

Unlocking the door, Riven reached over, scratching behind the dog's ear. "Go home with your mom. It makes her happy. She won't always have you by her side."

Chapter Twelve

"All the passageways to Earth are secure?"

Exhausted by a day of play and delicious food, thousands of dogs were waiting for evening story time on the Rainbow Bridge. One small Aussie was keenly interested with Josephine and Lea's conversation. She hid behind a butterfly bush as the angels looked down to Earth from the vast horizon of heaven.

"The only connection that has me concerned is the far exit, nearly to the Golden Meadow," Lea replied. "I hope no dog goes near it. Or else they'll end up in Merivelle."

Josephine leaned down and scratched Betty as she wiggled in joy.

The sound of all the dogs' commotion overtook the angels' voices. Barking and good-natured tussling filled the air as they waited for Lea's story.

"Remember Jiff?" Betty said, interrupting. "He was a Rainbow Bridge dog and did fine in Merivelle. With his friend, Bear! And then Henry—who doesn't love that good boy when he comes to visit from time to time?"

The two angels exchanged glances with one another, both concealing smiles.

"If a dog went to Merivelle, they could check up on things and come right back. Like Jiff when he was a corgi." Betty was panting in excitement, her pink tongue hanging out of her mouth as if she'd run for miles. "They could help. Cybil really needs someone these days."

Lea opened the palms of her hands as a book magically appeared. "Grab a blanket with your favorite scent from the pile, Betty. You can wrap up in it while I read."

"But I'm not even slightly tired. I have so much energy, I feel I could run to Earth."

Josephine chuckled as she lifted a blanket from the middle of the stack that dogs were sniffing through as they settled in for the evening. She leaned down, wrapping Betty in the fluffy blanket, setting her at the front of the audience. "You better stay here where Lea can keep an eye on you."

Betty burrowed in, her eyes on the horizon. The sky lit up with brilliant hues of orange, pink and violet, with the sounds of a celestial orchestra beginning to play as Lea began reading to the sleepy canines.

Chapter Thirteen

Driving home alone at the end of a long day at the co-op, Riven rubbed the back of his neck. He couldn't remember the last time he'd felt so exhausted. For the past couple of years, he'd slowly sold off his business interests so that he could visit his only granddaughter as often as possible. When he returned home to Merivelle after visits with Violet, he relied on Bear Bailey's for a social life. Only a decade before, he would have preferred the vast emptiness of his own home to the bustling beehive activity of the co-op. And now, he woke before dawn, watching the clock every quarter hour to count down the time before he could return to Mary's store on Main Street.

At the city limits, he checked his rearview mirror and turned in the middle of the highway. Almost instantly, the reflection of red lights caught his attention before he drove to the grassy shoulder of the highway. He put his truck in park and waited, tapping his fingers on the steering wheel as he waited.

"Riven Chapowits."

"Donkey."

The sheriff rapped his knuckles gently on the side of the truck. "Do you mind explaining something to me?"

Riven held a hand up. "I decided I need to go see Mary before Midsummer. But I shouldn't have whipped a U-turn in the middle of the road. Old habit."

Chuckling, Donkey shook his head. "If I pulled over everyone in Merivelle who made sudden highway U-turns, I'd never get home."

Riven wrinkled his eyebrows. "Did I do something else?"

"I think you did. And I wanted to have a word with you without everyone around at the co-op."

Riven leaned forward, directing the air vent to hit his face as he looked to Donkey.

A slow-moving car honked as they made their way into Merivelle. Once it had passed, the vast land around the pair gave way to sounds of distant meadowlarks, grasshopper legs whirring in the evening heat as they jumped among the tall, blowing grass surrounding the vehicle. A person could almost hear the insects land on the crisp stalks of the plants.

"Perhaps you could give me a clue, Donkey."

"I have a hunch that thanks to you, a summer Little League of no less than a hundred and fifty children has jerseys and new equipment."

Riven sat up, eyes fixed on the highway before he turned in question. "I thought manufacturers donate things like that all the time to promote their brand."

"You'd think that a company would love to include their name for advertising. Might send more than a card signed, *The Manufacturer*."

Riven winced.

The sun, beginning its downward slope for the day, cast a different sort of light, the clouds beginning to color with pastel hues. Donkey looked down the long highway leading outside and beyond the city limits before turning back to Riven. "You know, my old man always told me you weren't what you appeared."

An expression of remorse passed over Riven's face.

"When I was a kid, you scared me to death."

"I didn't mean to—"

"All men who aren't your own dad can terrify a kid." Donkey touched Riven's shoulder for a moment. "Then you grow up and realize life can be tricky. Now that I know about you and Katie, things make a lot more sense to me. How you always showed up at events. Even if you were grumpy."

"I could have been much more friendly. Especially with people or things that had nothing to do with the situation."

"Moving here in grade school when my dad took the sheriff's job, I wouldn't know everything that transpired before then," Donkey said, nodding to another passing vehicle. "But my adult brain has connected those times differently than my child-like memories. And as a father that gets to hug my children every night as I tuck them into bed, I don't know if I could have silently hung around in their lives without blowing my top. It took a lot on your part to show up."

"I appreciate you, Donkey. But there were others—"

"You have more children?"

"I meant others—people that I wasn't kind to. Didn't leave any meat on the bone with business deals over the years. I thought being successful was obliterating people. I caused a tremendous amount of hurt in my community." He glanced into the distance for a few moments, his eyes darting back and forth, before returning his attention to Donkey. "Any ideas you might have about my present activities in Merivelle, if you could keep it between us?"

"Why not let the town know the effort you're making?"

"A vow I made to my daughter," Riven said, sitting up resolutely.

"That doesn't sound like her. Anna says that when Katie visits, she talks all the time about how proud she is of you."

"Gave my word back when Katie and I were initially getting acquainted with one another. I wouldn't want to do anything to jeopardize her trust in me."

"Your life, your show." Donkey looked at Riven, a thoughtful expression on his face. "What do you think allowed you to find your way back into Katie's life after all these years?"

"Same as the whole town—Bear Bailey. That dog changed everything."

Chapter Fourteen

In the middle of a field, under a fading sun, the head of a small canine lifted above the sunflowers. Turning from side-to-side, Betty looked around cautiously. Expecting the airiness of the Rainbow Bridge, she took a few steps and fell, not used to the solid ground beneath her fawn-like feet.

In the distance, Bear rose from a seated position at the edge of Sagebrush Farms, a patch of earth worn away from his daily guarding of the area. Putting his nose into the air, he turned instinctively. A ripple in the field caught his attention as he ran toward the movement. In a matter of seconds, he was standing over Betty, who was cowering on her back as he towered over her.

"Bear Bailey!"

Jumping at the sound of the other dog's voice, Bear's eyes widened.

"I knew I could sneak away and find you if I tried," Betty said, wiggling in happiness.

"You speak?"

"Of course, I do. You should know that from your buddies, Jiff and Henry."

Bear's jaw fell open.

Jumping up onto her feet, Betty swayed as she continued to acclimate to the ground. "Everyone on the Bridge knows about you. You're the most requested story at bedtime."

"Everyone?"

"Well, when I say *everyone*, I mostly mean *me*," Betty said, smiling. "The others let me choose the stories, if I'll sit down and be quiet."

"You sure move around a lot more than any dog I've ever seen."

"I try hard to hold still. My body sometimes seems to have a mind of its own." Her backend wiggled, almost entirely apart from her upper torso. "So, Bear—I was wondering when you were going to fight some coyotes?"

"Coyotes?" Bear's ears went up in alarm. "Where did you see coyotes?"

"Nowhere, but that's one reason I'm visiting. I wanted to see some fresh Bear Bailey stories for myself." She looked around the sagebrush, her ear tilted to the wind. "Have you had any disturbances nearby?"

Confused by her request, Bear said, "We haven't had trouble with predators for a long time."

"Because you fought them all? Kicked them back to their Dark Dens?" Betty narrowed her eyes and growled at a sagebrush bush like it was a rogue coyote. "I bet you popped them right between the eyes and sent them on their way."

Bear sniffed the air. After a few minutes of silent observation, he looked at the petite dog. "We don't fight for no reason here in Merivelle. If there's a coyote, I'll take care of it. With good boundaries, there hasn't been a coyote that's passed through and caused trouble for years." He went to a nearby bush and lifted his leg. "But just in case."

Betty's face wrinkled when she caught a whiff of the moist dirt. "What is that smell?"

Walking from the spot, Bear looked at her. "I just marked our territory to make sure no coyotes come near."

"Now it feels like I'm holding a lot of water inside of me. What's going on?"

"You probably need to go potty."

Giggling, Betty snuck behind a bush. "I don't know why, but a giant dog talking about pottying makes me laugh." The sound of liquid hitting the ground made Bear turn his back as he waited. Once Betty was done, she reappeared, ready to talk again.

Going over to where she'd done her business moments before, Bear lifted one of his back legs.

"What are you doing?"

"Protecting you."

"How?" Betty asked with a disgusted look on her face.

"I cover your smell. So coyotes aren't tempted to come near you. I pee on top of all the other small animal's business at Sagebrush Farms. To keep them safe."

"Good to know, Bear. I'll stay out of your way when you're concerned about my safety."

Twilight continued its leisurely summer pace. In the distance, a pair of bright meadowlarks sitting on top of a fence-post warbled as sunflowers swayed in the evening breeze.

"This is the most beautiful place," Betty said breathlessly. "I don't know why I was so scared to come here."

Bear turned away from the horizon.

The smaller dog ran to the front of him, blocking his movement forward. "Where are you going?"

Bear's eyes were on the house in the distance. "To spend time with my favorite person."

Nodding in a knowing manner, Betty said, "I love Mary. She took you in when you were a pup and that young guy—what was his name? I can't remember. But anyway, he bought you for his girlfriend. And then when they broke up, you came to live with Mary. Who didn't want you at first, but then she fell head over heels for you. And now the two of you are best friends ever since."

The Great Pyrenees stopped and looked down at Betty. "How do you know we're best friends?" His eyes became glossy with emotion.

"She'd do anything for you. Everyone on the Bridge knows how much she loves you."

"Excuse me," Bear said, clearing his throat. "I gotta get home now." He ran through the sagebrush, jumping over the bushes as if they were hurdles.

Mary opened the patio door. "What on earth just got into you?"

Bear stood on his back legs, hugging her waist with his front paws as he whined.

Planting a kiss on top of his head, Mary released his paws from around her and guided him into a seated position.

Theodore came around the corner from their bedroom, putting on his watch as he looked at his wrist. "If we leave in the next ten minutes, we'll be fine." He stopped, surveying the scene. "You and Bear make up?"

Bear hooked one of his front paws onto Mary's arm, the breed's signature *Pyr paw*.

"Am I forgiven, Bear? You only missed out on a lot of meetings and Violet's rescue cat. Hobo gets grumpy with dogs. Which is understandable when he's missing his tail and the tip of one ear."

Bear leaned in and sighed.

"But if I could have taken you—I would have popped you in my suitcase." She smiled thoughtfully. "My mom used to say that all the time when I was a girl."

"Where did this little dog come from?"

"What dog?" Mary scanned the land beyond the house.

"That one," Theodore said, pointing. "Hiding behind your giant dog."

Mesmerized by both humans, Betty blinked rapidly. "*Theodore and Mary*—they're like meeting movie stars."

Bear groaned as Mary reached out and stroked the dog's fur.

"I'm so happy to meet your mom," Betty said, wiggling at Mary's touch. "She smells wonderful."

"What an adorable puppy!"

"And she called me *adorable*."

Theodore knelt beside his wife to examine the predominantly black dog with tan and white markings. His face softened. "What a beautiful dog," he said, reaching out to scratch her ears. "She's going to be a real Betty."

"That's my real name!" Betty circled Theodore's legs in excitement. "How did he know?"

Bear closed his eyes and yawned dramatically.

"Honey, what on earth are you talking about?" Mary said, laughing.

"She's a Betty. It's slang for a beautiful woman. Used in a sentence, '*Mrs. Bailey sure is a Betty.*'"

Mary shook her head and smiled at her dog. "He's being goofy, isn't he, Bear?"

"She's much smaller than other Australian Shepherds I've seen. Maybe a third of the regular size?" Theodore said, undeterred. "What a pretty face she has. And her markings are perfectly symmetrical."

Betty fairly melted. *"Theodore,"* she said in a happy manner. "He smells like the moist earth and moss in the most beautiful forest. Like everything is going to be okay as long as he's around."

"The sun is starting to set." Mary rose to her feet. "We need to go, but we can't leave her here alone."

"Oh, yes, we can," Bear said, leaning back to lick one of his hips. "Go back to whatever farm you came from."

"I have no idea how to get back to where I came from. If I could just stay—"

"No room."

"But Mary loves helping strangers. You do too, Bear. Remember how people that used to be strangers are now your best friends?"

"Mary's super busy. No need for her to be distracted by a second dog."

"Lots of people have more than one dog. It's highly unusual that you live on a farm and you've always been the only one," Betty replied, not at all fazed by Bear's grumpiness. "And I'm much smaller than you. The Baileys wouldn't even know that I'm here. I could even help out."

"I have everything under control," Bear said, huffing.

A trio of bleats interrupted the interchange.

Groaning, Theodore looked at his wife. "Did Pavi leave the gate open again? These goats drive me crazy! One of them tried to headbutt me the other day."

"Skittles bumped into you."

"Skittles bumped into me *forcefully*."

"There's nothing we can do. Bear has tried for years. I would love my flowers to grow the entirety of one season. Pavi's always in a hurry these days and forgets to latch the gate between our house and the barndominium. Make peace with the goats, Theodore. It'll be easier on everyone."

Theodore narrowed his eyes. "They're on my last nerve." He stood up and met Mary's gaze. "I'm serious. I need the goats gone from my general proximity. Now."

"Watch what I can do around here," Betty said, jumping down the patio steps.

Bear started barking. "There's nothing you can do about the goats. They're hopeless."

The Great Pyrenees' words blew away with the evening wind. Betty had already surrounded the goats, barking as they looked up, braying in confusion. Skittles put his head down, taking a few steps forward to the dog. Not fazed, Betty ran a circle around the goats, nipping each at the ankles before backing up and nodding her intent that they vacate the area. She continued circling the confused livestock, who looked at each other and then at the porch where Mary and Theodore stood in amusement.

"Move-out-to-the-sage-brush," Betty barked in quick syllabic bursts.

All three goats stopped; Pandora brazenly finishing the flower she had torn from a plant, chewing in a slow and defiant way.

"*No more eating.*" Betty growled, launching forward. "Let's go. Now! Now! Now!"

The goats lined up and walked in front of the Aussie, who wove around them as they moved forward.

Theodore's mouth was wide open. "What miracle are we witnessing?" he whispered.

In an impressive short time, the three goats were ushered down the walkway, past the barn and outbuildings, to an area brimming with weed overgrowth. Barking again and nodding her intent that they stay put, the goats turned their backs. Satisfied, Betty fired back to the house, halting at the gate.

Bear looked up at Mary, a questioning expression on his face. Theodore was radiant in admiration.

Going to the back side of the gate, Betty pushed it with her nose, running around it before it closed, clanging behind her. Rushing up to the porch in exhilaration, Betty looked at Bear, waiting for him to speak.

"No need to show off. Just do what needs to be done." He turned his back on the Aussie and faced Mary.

"Don't be upset, Bear," Mary replied as Theodore leaned down and scooped the little dog into his arms. "We can use all the extra help we can get—friends and strangers."

The doorbell rang as the two dogs eyed one another and raced to the front door.

Chapter Fifteen

"I'm concerned about the young man that's come to town," Riven said, crossing the threshold of the front door. "But I can't put my finger on why."

The Bailey's looked at one another as Bear lumbered forward to greet Riven, backing into the man and sitting on his feet, tilting his head almost completely back towards him. Riven took a deep breath, his countenance calming.

"Why don't you come in?" Mary asked. "You look pale and like you're trying to catch your breath. Have you eaten, Riven?"

The old man shook his head. "I got busy."

"Say no more, my friend!" Theodore said, going to the kitchen.

"I won't eat before the concert. Too hot."

"Then I'll add a sandwich to our picnic hamper, and then we can all be off."

"I don't want to bother you. Especially since Mary just got home."

"Nonsense," Mary said, motioning Riven forward. "We'd

love to catch up before the event tonight. I'll even introduce you to a new friend."

Bear groaned expressively, before letting his full body weight fall to the floor like a big sack of potatoes.

Theodore ducked out of the kitchen. "Is Bear hurt? He sure whimpers a lot lately."

Shaking his head, Riven said, "That's the sound he makes when he's exasperated."

"That's exactly right," Mary said, a look of amusement on her face. "You speak *Bear* fluently."

"What's bothering you, old man?" Riven bent down, grimacing as one of his knees popped. "Can't let things get under your fur."

"Funny enough, you and Bear both seemed agitated with our recent visitors today."

Riven paused, wrinkling his brow in question.

"Over there," Mary said, nodding toward the living room. "A puppy showed up out of nowhere. I always thought Bear would be happy to see another dog after Jiff and Henry."

"Those were full-grown dogs. He probably had a sense they belonged to someone else. Besides, sometimes old dogs aren't fans of puppies. Makes them think they might be replaced soon."

Mary's face dropped as she looked at her dog. "You are irreplaceable. But we do welcome new people and dogs, don't we, Bear?"

"Does she have a tag?" Riven asked.

Theodore came in from the kitchen. "No tag. I named her Betty."

"Perfect name for such a pretty canine."

"You can't believe how sweet and friendly she is," Mary said.

Riven reached behind the couch, extending his hand gently as he knelt down. "Hello, Betty."

Suddenly, the docile dog's demeanor shifted. She growled, baring her teeth as she backed away from Riven's open hand.

Mary and Theodore looked at one another in puzzlement.

"Don't act like that," Bear said, standing protectively beside the old man. "What's gotten into you?"

Betty growled again, backing away from Riven. "He was mean to you, Bear. Remember? Back in the beginning?"

"That was a long time ago—almost seventy years ago, if we're counting in dog years."

Betty turned her head in question. "Are you sure?"

"Absolutely positive."

"You mean *paw*sitive?" Betty said, her backend beginning to shake in joy again.

"Get out here and be nice to Riven. He's made some big changes in his life."

"For you, Bear—I'll do anything." Betty jumped forward and stood on her back legs, her paws on Riven's knees, wiggling as she licked his outstretched hand.

"Well, that was an about-face," Theodore said. "Look how fast Betty's mood changed."

"I'm sorry, what?" Mary looked up from her phone. "I got a text. What are we talking about?"

"Betty's *volt-face* with Riven."

"*Word of the Day,*" Mary said, still focused on her screen as she rapped the counter with her knuckles. "Abrupt reversal of opinion—a *volt-face.*"

Bear nodded toward Riven. "He doesn't even smell like when I first used to know him. Have a sniff and see for yourself."

Betty leaned into Riven, squinting. "You're right, Bear. He smells like old books in a giant library waiting to be read in a

77

leather chair next to a fireplace." She licked Riven's hand and panted happily. "An old scent. But a very nice one too."

"What about near his heart?" Bear asked. "Notice anything there?"

Betty buried her nose near Riven's chest and whined. "There is another smell, isn't there?"

"The closest I can think is when oil spills from vehicles in the parking spots in front of the co-op," Bear said, thinking for a moment. "Like something's breaking down."

"Poor Riven," Betty said mournfully. "I like the book smell so much more."

"It's why I don't want to leave him alone." Bear looked at Mary. "But it's hurting my best friend's feelings."

"I could go with him, Bear."

"What's a puppy like you going to do if something happens?"

"What would you do?" Betty turned her head as she spoke, sincerely puzzled.

"I could brace him up. Until help comes."

"What about bringing a phone to him if it's out of his reach?" She looked at Riven and barked. "And that's only a start. Let me show you all I can—"

With the sudden barking, Riven startled for a moment.

"You must be a young person's dog. I think you have way too much energy to be around Riven," Bear said, sighing. "You've got to calm way down."

Betty stopped mid-bark. "Yes, sir."

"You don't have to call me sir. I'm a dog."

"Yes, dog-sir." Betty giggled. "I'm sorry. I'm just super happy and excited to be here." She arranged her face in a serious expression. "Whatever you say, Bear. Now what do we do?"

"It's a lot to explain, and we're getting ready to leave."

"I'm current on all things Merivelle from Rainbow Bridge stories," Betty said, sitting up. "I know everyone's name. We can get this figured out. Like the goats."

Taking a deep breath, Bear said, "Mary's super busy with a new project—she's humming all the time in happiness. Theodore's content because Mary's excited. Even if he felt left out in the beginning."

Betty nodded solemnly. "Riven needs someone, in case the smell around his chest gets worse. What else, Bear?"

"Lupe's worried about her kids. Pavi always running around with friends she doesn't know. Reyna's still in Chicago, trying to figure out what she wants to do now that she's graduated. Cybil isn't remembering things like she used to. And now she's had a surprise visitor who Lupe thought was her nephew."

"You don't think Gavin and Cybil are related?"

"I don't think so. Two entirely different smells." Bear shrugged. "Our job as dogs is to be calm so everyone can figure out what's going on with all the new things in their lives."

"*Lord, what fools these mortals be!*"

Bear turned his head in question. "Shakespeare?"

Betty panted happily. "I thought I'd never get here to say it."

"Reciting Shakespeare?"

"No—it's what you always said with Jiff and Henry. '*I don't know how I know that, but I know.*'"

Mary gathered up her keys and purse, talking to Riven and Theodore as she motioned for the dogs to follow.

"We also can't forget to lean in and listen. That's a Bear Bailey hallmark move," Betty said. "Isn't that right, big guy?"

"Don't try to butter me up, Betty." The Great Pyrenees shook his head, barely concealing a smile, as he and Betty followed the humans out into the warm summer evening. "We still need to find out who you belong to."

Chapter Sixteen

"Do you think Betty has any idea that she's in Merivelle because we guided her?"

"Absolutely none, the little rascal." Josephine smiled as her eyes glimmered in delight. "She has the mind of most humans. She thinks she did it all on her own."

Lea looked down and focused on the small Kansas town. "Midsummer always seems to come with a bit of mischief on Earth. Are you sure that's the best spot for Betty?"

"The absolute best for everyone involved."

Chapter Seventeen

Merivelle's city park was brimming with traffic. Vehicles were bumper-to-bumper, the majority with windows down as passengers in cars spoke to people walking up on the sidewalk parallel to the road leading to the entry gate where a woman handed out parking tickets for entry. Words of familiarity floated through the air as the evening light gave everyone present a dreamy, soft hue as they walked through particles of dust dancing in the rays of the setting summer sun on the longest day of the year.

"We should have parked and walked," Theodore said, eyeing the rear-view mirror before glancing ahead at the long line of waiting cars and trucks. "We might not get there before sunset. Then you'll miss out on all the fun."

"I'm too tired for fun," Mary said, eyes glued to her laptop. "And I have a ton of work to do before Clay's people show up tomorrow."

"There's no way you can work on that later? I haven't seen you all week. And neither has Bear."

"Nor have I," Riven added from the backseat. "If you

twisted my arm not to take my own truck, the least you can do is talk to us."

"Look how still I'm being, Bear. It's hard, but I'm doing it." Betty's bottom jiggled in place, the suggestion of staying still more than her small body could handle.

Mary closed her laptop. "What do you want to talk about?"

"Let's gets back to Riven," Theodore said. "He doesn't like Cybil's nephew."

"How do you *not* like someone you just met?" Mary asked.

"It's a feeling that comes over you," Betty said, nodding knowingly. "Instinct. Right, Bear?"

Pointedly ignoring her, Bear turned his attention to the humans talking.

Riven cleared his throat. "This has nothing to do with liking someone. It's more important than that."

"How's that?" Mary asked, raising an eyebrow.

"We have to be more careful where Cybil's concerned. She would have burned her house down if Bear hadn't alerted us when we took her coffee this morning. Right, Theodore?"

"You are such a good boy!" Betty barked, then shrunk back when Bear growled.

"Cybil's fire was *this morning*?" Mary asked, rubbing her temples. "This certainly feels like the longest day of the year." She stopped for a moment. "Wouldn't it be a good thing if she had Gavin there to keep an eye on things?"

"Cybil's house is filled with all kinds of valuable things. Art, antiques, collectibles," Riven answered. "And apparently, a lot of money."

"Money?"

Waving at a passerby pushing a stroller as their spouse pulled a wagon with two other children, Theodore looked at Mary. "She had piles of money strewn everywhere. When did that start?"

Mary wrinkled her forehead. "I've only recently noticed that her house has become cluttered. Things she can't seem to throw away for whatever reason. But money everywhere? I don't recall that."

"When we asked her about it, she matter-of-factly grabbed the money and shoved it in a book, putting it on a shelf. She may have a small fortune stashed in her reading library," Theodore said, drumming his fingers on the steering wheel.

"That money should be safe in a bank." Riven leaned up between the two front seats. "I feel we should monitor her. Not hand over her house keys to a nephew we don't know."

"I guess I was stuck on the fact that Cybil finally had a relative to visit her. I wish my mom was here to ask." Mary turned in her seat and looked at Riven. "Do you remember anyone visiting Cybil before I came home to Merivelle?"

"Both she and Honey were new teachers at the high school, when Katie's mom and I were graduating. At that age, you don't think to ask a lot about your teachers. Even with a few years' age difference. And I guess after that, I didn't really pay attention. I wish had though."

"Can you smell all the book scents when he talks, Bear? He sure has a lot of stories." Betty closed her eyes as Riven chuckled and scratched her head.

Mary took a deep breath, a concerned look on her face. "What do you think we should do? Tell Gavin to get lost? Make him provide a birth certificate? That's not very Bear Bailey-like. We forgive, move on and include."

"With all due respect to what you and Bear have accomplished, Mary. Sometimes you can't let a strength become a weakness. Maybe Riven's right," Theodore said.

The old man put his arm around the bigger dog. "I realize the hypocrisy of this coming from me when I've been the on the receiving end of extraordinary kindness and undeserved forgiveness."

"Riven," Mary said, exchanging glances with her husband. "We believe you. But we aren't sure how to proceed without possibly alienating the one family member we can remember coming to visit Cybil."

Theodore continued to drive the truck forward, inch by inch, until they were one vehicle away from the gate. "We'll keep an eye, Riven."

"I could be wrong."

"You have good instincts on most things," Mary said. "Like your idea years ago when you brought Henry back to Katie at the co-op with one of your ties around his neck. Remember that?"

Riven leaned forward.

"You told me to stock dog collars and leashes," Mary said, a smile on her face as she turned around and hit Riven's knee gently. "Do you have any idea how much we're able to donate to the local shelter?"

"An off-hand comment from me that *you* turned into a reality."

"We'll argue that point another time, but for now—know that we trust your instinct. We also need to be open until Gavin's actions show us otherwise."

"It's a good lesson for all of us. Trust in the goodness of people you don't know," Theodore said, pulling the truck up to the gate attendant and smiling. "How are you tonight?"

"Five dollars," the woman said, yawning.

Searching through his wallet, Theodore passed a twenty-dollar bill to the woman. A gust of wind blew the money out of her outstretched hand and into the walking crowd.

"That was on you! I didn't have a good hold on it!" The

woman's tone was accusing. "You should have been paying better attention instead of talking!"

Everyone in the truck watched as a man reached down and picked up the paper bill.

Riven and Theodore locked eyes as the man contemplated his find. He looked behind each of his shoulders and then put the money in his pocket before walking away quickly. Theodore groaned as he threw his hands up in defeat.

Mary grabbed her purse, handing over more money. Theodore took the five-dollar bill from his wife as he glanced back into his rearview mirror.

Riven raised his eyebrows. "Go ahead—you were telling me about the goodness of strangers."

Chapter Eighteen

Once the sun had set for the evening, Steven's Park came alive with music and dancing. Many Merivellians had specifically dressed for the occasion of celebrating the summer solstice, wearing colorful clothing more akin to costumes as they danced under the tall city lights flickering on at twilight. In the middle of the park, rows of benches sat in front of an impressive band-shell. Over the years, the space had been used for nearly every holiday, school band and orchestra performances and other Merivelle celebrations. Children frolicked at the edge of the stage, lost in their own playful imaginations.

Behind the rows of seating, families laid out picnics on the lush summer grass. A handful of food vendors had come to the event, the lines in front of their concessions overflowing with children dancing in place as they waited their turn for snow cones and ice cream.

Seated on the large blanket Mary always carried in the back seat of her truck, Theodore opened the cooler he'd packed. Merivelle orchestra members filled the stage chairs, instruments in hand, as the playing children scurried off to their families.

"Here, you need to eat, Riven." Mary placed a sandwich and chips on a paper plate. "You're even more pale than back at the house."

"Maybe that's why you're grumpy with the new guy," Theodore said.

"I am a little woozy, truth be told," Riven said, nodding his thanks as he took the plate of food.

"Do you want to sit on a bench closer to the stage?" Theodore asked. "You wouldn't have to get up and down off the ground during the evening."

"I can stay here with the dogs," Mary offered.

"You two forget my yoga. It comes in handy for times like this," Riven said, crossing his legs and lowering down with one hand balancing a plate and the other reaching for the ground. Once seated, he looked up. "Alicia always says there's nothing I can't do if I put my mind to it."

The orchestra began to warm up. First, small plucks on the strings of violins, violas and cellos, followed by the horn and percussion sections. The sound of the collective instruments filled the air as a conductor in costume walked onto the stage to applause and cheers.

"Must everyone look like they dressed out of a thrift-store, grab bag?" Riven asked. "Why does the conductor look like a tree from a grade school play?"

A wiffle ball hit Riven on the knee. A diminutive girl, dressed as a ballet fairy, ran to the blanket, stopping short when she saw where the ball landed. Her eyes were wide as she gave a small shriek.

Riven reached over to grab the ball, holding it up. "Is this yours, sweetheart?" He tossed it to her in a gentle manner.

"Thank you!" the girl said, barely above a whisper, catching the ball and running away.

"Why was she so scared?"

"Maybe the fact that you were being grumpy with everyone's clothes," Mary said, raising an eyebrow. "And she'd clearly dressed up for the occasion."

"Well, you never answered my question. Why *does* everyone look odd?"

"They're fairies—for Midsummer," Mary answered. "It's one of the key elements to the celebration."

A look of understanding crossed Riven's face. "The girls near Violet's age make sense." He scowled again. "But what about the others—why are they dressed so weird?"

"For the summer solstice celebration. Bright colors, funny glasses and headgear. I don't think that's much different from other places around the world that celebrate the longest twenty-four hours of the year."

Riven pulled some turkey out of his sandwich and fed it to Bear, extracting an equal amount for Betty before he shook his head with a look of contriteness. "Sometimes I seem sterner than I mean to."

Mary looked behind him and waved. "Cybil's here with her nephew."

Groaning, Riven closed his eyes.

Bear put a paw on the old man's shoulder and nodded. Betty ran around him in circles as she barked excitedly.

"Can the new dog stop yipping?" Riven asked, though his voice was not unkind.

Turning, Bear lightly growled in warning at Betty.

"Sorry, Bear. I'm really trying. I don't know how you sit still with all this energy all around us. You can hear it, smell it, see—"

"Yes—all the things a dog senses. I get it," Bear replied, watching the crowd.

Every few feet, people stopped Cybil, hugging her and meeting Gavin. Slowly, they attempted to make their way through the crowd with Cybil pointing toward Mary and the others as her intended destination.

"Can we talk about how weird *A Midsummer Night's Dream* actually is?" Theodore asked as they waited. "I'm no English major, but I remember in a random class some weird conversation between the King and Queen of the Fairies—I forget her name."

"Titania," Mary said, smiling.

"And Obearon."

Betty wagged her stubby tail in glee. "Bear, that was going to be your name when you first arrived in Merivelle! King Obearon! Until Theodore said it would be silly, since Mary was going to call you Bear for short anyway."

Bear's face relaxed into amusement. "You really know that?"

"I love every one of your stories, Bear!"

"Theodore, remember there's no *Obearon* in *A Midsummer Night's Dream*," Mary said, laughing. "That was me tweaking the character's name to be clever for Bear. Remember?"

"Their names don't really matter to me," Theodore said, shrugging. "But why were they fighting over who got to raise the Indian boy?"

"Don't look at me," Riven said, staring at his half-eaten sandwich. "I'm no literary scholar."

"You want the long explanation or the Cliff Notes version, honey?"

"I'll give you one guess," Riven said, snorting.

Mary nodded. "The Indian boy was a changeling."

Holding one finger up, Theodore asked, "You're telling me that Shakespeare knew about American Indian tribes?"

"Seriously, Theodore?" Mary asked, putting her hands to her cheeks. "Of course not. Shakespeare said the boy was from India. I don't know that he would have even known about the culture. The important part of the story is who gets to love a child and why."

"Sorry for asking," Theodore said. "I was just confused."

"Titania wanted to raise the boy as a real testament to her love for his mother, who died giving birth to him. Her motives were kindness and protection."

"What about Oberon?" Riven asked.

Clearly pleased at the old man's interest, Mary continued. "Oberon wanted the boy to be a servant in his court. But mostly because he felt excluded by Titania's affections for the boy. Power and pride motivated him. One boy—two different motives where his upbringing was concerned."

"That's the play? An arguing couple?" Theodore asked, yawning.

"The subsequent fallout between the pair caused chaos in the natural world. Seasons are thrown off, animals act strangely and humans suffer." Mary looked up at the sky beginning to darken behind cumulus clouds as dots of stars appeared in the expanse. "The whole world fell apart because two magical beings couldn't decide who should raise a child."

Betty looked at Bear with her mouth wide open. "Is everyone in Merivelle an excellent storyteller? I love this place."

"Well, thanks for clearing all that up," Theodore said. "So that I'm sure to use that information never again for anything in my entire life."

Riven was quiet. "I appreciate the knowledge, Mary. Two

people, two different motives with raising a child, causing chaos to those around them. Good to remember."

"Thank you, *Riven*," she said, shaking her head at her husband good-naturedly.

Cybil had slowly made her way to the blanket, Gavin in tow. "We lost Pavi somewhere on our way in. That kid is friends with everyone."

"Sit down, sit down," Mary said, before hitting her palm to her forehead. "I should have brought you a fold-up chair, Cybil."

"Pavi told us your news, Mary. As if you had a spare moment with my *Ms. Barnes*, the co-op and the rest of Merivelle. Now you added a few country music video shoots." Cybil beamed at her former student.

Gavin extended an elbow to Cybil, lowering her to the ground in a gentle manner.

At the gesture, Theodore whispered to Riven. "*Helpful.*"

"You have a seat here, Gavin. Riven will scoot over," Mary said. "And so will both dogs," she laughed, rearranging the food and drinks.

Gavin looked down at everyone already on the blanket. "I I don't want to b-bother. I'll stand for a few minutes."

The orchestra warmed up, playing runs of notes. A slight breeze blew into the area, ruffling the pages of music in front of the musicians. The conductor held up her arms, vines dangling down as laughter filled the area. She tapped the music stand in front of her. The entire area was suspended in a quiet hush of waiting. Four distinct chords from the woodwinds section played.

Gavin knelt down, turning to Cybil. "M-mysterious, building expectation."

Cybil beamed, nodding her head.

"Your sm-small-town orchestra plays Felix Mendelssohn?"

"They've been practicing his *A Midsummer Night's Dream* overture since spring," Cybil answered. "I could hear the music at my house."

"There's m-more going on in Merivelle than meets the eyes," Gavin said as the music picked up tempo with children dancing around like swirling fairies. "M-mind if I get a closer view of the orchestra?" He reached down to readjust the shawl that had fallen off Cybil's shoulders.

"Oh, look!" Theodore said, waving. "Here's Donkey! With Anna and the kids." He looked at Gavin. "Our town sheriff. One of Mary's best friends from childhood."

"Theodore, I already told you that Gavin met Donkey down at the train station. Remember?"

"Are you sure you don't want to stay and eat?" Cybil asked, gesturing to the food. "You barely ate at home."

"I-I think I'll walk." Gavin looked down at everyone already on the blanket. "It'll give you more room. Unless you need any-anything, Cybil?"

"I'm fine. Among friends and ready for the magic of Midsummer to begin the season. You have fun. Go meet new people."

Making his way down the aisle, Gavin politely moved through the crowd to sit in one of the front rows near the stage.

"I love how he fusses over you," Mary said, turning to Cybil.

Cybil smiled, her face one of contentment. "I'm sure you've heard about this morning's jam incident. Gavin saw the pan soaking, scoured it and got it nice and shiny again. I was afraid I was going to have to throw it away. But he said it's important not to forget old things—most only need extra time and attention to be useful again."

"*What a jerk,*" Theodore whispered to Riven, stifling a laugh.

92

"He also told me the money I have all over the place would be safer somewhere else. Especially considering my proclivity to burning things. He's taking me to the bank tomorrow." Cybil chuckled, shaking her head. "You get used to silly habits every day and forget. That's why Honey and I got along so well. She took care of financial matters and let me paint and create."

Mary thought for a moment. "Is Gavin from her side of the family?"

"Enough about me," Cybil said, reaching forward on the blanket to pat Mary's foot. "Tell me all about the new people coming to town." The music swelled and drifted onto the breeze and into Merivelle. "Your mom would be over the moon with all you're trying to accomplish."

Chapter Nineteen

A short time before sunrise the next morning, a line of semi-trucks made their way into town. Merivelle was no stranger to large trucks and trailers passing through and around the city each day—the noise of squeaky axles and straining loads long ago becoming daily background noise. But this convoy differed from the manure-stained, livestock trailers or tarped, over-flowing beds carrying harvested wheat to be weighed at the grain elevator. These were white and shiny—impressive stallions among plow horses. And although they were unlettered, with no logos giving a clue to their identity, the mirror-like, decorative, gleaming chrome gave a hint that something exciting and out of the ordinary had arrived.

Mary stood at the edge of town, both dogs by her side with Donkey. All waited in the early morning light on the frontage road of an old gas station plaza just north of the city. The multi-acre property stood abandoned, a victim at the crossroads of an ambitious growth vision for Merivelle intersecting with constructions delays and dried up financial loans. Random sunflowers and grass pushed through the spiderweb cracks of the concrete parking lot. Over parts of two decades, the summer winds, often giving way to tornadic downdrafts, pulled away the metal roof above what would have been rows and rows of gas pumps that had never been installed. Instead, the concrete pedestal footings in which they were to sit became not unlike gravestones, marking the death of a dream for the area. A spotted snake slithered onto one of the end curbs, seeking any remaining warmth from the day before.

"Thank you, Donkey," Mary said, her face child-like in excitement. "We couldn't have done this without all your help."

"You're the one who ran all the permits through town. All the meetings and mountains of paperwork you must have worked through."

"That part is all Katie. Thank goodness for remote working. Sometimes, I forget she's not here in Merivelle with me every day."

"Still, I saw you running back and forth between the co-op and the courthouse a hundred times over the past six months," Donkey said. He nodded to the first driver entering the space, directing him to one of his deputies at the opposite end of the plaza. "How did you keep this quiet? The town won't know what to do when it wakes up."

"Lots and lots of signed NDAs," Mary said, laughing. "You know, I didn't even tell Theodore until yesterday."

Betty turned her head in question. "What's an NDA?"

"*Never discuss anything,*" Bear said solemnly. "I know that from living with an attorney."

"I don't know how I know. But I don't think that means what you think it means, Bear."

"*No dogs allowed?*"

"You're so silly," Betty said, laying on her back laughing. "I just love you, Bear!"

Donkey walked backwards as more trucks turned into the

lot. They drove slowly around the abandoned convenience store centered on the property and towards the back parking lots, once constructed in anticipation of nightly armies of truckers sleeping in their cabs before continuing on their journeys. "How'd Theodore take that? He sure loves to be the first person to hear news."

"You know Theodore. He's a chatterbox down at the diner, but where work is concerned, he respects confidentiality." Mary stroked Bear's head as he surveyed the activities with her.

The Great Pyrenees nodded to the smaller dog, a solemn look on his face. "Stay back behind me. You're getting too close to the vehicles."

Betty barked and spun in circles. "I can't believe I'm here in the middle of everything with you, Bear!"

Looking down with a charmed look on his face, Donkey asked, "The Aussie still hasn't found her owner?"

"Everyone thought she was adorable at Midsummer last night, but not one person came forward to claim her. I thought for sure a farmer in the area had lost her."

"I wonder where she came from?" Donkey said, motioning another truck forward.

"I dropped from the sky," Betty said. "Like Jiff."

"It feels like she literally dropped from the sky," Mary said, laughing.

"Hey! I just said that! Isn't that funny how humans repeat what we're saying sometimes? At the same moment, Bear?"

"Settle down. It was a coincidence."

"Josephine says there's no such thing as a coincidence."

Bear's head snapped. "Who?"

"Josephine, who oversees the Rainbow Bridge. She says coincidences are great love and miracles coming together. You wouldn't know that because you were—still are—on Earth. But

I tell you when Lea gets to that part of Jiff's story, there's not a dry eye in the whole Golden Meadow."

"Where is Jiff now?"

"With his owner from when they were both young. A nice man named Franklin."

Bear barked, running around Mary and Donkey as they tried to talk while directing traffic.

"He gets the zoomies at the strangest times," Mary said, laughing as she stepped around the dogs. "Sorry, Donkey. Go on about the overnight parking and security."

Bear suddenly stopped. "There must be more than one Franklin with a dog on the Bridge though."

"Oh, no," Betty said, sitting down as she looked up at Bear in a solemn manner. "On the Rainbow Bridge, Jiff is a black Labrador, and Franklin is—"

"You have the wrong dog and human."

"No, that's the thing, Bear. Beyond the Rainbow Bridge, each soul gets to decide at any moment how they want to spend time. Sometimes when Franklin comes to visit us on the Rainbow Bridge—" she paused, adjusting her tone to one with extra, special information to be shared. "—*because Franklin loves bridges.*"

"Franklin *doesn't* love bridges or deep water. It's one of the reasons he came to live in Kansas."

"Yes, when he was a boy and almost drowned. Until his loyal Labrador saved him." Betty jumped around in celebration before stopping, a serene look on her face. "In Heaven, all fears transform into something happy."

"No Dark Dens?" Bear shuddered before he sat up and looked around. "You probably don't know what that is. And I don't want to scare you. You're still a puppy."

"*Dark Dens.* I already know from your stories that Lea tells us. Everyone has their own Dark Den. A place their brain goes to when it's not occupied. It's why some dogs chew drywall and destroy furniture. Or they run away instead of sitting still and enjoying the love of their family. Dark Dens. When our brains show us things that may or may not be there. Then our imagination gets the zoomies."

"Yes," Bear said, blinking rapidly. "It's the worst thing when it happens."

"Like I said, there are no Dark Dens on the Rainbow Bridge, Bear. Nothing for any dog to be worried about. That's an Earth thing."

Bear took a deep breath, trying to calm himself. "Go on then with what you were saying."

"Well, some days Franklin comes to us as a young boy with a black dog and other days he shows up as an old man with a corgi."

"But how do you know it's Franklin and Jiff? If they're changing all the time?"

"Dog souls know, Bear. We see with our hearts on the Rainbow Bridge. And if you don't let Dark Dens get the best of you, you can do the same here on Earth. Open eyes and wide hearts can work miracles."

"You're very convincing," Bear said. "But maybe you use your imagination for stories, picked up from fragments you've heard from humans talking. A person can weave quite a tale, putting together puzzle pieces here and there."

"I wish there was some way for you to know," Betty said, turning her head. "I feel we could be much better friends if you believed me."

After directing the almost dozen gleaming semis with their trailers into the area, Mary and Donkey walked with the dogs to the front of the property's entrance as other patrol cars accompanying the caravan followed them through. The last vehicle paused as a pair of officers jumped out to close the giant steel gate, their patrol car parked against the width of the drive to deter any interlopers.

"Are you ready for the biggest week of your life?" Donkey nudged Mary with his shoulder. "Who would have thought when we were kids that we'd be standing here today trying to buoy the town you tried so desperately to leave?"

"I think it might be the very nature of dreams to take detours and wrong turns. Before you end up where you were supposed to be all along," Mary said, smiling.

"That gave me goosebumps," Betty said, her eyes wide in wonder. "Even if I don't understand exactly what Mary meant."

"Dreams don't always walk in straight lines. But the good ones bring you home," Bear said, gazing at the eastern sky.

Watching her dog's rapt attention on the horizon, Mary noted the imminently rising sun as she spoke to Donkey. "A new dawn. A new day."

Behind the humans, Betty also looked at the sky. "Daybreak," she said. "When all the dogs who left their owners on Earth the previous day return to the Bridge in the morning rays and then—" She opened her mouth to continue, before disappearing into thin air in front of the incredulous Great Pyrenees.

Chapter Twenty

Betty waited patiently as all the dogs arriving on the Bridge that morning ran to their humans. Joyous barking and humans' laughing filled the air. Putting her nose to the air, she breathed in. Every imaginable smell filled the air. Bacon, flowers, peanut butter, ice cream pup cups, candied apples and more mingled together in an olfactory symphony. On Earth, the aromas might have given humans pause if inhaled all at once—too overpowering for one moment. But on the expanse of the Rainbow Bridge, the scent was divine.

After Josephine answered all the humans' questions and helped them make their way through the Golden Meadow, she walked to the small Aussie sitting by herself.

Betty stared at Josephine with wide eyes. "I know I'm in trouble for sneaking to Earth."

"No dog is ever in trouble on the Rainbow Bridge."

"But I wasn't supposed to leave."

The next instant Lea appeared, a line of dogs behind her, barking with great enthusiasm as she was unraveling a long string of hot dog links to distribute—a way to keep their mind busy since their own humans hadn't crossed the Bridge with the sunrise. "Betty, you only leave if we allow it."

Betty looked between the two angels, a relieved smile on her face. "Really?"

Josephine nodded. "We thought it would be easier for you to finally go to Earth if you imagined it was your own idea. It was an overnight pass, so to speak."

"*Technically*, I wasn't a bad dog?"

Both angels laughed.

"It didn't go on my record?"

"We don't keep records here on the Rainbow Bridge," Lea said.

"In that case, could I still go back to Earth?" Betty asked, wiggling in anticipation.

"We should probably return you to Gheeta and Butterfly Academy. Remember the man that wants you for his lonely daughter?" Josephine asked.

Betty turned and looked down at Earth with a sentimental expression. "I feel I should be in Merivelle—Mary seems so busy. Cybil has a new guest who came to visit from nowhere. Pavi and his mom are working hard at the co-op. And then there's Riven. He's trying to help wherever he's needed. At first, I didn't think I'd like him. But if you sit next to him, he smells like leather and books." Betty paused, shaking her head. "But there's also another smell near Riven's chest. Bear's really concerned about it."

"It definitely sounds like Merivelle's humans could use the extra help," Josephine said as Lea nodded in agreement.

Betty sat up, her paw in the air as if she were ready to take a vow. "Then send me back. I'll assist anyone who crosses my path."

"Don't forget to lean in and listen," Josephine said. "Like our good friend, Bear."

Clearing her throat, Betty looked at the angels. "I have two tiny requests."

"Go ahead," Josephine said, the glimmers around her dancing playfully.

"Do you think when I go to Earth, you could arrange it so that I could read?"

"You mean the ability to read all the signs we send to humans? So they know we're watching over them in Heaven?"

Betty shook her head at Josephine. "I already know how to read those signs—all heavenly souls do. Only humans don't put together when a certain song plays on their radio or they happen across a coin on their path."

"Some humans read the signs," Lea said, reaching for a feather blowing in the breeze. "But it's very rare."

"But that's not what I mean. I'm asking if I can read on Earth like humans do. You know—*words*." She barked happily. "I just love stories."

"A dog who reads? That might scare the humans," Josephine said. "Give me a moment to think this situation through."

"What about reading to Bear? His imagination gets carried away. I could help him the same way Lea's stories calm all the dogs on the Bridge."

"Well, when you put it that way, I can see where the skill might be very helpful."

"That's an exceptional gift to bequeath to a canine," Lea said. "Betty would have to be extraordinarily well-behaved."

Betty sat up on her bottom and put her front paws together, looking up at the angels with pleading eyes.

"Very well then," Josephine said, the shimmering lights around her expanding through the meadow with the morning light. She reached out and put her hands on the dog's head before booping her nose. "Now you can read."

"Just like that? I don't want to get to Earth and have a glitch."

Swirling her hands in the air, Josephine traced out letters from the clouds above Betty's head.

Betty turned her head as she peered at the words appearing one by one until they formed a sentence. *"Help everyone you meet?"* she asked, a questioning look on her face.

"It's a statement. Not a question."

"Of course," Betty said, sitting up with a serious look on her face. "Can we try another one?"

Josephine held her hands up again, this time producing words in much quicker succession.

Betty recited the words as the angel wrote. *"Don't make trouble for the humans. Be kind when possible—it's always possible."*

"I think she already has the hang of it." Lea smiled, reaching down to pet the Aussie as Josephine continued writing in the sky.

"You need to return at twilight on the Fourth of July." Betty groaned in exasperation. "Why?"

"Let's steer you away from fireworks until next year," Lea said, redirecting Betty's attention to the other angel's next words.

"And don't forget to give Bear a hug from his old friend Josephine." Betty barked in excitement. "Bear will love that! But don't forget I have one more—"

The ground under Betty parted as her eyes grew wide before she disappeared beneath the clouds. Her laughter echoed throughout the entire Rainbow Bridge.

"What just happened?" Lea asked.

"It was her next request," Josephine said, smiling. "A slide right down to Earth."

Chapter Twenty-One

Riven unlocked the front door from inside of Bear Bailey's Co-op and Grocery and looked down through the glass.

Sitting at the entry of the store, Betty was blinking rapidly, studying the store's sign.

Opening the door, Riven looked around the street. "Where's Bear and Mary? Are you hurt?" He knelt, examining Betty from head to toe before wincing as he stood again. "No injuries that I can see."

Betty placed a foot on Riven's shoe to steady herself and panted.

"But you seem parched," Riven said, taking a few steps into the store. A bowl of water for visiting dogs sat right around the corner by *Ms. Barnes*. He picked it up, delivering it to Betty. "Here you go, girl."

After she drank nearly the entire bowl, Betty licked Riven's hand, wagging her tail in appreciation.

Propping open the double doors of the store, Riven chuckled. "It seems you've already been on quite a journey and the day's just started. Let's get you fed and then I'd love to hear your story."

"Riven Chapowits. Who on earth are you talking to?" Cybil was standing in the doorway, her hand on Gavin's arm.

Riven gestured at Betty, a slightly embarrassed look on his face.

"You old softie," Cybil replied, smiling. "Chatting to dogs like they're humans. Who would have ever thought such a scene would happen?"

Betty stood on her back legs, reaching up to Cybil as she tip-toed in place. She sniffed in Gavin's direction as he extended his hand in a gentle manner.

"I've always had good instinct where students are concerned. And this puppy seems very smart," Cybil said. "Let's see what she can do." She held a hand up. "Sit!"

Betty dropped her behind to the ground.

"Lay down." Cybil smiled at the dog's immediate obedience. "Let's try a few others." In under a minute's time, Betty shook hands, spun around, played dead, and barked when instructed to *speak*. Cybil looked at the two men. "Where in heaven's name did this dog come from? She's remarkable. I wouldn't be surprised if she could read."

Betty barked excitedly, spinning in circles.

"You deserve some of the bacon I brought for you and your friend, Bear." Reaching into his pocket, Riven pulled out a small plastic bag, giving the dog a hefty morsel.

"Where is Mary?" Cybil asked.

"She was getting a caravan of trucks situated before sunrise. Then she's giving a tour of the area to the production crew before they begin filming. I'm watching over Bear Bailey's, so Lupe's free to cater food on-site."

"That's a lot for you to handle," Cybil answered, putting

her purse down behind the counter of her booth. "You might have to find your own Gavin."

"H-happy to pitch in and help Riven any way I could," Gavin said, swallowing hard.

"I'm fine," Riven answered, almost brusquely. "Just need to get through this next week. Help Mary's big dream come true."

Gavin produced a chair that Cybil stored at the back of her booth for longer days, unfolding it and placing it in front of her. "You r-rest. I can unload the inventory fr-from your house. You can point where you want things."

Riven watched the pair closely. "Gavin, I can't shake the feeling that you and I have met before."

Opening his mouth a few times to speak, Gavin shook his head and tried again. "N-no idea."

Tilting her head, Betty went to the front door and whined.

The sound of a truck engine and a Great Pyrenees bark interrupted the conversation. Leaving her vehicle running, Mary opened her door to let Bear jump down as both ran into the store. Seeing the little dog inside, she stopped. "We've been searching all over for you, Betty!"

"She was here when I opened the front door this morning," Riven said.

"How did she make it into town before me?" Mary asked, over her shoulder as she ran toward her office at the back of the co-op.

Bear walked over to sniff Betty. "What happened?"

"Josephine dropped me here. I guess she wants me to be at the co-op helping."

"You've been back and forth from the Rainbow Bridge in the past hour?" Bear asked, his tone incredulous.

"Time works different on the Bridge than here," Betty said, clearing her throat in excitement. "And now I can read here on Earth!"

"All dogs on Earth can read."

"That's not what Josephine said, Bear."

"G-O. Mary spells it out all the time to Theodore, when she's trying to sneak into town without me."

"That's only two letters, Bear."

Bear puffed out his chest. "T-R-E-A-T."

"All dogs know how to spell that word. They teach us at Butterfly Academy."

"Well then, show me how you can read and spell better."

Betty's eyes focused on the back wall and the logo that Cybil had painted years before. "*Bear Bailey's.*"

"Too easy," Bear replied, acknowledging the giant likeness of himself. "Everyone knows those words spell my name."

"What about the smaller words underneath?"

Bear squinted.

"Go on."

"Bear Bailey's—*Mary's Best Friend.*"

Betty closed her eyes and laughed. "It spells, *Co-op and Grocery.*"

Returning to the front of the store, Mary held paperwork in her hand.

"Why don't you try reading the paper that Mary's holding?" Bear asked.

Betty put her nose a few inches from the piece of paper. Studying the words, she began reading.

"Clay Overstreet Video Shoot Locations—Arkansas River, Merivelle Train Depot, Bear Bailey's and Steven's Park Bandshell. Video shoots should last no more than two days, each with possible overlap, pending capability to move sets. In keeping with the narrative storytelling of Clay's vision for his next yet-to-be named album, videos will be recorded in order, the final being at Steven's Park."

Bear looked down at the eager dog, shaking in anticipation of his approval. "I believe you, Betty. That's a pretty neat thing you can do."

"I'll read to you when you have Dark Den moments. It really helps all the dogs on the Rainbow Bridge when Lea tells them stories while they wait for their owners to cross over."

"I don't want to think about dogs separated from their owners." Bear groaned as he pulled himself up off the floor and walked to Mary's side.

"I have another huge favor to ask you, Riven." Mary looked at her watch.

"I'm here for you. Whatever you need."

"Bear's already panting, and it's not even ten o'clock. I'm running back and forth between trailers on the concrete pad out at the old travel plaza. I'm afraid he's going to overheat. He's used to the sandy ground and grass at the house."

"Are you okay?" Betty asked. "It gets hot here pretty quick in the summer."

"I need to be with Mary. She needs me to help her keep track of things."

"It's okay to take a break sometimes," Betty said. "Let other people help you."

"Bear's always welcome in his own store," Riven answered. "I'd be happy to watch him."

"Thank you, Riven," Mary said, holding the paperwork by her side. She looked at Cybil and smiled. "You're here bright and early."

"We've already been to the bank and made a deposit. Now we're going to get to work on my stall."

"Why don't we take a pause with all things money and possessions," Riven said. "You certainly jumped in full throttle on your first day."

"Of course," Gavin said, clearing his throat. "I just wanted to h-help."

"Don't mind, Riven." Mary walked towards the door. "He's actually a rough, tough cream puff."

"Ask around town. Plenty of old enemies." Riven raised an eyebrow at the younger man. "I don't think anyone would want to cross me or one of my friends."

"Let's guide Riven to the back of the store for a bit. His chest has that smell again when he's talking," Bear said.

Mary's phone rang. She answered it, listening while she nodded her head. "Happy to pick them up. I'm leaving now."

Chapter Twenty-Two

Watching from inside Merivelle's small airport waiting lounge, Mary scanned the runway through the large windows. A regional hub for air traffic, the one-room terminal had a single gate inside, used for both arrivals and departures. A lone security lane was situated beside one wall, the opposite side of the building lined with vending machines with rows of seating for waiting passengers in between. In addition to regional commercial flights, a surprising number of private planes landed daily, almost always associated with agricultural business. A Grammy-winning country music star getting off a plane was a rare exception. Two employees watched in frozen amazement as the man shook Mary's extended hand before the pair exited to the parking lot.

"I hope you didn't go too far out of your way. Most of the time, the easiest way for me not to disturb is to sneak in with no fanfare," Clay Overstreet said, standing outside Mary's truck.

"Let me assure you, there are texts and phone calls going on inside right now." She unlocked the vehicle and sighed. "And somehow, despite all our best efforts with NDAs, a

Kansas City outlet broke the news that you were headed this way."

Clay opened the door and got in, pulling his seatbelt on. "Can I be honest?"

Mary nodded as she started the engine.

"The article was from my publicist. Looks like a leak but still gets word out. Good promotion for the tour dates I need to makeup when I'm done in Merivelle."

"That saves me all kinds of rehearsed apologies and explanations why there's a small army of people with Clay Overstreet signs parked out on the highway across from the travel plaza with all your tour trucks."

"Never complain, never explain. I have full trust in you, Mary Bailey. Otherwise, I wouldn't be here," Clay said, swatting at white hairs floating in the air. "Appreciate the ride."

Mary reached over to the glove box and produced a lint roller. "We'll see if you still feel that way after you get out of the truck with a thick coat of Great Pyrenees hair."

"No need. I always say you can tell a lot about a person by the amount of dog hair they have on them."

"We're going to get along fine then," Mary said, putting the item back before she began driving. "Sorry about my old truck. I was the closest one to the airport and didn't have time to detail it. Surely, you're used to much more extravagant vehicles."

"I prefer low-key vehicles. Sometimes the more battered, the better."

Mary put on her sunglasses, turning her head in question.

"People expect fancy with famous. An old truck and people are none the wiser. I can get right to work doing what I love."

"The best place to hide something is in plain sight."

"Did you just come up with that?

"I did not. A Sherlock Holmes quote, maybe?"

"Percy told me about Merivelle and everyone's love of learning. My entire crew has already signed up to learn a new word of the day in anticipation of meeting Lupe. We're bantering around words like *Brobdingnagian*."

"Huge size, gigantic, tremendous," Mary replied, smiling. "Always spelled with a capital B."

"I just know the word. What does it even mean?"

"It's an imaginary country from *Gulliver's Travels*. Based on Jonathan Swift's disbelief in some of the era's travel journals. Explorers went off, came home and brought tales from lands that were unverifiable."

"You talk like a polyhistor."

"Last Wednesday's *Word of the Day*," Mary said, smiling as she put her blinker on when they came to a four-way stop. "You have to meet our town's teacher. Cybil taught the older generations of Merivelle and still fills us in on almost everything there is to know."

"I've heard about Cybil from Katie. You both sound very close to her. Almost like family."

"*Better than family* is what another old friend used to say," Mary said, nodding in agreement. "Truth be told, I've been so busy with the project at hand, I've lost track of Cybil. She has a booth at the co-op. She's like everyone's aunt. You'll love her."

"I'm sure I will," Clay said, as he studied the horizon as they drove. "Funny how the same state can be so different. Even though it's flat, it sure is pretty out here in the middle of nowhere."

"The dust and open views will knock your socks off at the beginning and end of each day. There's nothing like a western Kansas sky at sunrise and sunset." Mary's phone rang. She looked down as Theodore's name appeared on the screen for a moment before it disappeared.

112

"You can take the call. I'll sit here and hum while I think," Clay said, watching the landscape.

"He must have got another call." Mary smiled as she gripped the steering wheel with both hands. "My husband, Theodore, has been counting the days to meet you."

"I'm excited to meet Percy's buddy and your dog too." He nodded at the mostly dried-up bank as they crossed a bridge. "What happened to all the water?"

"The river used to be so full when we were kids, sometimes you couldn't even see the bridge we were standing on. Katie and I thought it looked like we were walking on water."

Clay drummed his fingers on the side of the door, humming for a few moments. "You know my wife and I love your cousin. It's hard to picture Katie here in Merivelle. She fits in so well in a bigger city."

"I guess that's the good thing about a well-rounded person. They seem at home anywhere they go."

"Have you two always been so close?"

Shaking her head, Mary said, "Typical teenage nonsense. I moved away and we had no opportunities to mend our childish ways. But when my mom was sick and died shortly afterwards, Katie was with me as I figured everything out. Thought I was crazy for naming the store after my dog and she still supported me."

"Yes—*Bear Bailey*. The wonderful dog who's brought the whole town together. Percy tells me stories," Clay said, humming again. "Truth be told, I've been more interested in meeting him than all the humans in town."

"Bear loves everyone. He'll be honored to meet you." Mary looked at Clay as they came within eyeshot of the production camp. "I have a small request. Concerning my husband."

Clay sat up as tall, scooting into the passenger door. "Yes, ma'am?"

"Don't act like you're more excited to see Bear than him. It hurts Theodore's feelings in the worst way." She paused for a moment. "I'm kind of kidding," she said, grinning.

"Of course. Theodore's the star when we meet. Anything else?"

"Katie's dad, Riven. He's the biggest help to me. I don't want him to feel left out with all the activity. Especially while he's filling in while I'm gone."

"I hear there's quite a story between your dog and Riven. Old enemies, new friends," he said, trailing off as he hummed, nodding his head. Lost in thought for nearly a minute as Mary drove, he finally shook his head. "A small tic of mine. I hear words and then listen for the music that follows."

Chapter Twenty-Three

A few days into Clay Overstreet's week-long video shoot, Merivelle had come alive with the pulse of celebration. Though shooting sites were cordoned off with strict security measures, Clay assured Mary that he enjoyed the small-town excitement generated with the crowds. As long as everyone maintained a noise level that didn't interrupt production, Merivellians were welcome to watch. With social media posts and hashtags giving the production a fun and approachable feel, outsiders descended from other parts of the state and beyond. Along with every other store on Main Street, Bear Bailey's foot traffic increased. Working non-stop, Riven had overseen the co-op to great effect. Pavi assisted his mom in the kitchen, where they prepared food non-stop with help from a few culinary students from the community college.

Mid-day, after a busy morning at the co-op, Riven approached the front door and flipped over the *Open* sign, much to the disappointment of a young couple and a few other people about to enter. "If you hurry, you can sneak in to look around," he said. "We're closing early for an event."

"*A Clay Overstreet event?*" A young woman in a cowboy hat asked, giggling in excitement.

Riven shrugged in a good-natured way as he rested his hand on top of Bear's head.

"I saw a piece of paper on the truck seat when Mary was driving us in this morning. The music people are going to be at the co-op this afternoon. *That's* why we're closing," Betty said, still clearly delighted at her ability to read.

The rest of the crowd inside the store had dwindled as customers paid for their goods and moved on. On the way out the door, a friendly couple stopped to greet Betty. She growled at them, narrowing her eyes as she backed up.

The Great Pyrenees put a gentle paw on Betty's shoulder. "Do you need me to talk to you about growling again? We welcome everyone here at Bear Bailey's. Strangers are only friends we haven't met yet."

Betty hung her head. "Sorry, I'm still learning."

"They look like they're having a conversation, don't they?" the woman said, laughing as she took photos of the two dogs.

"Is it like this everywhere you go?" Betty asked. "You're like a celebrity."

Bear extended his paw to the young woman as he turned to her phone and grinned.

"How do you look in the camera the way you do?"

"What are you talking about?" Bear asked, pausing as the woman moved to the other side of him to resume photos from a different angle.

Betty shuddered. "I don't know. They just freak me out. I don't even want to look at them."

"Don't be ridiculous, they're just cameras," Bear said, turning so the customers could take stickers out of his backpack before they exited the store.

"Maybe I could get a backpack like yours. I could run around and reach the people you can't."

"Sure. Let me ask Mary to order you one. What size?"

"Extra small. Maybe even a size up after all the bacon Riven's given us while he's dog-sitting."

Bear gave a heavy sigh. "Please explain to me how I would ask Mary to get you a vest."

"True," Betty said, nodding her head.

"Besides, you can't be a Bear Bailey ambassador with your attitude."

Betty's mouth fell open.

"You gotta stop growling at people. It's rude."

"I'm sorry, Bear. I think it's an old habit. From when I didn't want to come to Earth. The past few days, I really do like meeting new people."

"It's okay to feel nervous. But try your best to see the good in people. Almost everyone wants to be a kind person." Bear looked up and gazed through the store's picture windows. Mary was walking across the street, talking animatedly with people. A sizeable crowd gathered outside Bear Bailey's.

Riven also caught sight of Mary's arrival. He walked to the front of the store in anticipation of her walking through the door.

In the *Ms. Barnes* booth, Gavin was writing in a journal. Riven gazed around. "Where did Cybil go?" His sharp tone matched his expression.

Gavin froze, holding his pen in the air. "She—"

"Well?" Riven asked, leaning his heard forward.

"Cy-bil went h-home a little while ago."

"Hold on, Betty." Noting the younger man's shaking hands, Bear went to Riven and put a paw on his leg. He whined until Riven looked down at him. Getting his attention, Bear lowered his head in a soft manner, almost perfectly emulating the energy from the young man. Riven looked between the Great Pyrenees and the Gavin, nodding his head. He took a step in Gavin's direction, clearing his throat. "What are you always writing?"

"Nothing im-important."

Bear looked up at Riven, a pleading look on his face.

Riven studied the young man's face. "Why do you say it like that?"

Gavin eyed the words in the open journal. "Just th-thoughts. Nothing inspired."

"I'd imagine thoughts on paper are much better than rolling around inside a man's head."

"They're jum-jumbled words. Meant to be song lyrics. They make sense in my head, but not on paper," Gavin said, holding the journal. "Em-embarrassing if-if anyone read them."

Approaching Gavin's side, Betty studied the words, wagging her tail in excitement. "Your name is all over the pages, Bear. He really likes you a lot. Calls you the old dog."

"Old?"

"Not in a bad way." Betty peered at the pages again. "Like you're wise. With life experience. You know how to help everyone." She put her nose near the journal and began reciting what she was reading. "*He rises with the sun, rests under the stars. Carries old stories and a couple of scars. A heart full of memories, a back full of weight. He's makin' his peace with the slow hands of fate.*" Betty looked up at the Great Pyrenees, clearly moved. "Imagine those words with music, Bear."

Bear looked between Riven and the younger man, whining before going to sit beside Gavin.

"You're telling him to be kind. Look for the best. Aren't you, Bear?"

"He'll get it. It usually takes Riven a few tries. He's still learning too." Bear extended a paw to Gavin and panted.

Taking the dog's paw, Gavin held it for a moment, clearly moved by the Great Pyrenees' attention.

"Is he going to cry?" Betty asked. "He looks so appreciative. You'd think no one had offered him a kind paw of welcome before."

Without a word, Bear leaned into Gavin, calming the young man's shaking legs. He looked at Riven, waiting for the man's next words.

After several moments, Riven spoke. "I never enjoyed hearing advice from old men when I was your age. Or if I'm honest, I didn't like getting advice from anyone."

Gavin looked up from stroking Bear's fur.

"What you hide about yourself is almost always the gold that you're seeking."

Mary approached the booth, a smile on her face. "That's very poetic, Riven." She stopped, looking between the pair. "I'm sorry. Did I interrupt something?"

"Hearing some pearls," Gavin said, touching to the top of Bear's head. "Can you keep an eye on the b-booth? I'll be right back. Quick bathroom break."

"You think Gavin's okay?" Betty asked. "Should we follow him?"

"Sometimes humans need some space to sort things out," Bear replied.

Mary looked down and scratched the top of Bear's head. "Thanks for keeping track of these two, Riven. I couldn't manage this without you."

"I've been thinking about my past actions and how you're wearing yourself out to help the town. The Rural Initiative grant would have helped the downtown without you exhausting yourself for the better part of the year. You and Katie missed out. All thanks to me."

119

"Your motive was not to lose grant money for the co-op. You wanted to be close to your daughter."

"But I still caused damage. I can't act like I didn't."

"Remember Franklin," Mary said, tilting her head as she thought. "If you're assured of someone's motives, nothing they can say or do would ever hurt you."

"He used to say that?"

Mary nodded. "Here comes Gavin. I don't want you talking bad about yourself in front of other people. Head high— you're an integral part of the team."

Chapter Twenty-Four

At the end of the long day of shooting at the co-op, Betty sat on Clay's lap, wiggling with joy every time she looked up at him. The country singer's crew ran about the co-op, packing up equipment as the lingering scent of earlier-brewed coffee and Lupe's finished cooking hung in the air. Bear sighed as he laid at Clay's feet. The comforting aromas of finished food and drink and the low tone of humans speaking after the sun had set was always his one of his favorite times of the day. *Campfire time* had been the term Henry had used years before in explaining to Bear the intrinsic, magnetic pull that brought souls together at the end of a day.

"You certainly have a fan club with both dogs," Mary said, her face lined with exhaustion. "I can't remember when I've seen Bear so at home with a new person."

"You already know what a big fan I am of your Great Pyrenees," Clay said, chuckling. "What's the Aussie's story?"

Betty practically swooned with the attention, batting her eyes with a dreamy look on her face.

"We say she popped out of thin air," Theodore answered. "It happens when you live in a rural area."

"My kids would flip over these two. Does Bear like children?"

"When Violet comes to visit, he's very protective of her." Mary nodded toward the kitchen. "And he's loved Pavi since he was a small boy."

"Protected him from a rattlesnake," Riven said, walking up to the group. "Out here in the middle of nowhere, without anti-venom, things might have been much different for the Posadas. This old dog has literally saved lives."

Hearing the words, Bear groaned as he pulled himself up off Clay's feet and went to lie down in front of Riven, sighing as he dropped on top of his feet. Clearly touched by the gesture, Riven smiled, leaning down to stroke the dog's mane.

Clay watched the pair, drumming his fingers on the table as he hummed. He stopped for a moment, thoughtful in his expression. "Do you think you and Bear are near the same age? If you counted dog years?"

"I've never thought about it, but I think you could be in the right ballpark," Riven answered. "We're both old dogs, aren't we, boy?"

Mary looked up at all the activity gearing up outside the co-op. "I'm going to see if Lupe needs any help so she can get to bed." Outside, the streets had become loud with festivities, the crowd playing Clay Overstreet songs at a high volume.

"I'll help you, Mary. Leave you two guys to it," Theodore said.

The dogs stayed in place, both clearly content and worn out from the day's activities. Betty yawned. "I'm too tired to talk. And you must be really exhausted, Bear."

"Listening to humans talk late at night. It's sort of its own kind of music," Bear said, sleepily.

Clay watched his crew continue to roll up cords, dismantling for the day. "I hope you don't mind me asking, Riven. But I understand you and Katie have only recently become close."

Bear opened his eyes and looked up to Riven, his nose twitching in question.

"I could have handled things much differently when she was growing up. I missed out on a lot."

Studying the older man with great thought, Clay said, "Katie thinks you hung the moon.

Not those exact words, but it's clear when you come up in conversation."

"That's nice to hear. Undeserved, but appreciated." Riven's face was one of gratitude. Bear laid back down again, closing his eyes.

"Violet talks about her Grandchaps all the time."

"If you would have told me a decade ago that I'd have a granddaughter who wants to spend time with me—"

A woman from the video production team approached the table. "We can sneak you out through the back alley door, Clay."

"Thank you. I'm almost ready," he said, returning his attention to Riven. "A few more words with my new friend here."

Riven looked down at his hands. "Feeling left out can make a person crazy." He looked at Clay. "Someone like you, popular and well-loved—you wouldn't know."

"We all have times we feel the odd man out."

"The thing is when you're in those situations, especially year after year of your life, it's hard to imagine a different role you might play. I let myself get so wrapped up in revenge and anger, I nearly missed the Grandchaps portion of my life," Riven said, choking on the last few words. He shook his head. "Don't mind me. Apparently, the older you get, the more emotional a person can become."

"You're sharing from your heart," Clay said, leaning toward the older man. "Nothing wrong with that."

Riven looked at the *Ms. Barnes* booth. Pavi had joined Gavin, pointing to his journal and almost imperceptibly nodding to where the older men were speaking. "Cybil once told me—"

Clay held a finger up. "One second. I want to keep everyone in town straight. Who is Cybil?"

"I forgot she wasn't here tonight. That's her booth. A real success story," Riven said, motioning towards *Ms. Barnes*. "Her nephew is helping her out for a bit."

"Gotcha. Go ahead."

"She once talked to me about old, tribal initiations for boys when they came of age."

Clay sat up and leaned towards Riven. "To show they were ready to become men."

"Yes, but before Cybil explained further, I thought that was the summation of what was accomplished. Leave the village a boy, go out into the darkness of night, show you can make fire or some other important tasks showing courage, strength or wisdom. Then a man, not the child, comes back to the tribe with a new identity. But that wasn't the only benefit."

Clay turned his head in question.

"Most importantly, it was a way to show a young man they were part of something bigger than themselves. Which preserved the safety of the tribe going forward."

"Because the tribe added another man to hunt and protect the members."

Riven's eyes were full of light. "Yes, but also, when people feel part of something bigger than themselves, they naturally seek to contribute to it and promote its success. Only a psychopath would destroy a community when given a chance to join."

"I like that very much," Clay said, drumming his fingers on the table as if he were playing the piano.

Gavin approached the table, journal in hand. "Excuse me, Mr. Overstreet. I was wondering if—"

The production assistant returned to the table. "Clay, your wife called, and she wants you back in your trailer, getting ready for tomorrow. We're all going to be in trouble with her if you don't head out."

"Give me a few minutes," Clay said, raising his eyebrows. "I'm going to put to use some wisdom from Katie's dad and give this young man—" He paused. "I don't know your name."

"Gavin Ring."

"I'm going to spend a little time hearing what Gavin has brought me to look at in his notebook."

The assistant nodded as Riven excused himself, patting Gavin on the back as he left him with the country singer.

"Don't be nervous. Every song you know originated from a writer sitting where you sit."

Gavin's hands shook as he opened his journal. "Sorry, Mr. O-over-s-street. I get nervous. Tr-trying to explain my thoughts."

"Deep breath. Pretend you're talking to someone you've known your whole life. Like your dad."

"I don't have a dad."

Clay's head fell forward in remorse. "That was thoughtless of me, Gavin."

"I mean, I have a dad. Everyone does. Just not one that showed up very much."

"And when he did?"

"It was loud," Gavin said, unconsciously wincing. "Better that he wasn't there. Ma-making my mom sad."

"There's some deep emotion there. Causes you some physical symptoms."

"St-stuttering. Yes, sometimes."

"Have you written anything about your relationship with your dad?"

"Not quite ready for that."

"You'll find the words at the right time," Clay said, sitting at the edge of his chair.

Swallowing hard, the tight muscles in Gavin's neck were visible as he tried to speak.

The look on Clay's face was kind. And though he was tired, he leaned forward. "Let's talk about what you do have written that you'd like to share."

Gavin handed Clay his open notebook by the spine, the pages fluttering like bird wings with his nervousness.

Examining the lines of handwriting, Clay nodded. "Most writers' thoughts are much better expressed on pages than speaking."

Gavin looked around the co-op as Clay read. Standing inside *Ms. Barnes*, Bear stood on his back legs, nose-to-nose with Riven. Speaking animatedly to the Great Pyrenees (though Gavin couldn't hear a word), Riven looked like he was speaking to another human. Betty sat patiently at both their feet as she listened.

The assistant was back again with a phone in one hand, an imploring look on her face.

Immersed in reading, Clay looked up, blinking for a few moments.

Eyeing the country star playfully, the assistant tapped the time on her phone as she walked away within earshot.

"Tell my wife, two minutes!"

Holding his breath, Gavin waited.

"You've written before?"

"S-sold a few songs o-over the years. Sm-small jingles for ads."

"That explains that you seem to have more solid footing than most people who approach me with what they've written. I can tell you've really studied other songwriters. But you can't copy other artist's style and expect to have a deep emotional connection with someone who hears your words."

Gavin nodded respectfully.

"That's not to say you don't have a thoughtful way about seeing the world. Look what your wrote here—*It's a good life. Adventure in your home and home in your adventure.*"

"You l-like it?"

"I do. Hits me right here," Clay said, patting his chest.

"Mary Bailey said something like it. On the train."

"Then she inspired you. Nothing wrong there. But you'll need to dig from within. What moves *you* in a deep and inspiring way? Brings a tear to your eye? Or makes you laugh until you don't think you can take another breath?"

"I-I don't think I've lived that interesting of a life."

"Then look for something you've avoided. And get curious about yourself. It takes a lot of courage to stare at the dark parts of your life. But I promise you, that's where the creative treasure always is."

"And what if I c-cant?" Gavin asked, a sincere look on his face as he stuttered. "Do I st-stop writing?"

"Never, ever stop pursuing your own personal art. Especially when you want to. That's the biggest clue that you're close to gold." He stood up, signaling to his assistant that he was nearly ready to leave.

Gavin's attention went to Bear. The dog had landed back on all four feet, positioning his head under Riven's hand. The feathery tips of his white fur tickled the old man's fingertips. Riven's face wrinkled in glee as he leaned down to kiss the top of the dog's head. The Kansas wind blew the double doors open as both canine and human took an unconscious step into it. The smell of imminent rain filled the co-op.

"From what I hear, those old dogs didn't always see eye to eye," Clay said, extending his hand to the younger man. "Start there. See what happens. Everyone loves dogs and grandpas."

"Thank you, sir," Gavin said sincerely as he shook Clay's hand. "For the gen-generosity of your time."

Struck with the humble thanks of the young man, Clay paused. "Take a couple of days to find the story there," he said, nodding at Riven and Bear. "And then send what you have with Mary. I'll look at it before I leave town and we'll go from there."

Chapter Twenty-Five

Mary sat in a bath at the end of the day, propping herself up with one foot, soap bubbles of various sizes floating on the surface. She stared, without thought or movement, as slow-forming, single drops from the bathtub faucet fell, radiating circles out onto the water. Outside, a meadowlark awakened from the light of the moon. The evening breeze carried its song through the open bathroom window as Mary turned her head, listening to the bird's nocturnal melody.

"Why are you in the dark?" Theodore asked, picking up a book of matches and lighting the candles around Mary.

"Too tired," she mumbled.

"Hot water at the end of a sweltering day?"

"It felt like I had a thin film of dirt from the blowing wind today. Grit even in my teeth and hair."

Theodore watched his wife as the candlelight gave a soft glow to her face. It was one of his favorite times in their daily routines. The two of them, tucked away from the rest of the world. In the mornings, often the pace was brisk and the words encouraging—almost like a fun, pre-game pep talk for each other. At night, though, the emotion shifted into one of sharing instead of expectation. He sat down on the square ottoman beside the tub. "Has this adventure been what you imagined?"

"In some ways more. In some ways less."

"I think that's true with most dreams."

Mary sat up in the tub, wiping her face. She looked at Theodore and sighed. "You know what I'm thinking about mostly while this whole thing is going on?"

Theodore waited for her to continue.

"How quickly the day can be done, and I can be home with you and Bear." She mindlessly popped some of the remaining soap bubbles with her fingertips. "I wonder if all the work is even worth it."

"Of course it is. Don't forget you're doing this for Merivelle."

Mary closed her eyes. "You're right."

"So you feel justified when you leave."

"What do you mean *when I leave?*"

Leaning into the tub, Theodore said, "Traveling like you love. After Bear dies."

"I can't believe you brought that subject up. Not this week."

"Bear's not imminently ill. He may be old and getting slow but he still has a couple of years left in him."

"*A couple of years?*"

"Honey, take a breath and hear me out."

She splashed the water in annoyance. "You better talk fast because you really hit a nerve."

Theodore swirled the water around her knees. "I think you're moving heaven and earth so you don't feel bad that you still want to travel. The town and your giant dog make it hard for you."

Mary flicked water at the candles, causing them to hiss.

"You've hidden out from life under the umbrella of service to Merivelle and taking care of Bear."

"What are you talking about? I'm out and about all over Merivelle. Every day."

"Your new passport that you renewed after we moved here doesn't have one stamp in it. It's wonderful to be of service to those you love. But not at the expense of your dreams."

Mary sunk back in the tub and took a deep breath. In silence, she traced one of her big toes under the faucet. "Bear touched parts of my heart that I feel would have made me a very calloused, unkind woman without him. I don't even like to think about how I was in Chicago. And I don't think you do either."

In the low light of the small room, a shadow of emotion passed over Theodore's face. He reached into the water for Mary's hand as he listened.

"I can't travel at this point in Bear's life. He won't understand what's going on. It's hard enough that Riven has him this week so I can work with Clay."

"He's a Great Pyrenees. His breed is used to being alone, guarding boundaries. And now he has Betty. I think if you're honest with your feelings, you may have sent Bear so Riven wasn't alone."

"Why do you say that?"

"I think you don't want Riven to feel left out and forgotten, so you sent your dog in proxy."

"That may be one of the reasons." She rubbed her eyes, blinking from the sting of the soapy water. "You know, if my dad was still alive, he'd be near Riven's age."

Theodore was solemn as they sat in the silence, the breeze continuing to blow through the window. He reached over and tucked a loose strand of Mary's hair behind her ear.

"This town has my mother's signature on it everywhere. I

have strong and distinct memories of her. But my dad—those memories are scarce for me.

"I wonder if I may use this new-and-improved version of Riven as a stand-in father figure in my mind. It gives me confidence when he gets behind me at every turn." She watched the water as she spoke. "When people want to grind in and keep track of petty, old grievances they have with Riven, I want to let them have it. But he won't let me. Says that he has it coming."

"He does roll with the punches."

"I think he does it for Katie. I would bet they have some sort of arrangement that he can't say all the good he's done."

"Is that what Katie told you?"

"I'm guessing. Based on the entire Little League having new uniforms and equipment. This week, Frannie unpacked new outdoor canvas umbrellas for a sitting patio. They're so pretty, Clay's people added her diner into one of the videos shoots downtown. And then, think about the train depot refurbishment."

"You still think that's Riven too?"

"You and I have talked about it. The whole town saved spare change for years to update the depot. Then suddenly, after he and Katie established their relationship, we receive a grant that no one remembers applying for? And just like that, Merivelle has one of the best train depots in the country. Clay literally told me they would have picked another town without it."

"It all came down to the train station?"

"That close. All the work Katie and I put in and it was actually Riven's secret generosity that saved the day." Beads of sweat collected at Mary's brow as she wiped them away, turning her face to the breeze fluttering the curtains through the window.

"The train depot had to be a multi-million dollar restoration. Business-wise, it makes no sense to renovate it for a town the size of Merivelle," Theodore said. "Do you think it's a connected to his dad being a hobo?"

"It's very touching. Taking up a task when his dad's been gone for decades." She pulled the stopper from the drain, draping the silver-beaded chain around the faucet head. "Because of Riven, I think about my dad more over the last few years. He was the backbone behind all my mother's plans, hopes and dreams." She thought for a moment before speaking. "*Parker Webb*. When's the last time you heard that name in town?"

The water had cooled, the bubbles merely a sheen of soap on top of the water, bobbing around as Mary gestured. Theodore reached for a towel from a basket from under the sink, unfolded it, shaking it in the air before extending it to his wife.

"You were talking about wishes coming true—what I wouldn't give to hear one story about my dad again," she said, standing as she took the towel from Theodore's grasp and wrapped herself in it. She leaned down and blew out the candles.

Chapter Twenty-Six

"I was thinking last night back at our travel site north of town." Clay was sitting under the new canvas outdoor umbrellas installed at The Hen's Nest. Local Merivellians went about their breakfast seemingly unfazed, though the energy of each table hummed in excitement once they recognized the celebrity. "What if I offered a community concert to Merivelle at the end of shooting? As a thank you for putting up with us disrupting the town."

"That's very generous of you," Mary replied, looking to Riven seated to her right. "Don't you think?"

Caught with his hand under the table, feeding both dogs, Riven blinked several times. "Yes, it sounds very nice."

"They tell us at Butterfly Academy to take it easy with bacon." Betty licked her lips under the shade of the table. "Is Mary okay with us eating this much?"

Bear put a paw on Riven's knee and waited for the next morsel. "She says I'm supposed to live forever. Bacon's a treat on special occasions. But Mary also never wants to hurt other people's feelings. Being thankful is very important to her."

"How would you even say thank you to a human?"

"Many ways. You give them a gentle Pyr paw. Or a small *woof*." Bear turned his head, demonstrating the sound in a low decibel. "But if you're feeling especially grateful, you give them a big, slobbery lick. Right in the face. They say they don't like it but watch—"

"Bear, do not lick Mary in the face while she's trying to talk to Clay Overstreet."

"Why not?"

"A girl needs to look her best around this kind of star." Betty stood on her back legs and looked at the singer with a mesmerized look on her face.

Bear groaned and shook his head. "Mary only looks that way at Theodore. She won't mind. Trust me on this subject." He put a paw on Mary's arm and leaned in, breathing in her face as he panted. "She's going to love it."

Mary sat up in her chair, laughing at Bear's hot breath on her cheek. "Do not lick my face, Bear." She sat up and giggled, turning to the two men at the table. "I don't know what gets into him sometimes. He gets goofy and overly affectionate." She gently put his front paws on the ground and kissed the top of his head before returning her attention to the table. "Go ahead with your idea, Clay."

A passing car honked. Someone in the backseat yelled, "We love you, Clay!"

Nodding modestly, Clay kept his focus on the conversation at the table. "I wanted to thank everyone for their hospitality. We've been to a lot of pleasant towns all over the country, but Merivelle might be one of my favorites."

"I appreciate you being patient with us as we learn," Mary said, crossing her fork and knife on the plate in front of her and pushing it forward. "You took a chance with Merivelle and we're so thankful."

The door to The Hen's Nest opened, the miniature bell at the top ringing with the movement. Frannie walked out with a coffeepot in her hand, filling the cups of the tables closest to the door as she winked at Riven. He watched her speak with ease with each table, thoughtful questions reflecting her recall of minute details and genuine interest in whatever was going on in the lives of her customers.

Riven cleared his throat as he re-focused his attention. Clay and Mary were waiting for his answer to a question he hadn't heard. Bear put a paw on his forearm. "I'm sorry. What are we talking about?"

"Clay asked about Katie's grandfather."

At Mary's words, Riven nodded. "What do you want to know?"

"Did Katie tell me your own dad wasn't around much?" Clay asked, a sincere look on his face. "She thinks her grandfather had PTSD before anyone called it that?"

"In his day, they called it battle fatigue or combat stress. My dad dealt with it by moving before the feelings could catch up with him. He left notes that he'd gone fishing. And then I'd be home by myself for a stretch of time."

Drumming his fingers on the top of the table, Clay rocked in his chair, listening to Riven speak.

Mary looked to Riven as both dogs became still. Betty jumped on his lap and snuggled in as she waited for him to speak. A sudden breeze blew the umbrellas, spinning them in a pretty way. Betty looked up; her face was incredulous. "It's Wendell!"

"I don't know any Wendell," Bear said, scrunching his eyebrows.

"But you know Wendell's dog—Henry."

"Henry was Katie's dog before she married Percy and had a baby. Then when he died, she got a cat for Violet."

Betty looked down from Riven's lap. "I forgot you don't know this part!"

A group from a nearby table stood up before politely excusing their interruption to tell Clay how one of his songs was the first dance at their wedding and another had special significance with their children. The two dogs kept talking to one another.

"Riven's dad's name is Wendell!"

"It was?" Bear asked.

"Yes! Riven's dad was a wanderer. That's what his name means! Never let a human name a dog Wendell. Or they'll never see the front end of that canine again."

Bear sighed contentedly. "It makes me happy Riven had a dad. I don't remember my own. I think he looked like me. When we're taken away when we're puppies, we almost never know what happens to the rest of our family."

"That's one of the saddest things I've ever heard," Betty said, hiccupping.

Bear's eyes were wide as he trembled with emotion. "You hope your puppy siblings are safe. That they found wonderful homes like Mary's, but sometimes late at night when I start to think—"

"No Dark Dens this early in the morning. Only think happy thoughts, Bear."

"You're going to have to talk about something else because right now I feel sad wondering about my family and what might have happened to them."

"Then listen, Bear! Here's what I was telling you. When it's super windy here in Kansas—"

"Mary says it's always windy here in the western part of the state. Worse than the Windy City—Chicago, where she and Theodore came from."

"This wind is different. Like when it swirls around Riven's

feet when he mentions feeling all alone. Or a feather lands in Katie's hand when she's showing her little girl something. The scent of flowers, even though there's none growing nearby—that's all Wendell and Henry trying to show Riven and Katie that they're still with them."

Closing his eyes, Bear let out a slight humming sigh. "It sounds nice when you say it like that."

"Which part? So I'll know what to say when you get in one of your Dark Den depressed states."

"That the people you know and love are already there—waiting for you. That would be my idea of Heaven. To see Mary's face when I get there." He sighed again. "Then I wouldn't be so scared."

"The Rainbow Bridge is the exact opposite of Dark Dens, Bear. You shouldn't ever be fearful of it. It's the most beautiful place in the entire universe."

"Then why are you here and not there?"

"Because I loved all the stories from Merivelle. *Your* stories, Bear. You're one dog, but you changed the whole town."

"Mary changed the town. Riven's helping her."

"They wouldn't have ever done it without you, Bear." She stopped for a moment and listened as the Clay outlined his plan for the concert the last day of his visit. "And you know what?" Betty jumped off Riven's lap and put her nose up to Bear's. "I didn't realize it until this exact moment. But maybe I'm here to help you with a few loose ends in Merivelle. Before you continue on your own journey."

"Wait—where am I going?" Bear asked as he and Mary's eyes met.

Seeing the shared moment between the Bear and his favorite human, Betty's face softened. "Nowhere yet, Bear. Let's just attend to the humans who need help."

"Cybil?" Bear asked. "She seems more and more forgetful."

"And don't forget Gavin."

"He's helping her," Bear said, nodding knowingly. "Everyone's so busy right now. It's perfect timing that he showed up."

Betty looked down the street, onto the next block as Pavi opened the co-op door and swept in front of the store. "And let's not forget the Posadas. Something tells me they need more help than they're letting on."

"How do we let the humans know we're trying to assist them?"

Betty sighed, licking Riven's hand, dangling from his knee. "That, my big furry friend, is always the trick with humans and heavenly things. We have to wait for them to catch up and read all the signs sent to help them."

Chapter Twenty-Seven

The phone rang at Cybil's house. Under the stairs, sitting in an old cutout space, the small, wood-trimmed nook had housed a variety of phone incarnations over the years. Cooking breakfast in the kitchen, Gavin looked at Cybil sitting at the breakfast table. "You still have a house phone?"

The phone continued ringing.

"Probably a tele-marketer." Cybil pulled a napkin off the table and settled it in her lap. "All my friends use my cell phone."

"Then why do you still have a house phone?" Gavin asked, holding a copper skillet as he lifted two eggs with a metal spatula.

"I love the sound of it."

"You pay an extra bill each month because you love the sound of something?" He placed the eggs on Cybil's plate.

She nodded her thanks as she picked up a fork. "It reminds me of a time when love and music filled my house. Honey used to get so excited to get phone calls."

"Like the dogs and Pav-lo—" Gavin stumbled on the word.

He took a breath and shook his head. "Sometimes I get caught on words. I feel so stupid."

"Nonsense. You made a keen observation about the Russian physiologist, Ivan Pavlov. Whose name is a bit of a tongue twister itself." Color filled Cybil's face as she spoke, the light making her radiant in the morning sun. "He's renowned for his experiments in classical conditioning. It was an astute comparison, Gavin. Nothing at all to be ashamed of."

"Just trying to join in—" he said, trying to speak but further words eluding him. His face was flustered as he gripped his fork.

"Take a breath. Don't rush speaking. We have all the time in the world."

"I can't talk —" He nodded to his journal nearby on the kitchen countertop. "It's why I write."

"You have a myriad of talents, Gavin." Cybil gestured at the freshly cut blooms on the table. "Floral arranging, to mention one."

"My m-mom loved flowers." He blinked several times as if he'd come out of a trance. "Flowers and butterflies."

"Where's there's one, you'll usually find the other," Cybil said, nodding. She playfully startled at baked items on a cake stand. "Fresh muffins?"

"I saw all the in-ingredients on the coun-counter. Thought I'd give it a try."

"The day you arrived, I'd given up on trying to figure out an old recipe. Left things on the counter to figure out later." She reached over, selected a muffin and smeared butter on it, closing her eyes in delight. "These can't be healthy for me."

"I added all the-the chia and flax s-seeds and psyllium you had l-lined up on the counter."

The look of happiness at Cybil's reaction was radiant. "You

managed to get all those ingredients in these wonderful-tasting muffins?"

"Walnuts and canned pineapple. Hey-help the taste."

"Well, let's hide the muffins then. They're so delicious, I don't want carried away." She motioned to the chair next to her. "Relax and enjoy this breakfast you've whipped up for us."

Pulling a napkin from beside his plate, Gavin placed it on his lap.

"Good eggs, Gavin. Where'd you learn to cook?"

"My mom."

"You seem very fond of her."

"I would have done an-anything for her. She was the b-best mom you can imagine."

"It's a genuine joy to hear children sing the praises of their parents. Especially at your age. Sometimes it takes longer for some people."

"She made me feel im-important—" He paused for a moment as he took a deep breath and swallowed.

Cybil leaned in, reaching for a jar of homemade jam. "Tell me some of your favorite things about her." She leisurely twirled the fruit spread on to the half-eaten muffin.

"She was so fun and kind. She'd check me out of school. We'd go to movies. When I was having a hard time." His voice trailed off as his face became soft with remembrance. "She wanted to be a songwriter. Told me it was important to have something creative to leave behind."

"Is that why you carry a journal around? As a connection to her?"

Tapping his fingers on the table, Gavin did not speak. His eyes moved as if they were figuring out a complicated math calculation.

Cybil placed the spoon she was holding onto her plate, so gently the silverware didn't make a sound on the porcelain.

"You don't hesitate when you speak about your mom. I would wager it's an important clue to understanding your stuttering."

"I can't always weave my mom into conversation so people un-understand me."

"Honey thought music was the answer for everything. I specifically remember her addressing stuttering. How when a person listens to music, it's nearly impossible for them to stutter." Cybil reached over the table and put her hand on Gavin's. "Maybe your mom's memory is your music."

"I love that thought." Gavin's eyes searched past the opened French doors to Cybil's patio. In the morning light, butterflies danced on the sunflowers in Cybil's garden. "I would usually jump and scribble in my journal. But it feels nice to sit here with the thought of her."

"Then that's what we'll do."

The pair of them sat in silence. Cybil looked to the other side of the house, transfixed with the light dancing on the ceiling from the stain-glassed windows lining the back of the house. In contrast, the trees growing in the front yard shaded the rooms. Dappled light found its way through the leaves and onto the wooden floors inside.

Gavin finally spoke. "My whole life, pe-people try to help me by jumping in. Finishing my words for me. My stuttering makes them feel un-uncomfortable. It's terrible to know how I make people feel."

"Everyone has things about themselves that they feel unsettle others. But mostly, those are our own insecurities we attach to other people's perceptions of us."

Swallowing hard, Gavin continued. "When I arrived here in Merivelle, I was-was trying to find a room. And there were none."

"All the visitors for the Midsummer celebration."

"I travel all the time. Not unusual for small towns to have

no vacancies. This is the first time I've been offered a place in someone's home when there are no rooms."

"Good heavens, Gavin. Where do you sleep then?"

"In a park. Sometimes in a station, waiting to catch a train somewhere else. You find ways." He took a deep breath and let it out slowly before speaking, his words halting and slow. "When I arrived, I got ushered in to Merivelle. Sp-specifically by Lupe. She swept me in. More quickly than my stutter allowed me to explain."

"You mean you're not my nephew?" Cybil asked, her face comical.

"You knew all along?"

"Of course," Cybil said, laughing. "You know, Honey and I were called *Aunt Cybil* or *Aunt Honey* for years. It became a token way to express affection to each of us when people in our small town didn't know what to make of our relationship."

Gavin cleared his throat. "I'm so sorry. I never meant to—"

Cybil held her hand up. "I enjoyed pretending that somehow Honey was still alive here in Merivelle. The same way I pay for a phone that I don't use." Her voice was calm, her face momentarily unlined with age. "Our storylines collided, Gavin, and we let ourselves make-believe."

"You aren't mad at me?"

"I was a willing participant. I knew you could be trusted the moment you were wide-eyed with my money lying around. You couldn't get it to a bank fast enough," Cybil said, smiling. "It was a recent wish come true to have someone living in my house again."

"What about the other people in town? Mary and Riven? The Posadas? I should tell them."

"Let's get through the week with Clay Overstreet. Then we'll let them know. I told everyone I had things under control." Light touched the stain-glass windows above the

144

landing leading to the second floor, filling the room with rainbow-colored light. The aroma of honeysuckle filled the house.

"Do you ever think you see Honey? You know, in a restaurant? Or walking down the street?" Gavin sat up, his eyes bright as he gestured. "And your brain knows it's not her. *Knows it.* But your heart—it *wants* the vision," he said, clutching his fist near his chest. "It tells you to just *feel* and *love* the mirage of them. Even if the glimmer of their likeness lasts for only a few moments."

Cybil watched the flickering light, nodding through tears. "Strangers unknowingly gifting you with their likeness of the person you loved most in life."

Pushing his breakfast plate forward, Gavin put his elbows on the table. "I promise, my motive was not to deceive. It was nice to think there was someone waiting at home for me."

The pair of them sat again in stillness, the traffic outside Cybil's house picking up. Seen through the windows, early morning walkers passed by on the sidewalk in front.

"My dad wasn't at home much. He moved around towns. He used to visit us. When he needed money. She could never tell him no. And then we'd be without money. Even for food."

"Is that why you panicked with money lying around?"

"Probably," Gavin said, his eyes wide with the connection. "My stuttering drove him crazy. He was a fast-talker. And I'm —as you know—rather slow."

"You're thoughtful with your words. I see you writing in that journal of yours with the words spilling out on the page as fast as you can write them."

"It doesn't matter. I was still a disappointment to him. My mom tried to make me feel better. She told me he was more of a girl dad."

"You have a sister?"

"He had a different relationship with someone before my

mom. It was that woman's daughter. But he used to tell stories about her. She was really going to become someone, he thought."

Cybil put her hand over Gavin's and patted it. "Do you have any desire to see him?"

"I'm not really sure. My mom said he'd passed through Merivelle years before. When I saw the magazine article about you, I thought the town might give me a clue about him."

"And has it?"

"It's not how I remember him talking about it. But maybe when you're a kid, you don't listen well."

"Where is he now?"

"Not far. Amarillo."

"I get the feeling, if the opportunity presented itself, you'd like to see him again. Am I wrong?"

Placing his silverware on his plate, Gavin took a deep breath. "When I've accomplished something big. I think he'd be open to a relationship with me then."

Cybil stood up from the breakfast table, stacking the breakfast plates. "Don't wait until *you* feel proud, Gavin. Seize the opportunity the first chance you get so you can get clarity with your past. Life goes by so very fast."

Chapter Twenty-Eight

The weekend had done nothing to diminish the crowd numbers in Merivelle. If anything, more vehicles appeared, backing up the downtown area and beyond. Foot traffic was unprecedented, each shop crowded with customers weaving in and out of storefronts, multiple shopping bags in hand. One of Clay's superfans, with a large following on social media, had posted from inside Bear Bailey's Co-op and Grocery. The store was wall-to-wall with people.

Theodore watched filming down at the train depot during a closed set—his first chance to see everything in action since Clay arrived. Mary re-appeared at the co-op to help with the overflow of customers. Lupe had been nearly invisible, rarely leaving the kitchen. Using her son's athleticism, she had Pavi run food wherever it was needed around town. Lupe and Mary spoke briefly, but when their eyes met, both women smiled in excitement, an unspoken knowledge between them of the long road that had brought them to the celebratory week.

"I wish my daughter had her bookstore up and running for a day like this," a local woman said to Mary as she was checking out with groceries. "She has her heart set on a curiosity shop with antiques and books. Her dad and I have always told her it will never work in a small town like Merivelle. But on a day like this, I feel I should amend our thoughts on the subject. She's so passionate about opening it."

Mary placed two jars of honey with a loaf of sourdough bread into the basket that the woman brought in when she shopped. "Well, as someone who started a business in an old hardware store, named after her beloved dog, who she never thought she wanted—I say for Rose to follow her heart. You never know where it will take you."

The woman picked up her basket. "I know you're right. Rose is my only child. I'm overly cautious with her. She's nearly done with college and I act like she's still in grade school."

"Tell her to pop in next time she's home," Mary said, putting a sprig of lavender in the basket. "It seems like a lifetime since I've seen her."

"Maybe we can convince her to drive home to see Clay's Sunday Merivelle concert."

"Tell her that Katie will be here. With Percy and Violet." Mary let out a small shriek, causing another customer to turn in question. "Sorry," Mary said, beaming in happiness. "My cousin's visiting and I'm thrilled."

From under the register, a shady oasis from the heat of the day for both double-coated dogs, Betty panted. "Remember your puppy Pavlovian response to Katie's name? You would groan whenever you heard the word *Katie*."

"But she became a genuine friend to Mary. And whatever makes Mary happy makes me happy," Bear said, sighing with the coolness of the concrete.

"Then Katie's mom came to town and then you'd groan when you heard the word, *Julia*—"

"I still groan when I hear the word."

Betty stopped. "Why?"

"Julia's a non-stop talker."

"Sorry, Bear," Betty said, falling on her back submissively. "I get carried away because I still can't believe I'm here in Merivelle. Don't let me get on your nerves."

Bear swatted at her. "Get up. I shouldn't have been rude. My hips hurt."

"Again?"

"Always these days," Bear said, whimpering softly.

"You've got to tell Mary."

"She'll get back to all of us when Clay leaves town. I'll signal her somehow on Monday." He stopped for a moment. "She needs to rest for a couple of days and then I'll let her know next Wednesday. Possibly Friday."

The next moment, Donkey walked into the store, eyes wide when he saw the foot traffic. He spoke to people as he made his way to the co-op's center counter.

Mary glanced up as she passed one of Cybil's wind chimes over the counter to an out-of-town customer. "How's everything going down at the train depot? Is Clay happy?"

"He's more than happy. Not at all as I imagined. No hand-holding or crazy demands. Clay's a real musician."

"I thought so too," Mary said, leaning over the counter. "His requests are few and far between. You can tell he loves storytelling with his music more than headlines with his antics."

"If only all the fans were that way."

"Trouble?"

"Just how most people are when they don't have a stake in town. Stupid actions without regard to consequences." He looked over to Cybil's booth. A line of people formed, waiting to take their picture with her. Gavin held customer's purchases as they spoke with her. "Do we know anything more about that kid showing up out of nowhere?"

"He's seems to really be helping Cybil with whatever she needs. Which is a real blessing right now when I'm short of time."

"Do you think they even look like family?"

Both Mary and Donkey turned.

"They look as related as your two dogs here," Donkey said, motioning to Bear and Betty, gesturing at the disparity between their sizes and markings.

"You never know with families. There are nephews by marriage. Step-nephews, half-nephews." She nodded over at Cybil. "And how many times over the year have students claimed Cybil as their own family? Even if they aren't, she never seemed concerned."

"I'm shocked that out of all people, you aren't more worried."

"I took a cue from Bear here. At the beginning of the week, he didn't seem excited about this little dog and now they're good buddies."

"Did you hear that? They know we're friends now," Betty said enthusiastically.

Bear opened one eye. "You still talk too much."

"Is that you or your sore hips talking?"

Bear sighed, extending a paw out to her. "You're a good friend, Betty."

She wiggled in complete and utter joy. "Then can we have an adventure together? Everyone's so busy here at the co-op. Maybe we could go somewhere else."

"I'm needed here. To help Mary. Like I always do."

Betty wilted in disappointment. "I wanted to spend time with you, Bear. So I have a fun story of my own that I could tell when I'm back at Butterfly Academy."

The dogs turned their heads when Gavin's phone rang. He looked down, startling in surprise. He whispered something to Cybil before ducking out of the co-op and walking briskly across the storefront.

Groaning, Bear heaved himself up.

"Where are you going?" Betty asked.

"Let's see if we can find you a good story with a quick adventure."

Chapter Twenty-Nine

Outside the store, out of view of the large picture windows of the co-op, Gavin paced as he spoke on the phone, barely noticing the two dogs mingling with the crowd on the sidewalk. As he walked further, the pair of dogs were stopped by people petting them and trying to take photos with their phone cameras. Initially skeptical of being photographed, Betty imitated Bear's good-naturedness on the subject as they kept an eye on Gavin.

"Do you think he knows we're following him?"

Bear panted in the hot afternoon temperature, glancing up at the sky. "I wish he would have picked the shady side of the street to take his phone call."

"I thought Great Pyrenees had coats that protect you from the cold and heat. Like an insulation of sorts."

"When I'm on grass or dirt. Concrete is an entirely different thing. My paws are burning and I feel very woozy right now. Maybe we need to get back to the store so I can get some water."

"Can we please follow another block? I feel I'm so close to

my own Merivelle story." Betty barked, her excited puppy tone garnering attention. "I feel like we could be dog detectives. Unraveling whatever Gavin's on the phone talking about."

A girl tugged on her mom's sleeve. "The puppy sounds like a toy!"

Betty groaned.

"What's wrong?"

"I got overly excited and we're spying on someone."

"You're the only one who thinks we're undercover. We're the complete opposite of undercover. We're a bit of a spectacle."

Betty bared her teeth when a woman came near, bending down to be close to her.

"Don't growl. You don't want that part in your story—you're no coyote."

"You're right, Bear. I still get scared humans are going to hurt me. But I'm really trying."

The woman scratched Betty's stomach before moving on.

"We lost Gavin. Did you see where he went while everyone was taking pictures?" Panting as drool dribbled down his mouth and onto his mane, Bear said, "Let's take a quick break and get back to Mary."

"Whatever you say, Bear." The scent of roasted coffee beans filled the area. Betty's nose went to the air. "That smells almost as delicious as a library. What is it?"

"Tamru's store." Bear looked up at the sign, pretending to read. "*Mare Coffee Roasters.*"

"Mare? Like a horse?"

Bear shook his head. "*Mare*—it's Ethiopian for *my dear* or *my beloved.*"

"How do you know that?"

"He named his shop in honor of his wife. Tamru is a very

kind man," Bear said, a look of admiration on his face. "If he sees us, he'll probably bring out some Wishbones."

"There's a line out the door. Tamru's not going to bring us anything today."

Gavin exited the coffee shop holding a large drink, his phone to his ear with his other hand.

Betty growled. "Who needs a large coffee in this hot weather? He's trying to throw us off his track."

Bear swayed in place as he lifted his paws off the pavement. "It's so hot."

Still listening to his call, Gavin made a beeline for the dogs. Betty ducked behind Bear as they both listened to him struggling to speak to whoever was on the other line.

"I-I thought—"

Betty nudged Bear from behind.

Gavin paused and listened. "No, I under—"

"He's shaking. His voice *and* his legs."

"Because he's probably up to something," Betty said.

Gavin knelt beside the dogs, placing the large coffee cup in front of them.

"It's full of water, Betty. He knows we're following him." Bear hooked his paw onto Gavin's arm. "And he's still trying to be nice."

"I guess I messed that one up, huh, Bear?"

"You're a few hours' drive a-away, we-we could meet and —" Gavin paused.

Bear looked at Betty, his eyes wide with sadness. "Whoever is talking to him sure doesn't listen. He can't even finish what he's saying."

"Mind if I take a drink of water, Bear?"

Bear put a paw on Betty's head. "Sit still for a sec. This guy has a hard enough time speaking."

"It's a real-really friendly town. The people—"

Bear swayed in place, panting more heavily with each passing moment. "This poor kid. His heart rate is through the roof."

"—are helping me. A man named R-riven told Cl-Clay." Gavin pulled the phone from his ear. "No—I haven't said any—"

"Help me, Betty. He needs us both here." Bear leaned into Gavin's legs, looking up in encouragement. "Let's show him he's not alone."

Betty hung her head. "You always do the right thing, don't you, Bear?"

"Whoever he's talking to is a real Dark Den to him. I hate that feeling for anyone."

"I didn't m-mean—to upset—" Gavin shook his head. "A-another time. Maybe." Sweat spots showed through his t-shirt.

"We all need to get back to the co-op," Bear said, trying to catch his breath. "I don't feel so good and I don't think Gavin does either."

"A couple more minutes. Let's figure out who he's on the phone to."

"There's a concert," Gavin said, pausing. "Tomorrow Yes-the whole town." He swallowed, taking a deep breath. "I'm not sure—"

"Who?" Betty asked, barely audible.

"You don't have to whisper. We could shout and Gavin still couldn't hear us."

"The train de-depot?" Gavin looked south down Main Street, his eyes searching as he listened.

Dry heaving, Bear shook his head. "I'm not feeling good, Betty."

"I-I need to go now." Gavin hung up his call and knelt to Bear. "You're going to be okay. You're just shaken, Bear. Away from Mary."

"What's going on with Bear?" A woman approached the scene, a concerned look on her face.

"I'm going to nip this lady's ankles to move her along." Betty took a step toward the woman, knocking over the cup of water. "We don't need a crowd getting in the way."

"Do not bite anyone," Bear said weakly. "She comes into the store with her kids all the time—"

"He's panting pretty hard and his nose is dry," Gavin said, stroking Bear's mane. "Do you think you could run to the co-op while I stay with him? I don't want him to be alone when he can't tell people what's going on with him."

The woman nodded as she began jogging in the opposite direction.

"Hang on, Bear. Mary will be here in a minute," Betty said, trying to nudge the cup with a negligible amount of water left in it.

Bear put his paw out to Gavin and whimpered. "Mary loves me to be thankful. This young man is so kind. I wish I could tell him how much—" The next moment, the surrounding scenery swirled and the Great Pyrenees fainted on the sidewalk.

Chapter Thirty

When Bear came to consciousness, Mary was gazing down at him, with bloodshot eyes and tears streaming down her face. She cradled his head in her lap as she stroked his fur. "I'm on the Rainbow Bridge," he whispered. "It's Mary's face. Like I always wanted."

"You're not on the Rainbow Bridge," Betty said, sitting beside Mary, her voice gentle. "I already told you—there's no sadness there. You *are* at the vet's though. Everyone's worried about you."

Nuzzling Mary's hand, Bear pulled himself an inch closer to her. "Oh, good. I only said that trying to be brave." He looked around the examination room, familiar from years of annual visits. "Why am I here?"

"You fainted. Right on the sidewalk. A big, Clay Overstreet-sized crowd gathered around you," Betty said. "You're kind of even more famous now that you had something dramatic happen to you."

"My head hurts," Bear said, stifling a whimper. "But I don't want to worry Mary. She's all alone."

"Riven's on his way. I overheard her call with him."

"No Theodore?"

"He's on a closed set and can't be interrupted. Mary's going to talk to him as soon as he can take a call."

The door opened as Bear's tail wagged.

"You're not scared of the vet?" Betty said, backing into the corner of the room, her eyes wide as she growled.

"My vet is a friend that takes care of me. He can sort out anything. I once got my face stuck in a peanut butter jar. It would still be there if it wasn't for Dr. Luke," Bear said solemnly.

Betty took a step forward and giggled. "I don't think that's entirely true, but it's nice you give him so much credit."

Dr. Luke put an x-ray up on the wall, switching on the light box.

"Are those your bones?" Betty asked, the hair going up on her neck as Bear gazed at the film.

"We gave Bear some fluids and something through his IV to help relax him. You mentioned his hips, so I snapped a shot of his back leg. Have you noticed he's limping on it? Or is that something from when he fainted today?"

Pausing as she stroked Bear's back, Mary blinked back tears. "I've been so occupied. I've probably missed something very obvious."

"No need to feel guilty. We want to get your boy in tip-top condition. Especially at his age. He's an old dog now."

"I always tell Theodore not to say that because I don't want to think about it."

"Neither do I," Bear said, nudging Mary with his snout.

Dr. Luke pulled a couple of tissues out of a box on the counter and handed them to Mary. "Don't forget that one Christmas Eve, when Bear was a young dog. Remember how he limped after he went missing?"

"I think the best we sorted out together was that a vehicle had clipped his back hip in that terrible blizzard," Mary said, recalling the night that Bear had run into the snowy night when he thought he'd disappointed her. She choked back a muffled sob.

"That part of your Christmas adventure was real," Betty said, nudging Bear's chin. "Then Jiff showed you what everyone's life would have been like if you hadn't lived with the Baileys."

"How do you remember all that?"

"I love every bit of your story, Bear!"

"I wish that night had never happened. Sometimes I push it out of my mind entirely," Mary said, holding Bear tighter.

"Well, no sane person ever wants to think about their dog in pain. But for this conversation, old injuries have a way of popping up later in life. And I think that's most of what Bear is dealing with. We'll keep an eye on it. But the last place for Bear to be is out running on concrete during the summer."

"I don't know what happened. I looked up and both dogs were gone. Bear's never dashed out of the store like that in all the years the co-op's been open."

Betty put her head down. "Sorry to ruin your good behavior record, Bear. This whole thing is my fault. Josephine's going to be so disappointed."

"Now the other dog is an entirely different story."

"How so?" Mary asked, reaching back to scratch Betty on the head.

"I've never seen such a healthy specimen of a dog. Absolute, perfect health. Heart beating out of her chest like a drum."

"Did you scan her for a chip? Theodore would love to keep her."

"Your husband and every one of my staff," Dr. Luke said,

smiling. "She's charmed everyone here." He went to the counter and picked up an aerosol can.

"I'm trying not to growl here, Bear," Betty said, backing up. "But I'm about ready to freak out."

Dr. Luke shook the can several times.

"Is something bad about to happen?"

Bear tilted his head back, closed his eyes and opened his mouth. "Do what I do. Trust me on this subject."

Dr. Luke sprayed cheese onto Bear's drooling tongue.

"And here you go, little Aussie," Dr. Luke said. A whoosh of aerosol delivered cheese-flavored goo onto Betty's tongue, causing her to laugh as she pawed the vet for more.

Watching the other dog's joy, Bear licked her ears tenderly. "Since you've shown up, I've been cranky because I'm in pain. But I want to say thanks for staying with me."

The fur around her face half-drenched with Bear's saliva and cheese residue, Betty said, "Thanks, buddy. A gentle paw next time." She snuggled into Bear. "Or really whatever you want, friend. I'm just happy you're safe and sound."

Chapter Thirty-One

"I need you to stay as close as possible to me the rest of the time Clay is here." Lupe was chopping vegetables at the co-op counter as she looked over to her son, cleaning up tables at the end of the day.

"Mamá, please be reasonable. It's a party week. All my friends are out at night having fun."

Pointing to the front of the store with her knife, Lupe said, "These Main Street parties are going to spoil everything good that Mary has worked to bring to our town."

"They're having fun. It's the most exciting thing to happen to this old town."

"Pablito—"

"No," he said, turning his back to his mom, shaking his head. "My name is Pavi. Or I won't speak to you."

"*Pablito Marcos Posada*—never talk to me that way again." Lupe wiped her hands on a towel before coming to the front of the counter.

"I meant no disrespect. It's a small thing for me. A new name. For a new me."

Lupe studied her son's features in the light. "It's hard for me not to think of you as the boy playing in the dirt in front of the trailer we first lived in when we came to Merivelle."

Standing at a table, Pavi finished wiping it down, brusquely pushing the chairs back into place. "I always do everything you ask me to. No trouble at all. I ask one thing and it's a big deal."

"Please sit down for a moment, *Pavi*," Lupe said, taking the few steps to her son with her arms outstretched.

Instantly, Pavi's shoulders dropped. "*Lo siento mucho*, Mamá. I'm so sorry."

Lupe motioned to the table. "We've been too busy to talk. And that is not our way. Please sit down."

"But we're almost done for the night."

"A few moments with you. Before you fly away for the evening." The smile on Lupe's face was sincere.

Pavi looked at the table, still wet from his cleaning a few moments before. He took a napkin out of the dispenser and wiped it dry for the space in front of Lupe. Pulling the chair out, he waited for his mom to sit before he followed suit.

Outside the co-op, parties had popped up with Clay's time in Merivelle. Each evening, they grew in noise and music, starting earlier than the previous day. *An enormous block party*, Mary had called it. Pavi looked longingly at the scene from where he and Lupe sat.

"Your sister, Reyna—"

"Perfect Reyna, you mean. Works hard, graduates early, finds a temporary legal internship. I know, Mamá. You and everyone in Merivelle tell me all the time about Reyna."

"Let me finish."

Pavi nodded, folding his hands.

"Reyna is my reflection. She'll make a good life for herself. Because she works hard. If she hadn't gone to school, she would have taken that same energy and worked her fingers to the bone."

"You always taught us that hard work was the way. Don't wait for the iron to strike, strike the iron."

Hearing her words repeated by her son, Lupe smiled. "Luck is merely hard work meeting opportunity." She leaned in, her forearms resting on the table. "But that is *my* path. And the path of your *hermana*, Reyna."

All fight drained from Pavi's expression.

"You are the color of a different horse."

"You mean a horse of a different color."

"I do?"

"Yes, most definitely," Pavi said with an affectionate grin.

"English sayings—they get me every time." Lupe wiped her face with her hands before continuing. "Reyna and I will work diligently in our lifetimes. And we will be thankful for our opportunities. But you, Pavi—your life will differ greatly from ours."

"Sounds ominous."

"Very much the opposite. Good things—wonderful things will flow to you with ease. It is who you are. Miracles will always find you."

Sitting up at the table, Pavi rubbed his hand together. "That sounds great. Let me get this party started." He nodded to the street. "Who knows who I could meet the minute I step outside Bear Bailey's? My whole life could change in an instant."

"Do you understand how critical it is for me and our whole family to stay out of trouble? No issues of any kind or I will not become a citizen."

"We've been waiting for your papers for practically my whole life, Mamá. I know that."

At the stoplight, car horns honked, blaring music collided

with angry shouting before the squeal of tires started when the light changed. Pedestrians joined in, throwing cans as they laughed.

"Why would you risk getting into any trouble with people that don't even live in Merivelle?"

"It's only a bunch of trash and noise."

Lupe hit her hand on the table, her expression fierce. "Use the proper word. It's *vandalism*. The deliberate act of defacing property, especially when it is done in a manner that harms the aesthetic or usability of the area."

"I promise, nothing bad will come of it." Pavi's legs tapped in excitement.

"That is not the point. You are not to endanger our family's future with poor decisions." She stood up from the table.

Pavi opened his mouth to speak.

"No words from you on this subject. Commit mine to your memory, Pablito," she said before shaking her head to correct herself. "*Pavi*—do not get into trouble of any kind. Be especially careful the rest of Clay's visit. Do you understand?"

"Yes, Mamá."

Walking back to the kitchen, Lupe picked up her knife and began chopping again.

A young man came to the window, motioning to the hours of operation sign on the door. Pavi shook his head, turning his back on his friend, going over to the kitchen area where Lupe worked with her head down. The cadence of her knife work was rapid, her breathing heavy.

"You're turning the cilantro into juice."

"It's for salsa. It's fine."

"You always say to put good feelings into the food. Someone's going to choke on their chips and dip."

Lupe sighed. "You're right. I cannot put fear into the food."

"But you're angry."

"No, Pablito. I'm terrified. We have to be careful. You and I, and wherever Reyna is in Chicago. We are guests in this country until it is our own."

"I know that. You drilled it into our heads since before we met Mary and Bear."

"If something goes wrong, you will be the person with the most eyes on them. Not the other boys. You and your very brown skin."

"Nobody cares about that here. Our last name is practically Bailey."

Lupe picked up an onion, cutting off both ends before peeling away the papery tunic. "Do not get tangled up with people we don't know. No matter how innocent. Use great care, Pavi."

"No friends outside Merivelle? That's unreasonable. Maybe that's why Reyna is so lonely where she is."

"My papers could come any day. No surprises, *por favor*."

"Are you crying from the onions that you're chopping or what you're telling me, Mamá?"

Ignoring Pavi's attempt at levity, Lupe continued. "You wouldn't be here if it weren't for that dog." She pointed to Bear's mural on the wall. "Papers or no papers, we owe Bear and the Baileys respect. This catering job is a year's income for us. A big sum of money that could fix a lot of my past mistakes."

"What mistakes?"

"Ones that I made when I was a little older than you. Thinking that everyone with a smile was my friend and had my best interests at heart." Her voice trailed off.

"Tell me. Maybe parts of our lives before Merivelle would make more sense."

Lupe shook her head. "Not today. We just need to focus on finishing the catering. And then we're going to take a trip together. Lots of road time to tell you all the things you want to know."

"A road trip?"

"Do not mention it to anyone. I will tell Mary in my own way. Promise me, Pavi."

Noting his mom's shaking hands, Pavi went around the counter to put an arm around her. "Of course. Anything for you." He kissed her on the cheek, grabbing a chip from the counter. "Strangers can be as nice as the people we know. You shouldn't always be so worried, hiding out in the co-op all the time."

Lupe scooped up the cilantro and tossed it in a large, industrial-sized metal bowl, stirring the contents together. The smell of roasted tomatoes, onions, garlic and jalapeños intensified, blowing the scent into the rest of the co-op.

Leaning over to dip a chip into the aromatic salsa, Pavi said, "I was talking to Gavin. Cybil told him to find his dad. Reach out to him while there was still time. Which made me think how I should try to find my own."

Freezing mid-motion, Lupe looked at her son.

"Yes, Mamá—a son interested in his dad. Please tell me what is wrong with that? Katie knows who Riven is now. A stranger comes to town and within a few days, Cybil tells him to contact his dad to help him make sense of his own history. Why not me too?"

Shaking her head, Lupe avoided making eye contact with Pavi.

"And what about Reyna? She lost her chance."

Yes-"It was a terrible automobile accident, out of the blue."

"Yes, life happens. Even more reason for me to look

"Pavi—please. Do not search for him until I am a citizen."

"And once you're naturalized? I can search then?"

Lupe put her knife down and sighed. "Yes—only then. Carefully and away from Merivelle."

Chapter Thirty-Two

"Chaps! We found him!"

"One second, Katie." Riven sat in his home, on the bench at the end of his bed, groaning as he pulled off his cowboy boots and socks, tucking the latter into first. He picked up his phone again.

"Please tell me you aren't wearing cowboy boots in this heat."

"How did you know?"

"You make that sound all the time when you take them off. And now Violet does too. We think it's especially funny when she's taking off her ballet shoes."

Riven rubbed his eyes and smiled.

"We're driving and almost to Merivelle. I'm too excited to wait until we get there."

"Mary already told me. Percy's going to play drums at the concert tomorrow night."

"He is. But that's not why I'm so excited. We found Pavi's dad!"

Riven sat up, his eyes searching the room. "Where?"

"Wyoming."

"That's great. He's alive. Not like Reyna's dad."

There was silence on the other end of the phone for a moment.

Riven shook his head. "I can't even bear to think of her hearing the news. Her last visit with her mom and Pavi is a terrible image in my head."

"That crossed my mind a hundred times with all the dead-ends tracking down Pavi's dad. You'll never guess what the issue was."

"Tell me."

"Lupe and her partner are originally from Mexico."

"They aren't married?"

"Lupe always changes the subject. I don't actually know. But it's not their marital status that's important. It's their surnames."

"*Posada?*"

"Posada is Lupe's maiden name. In Mexico, children are given their father's surname, followed by their mother's maiden name. Reyna mentioned it to me when she was addressing Pavi in a playful manner. *Pablito Marcos Posada.* I assumed Marcos was a middle name. But it's his dad's last name, hiding in plain sight this whole time."

"Then let's bring him to Merivelle."

"Do you think that's a good idea?"

Riven leaned over, his elbows on his knees. "I talked to Cybil's nephew, who seems pretty wrecked about his own dad. Let's help Pavi get a better start as he goes out into the world."

Chapter Thirty-Three

"One more day of filming, honey. Hang in there."

Theodore rubbed Mary's back as they approached Riven's front door. People would have considered the house a mansion anywhere it was built. But outside of town, on the Kansas landscape, on the highest point of elevation on acreage, it was a startling sight. *A castle on the prairie* was Riven's vision when he'd first come into money. And he hoarded every cent he had to bring his dream to fruition. By the time he'd saved enough, the young woman he'd hoped to entice with his newfound wealth had moved on, their daughter in tow.

"This house," Mary said, yawning as she looked around the entry. "It never ceases to amaze me."

"It's so huge. I'll bet it echoes," Betty said, barking. She turned her head as the sound reverberated through the porch.

"We already know that without disrupting the peace of the scenery. By using our eyes."

"Sorry, Bear. I forgot you have a nasty headache."

After his collapse on the sidewalk downtown, Bear spent the rest of the day at home with Mary attending to his every need while she oversaw operations remotely. When Mary and Theodore moved to leave for the evening, Bear (with Betty beside him) stood resolutely at the door, determined to go.

"Why did you insist on coming to Riven's, if you're still not feeling good?" Betty asked, trotting alongside him.

"I wanted to see Katie." Bear put his nose in the air and sniffed. "Do you smell flowers?"

"The same scent happens when Wendell comes to visit with Henry!" Betty exclaimed.

The front door opened. Katie, smiling radiantly, threw her arms around her cousin as the two women hugged and laughed.

Mary pulled back first. "Where is our darling Violet?"

"Chaps has her mesmerized at the piano."

Hugging Katie from the side, Theodore said, "Who would have thought, huh?"

Kneeling, Katie looked into Bear's eyes. "I heard you had a time of it today. I didn't think we'd see you tonight." She buried her face in Bear's thick mane.

"Are you crying?"

"Yes, Theodore. I am," Katie said, wiping her eyes. "Without this dog, nothing I love in that home would have happened for me."

"That's kind of you to say," Mary said, beaming like a proud parent.

Katie rose, kissing the top of Bear's head. "Not to mention how wonderful Bear was to my hobo dog. He was always so gentle and patient with Henry."

"They sure love you around here," Betty said, her voice full of admiration.

Bear lowered his head as he sighed in memory at the mention of Henry's name.

"Don't be sad," Betty said, putting her small paw on top of his. "Henry's traveling around Heaven with Katie's grandpa,

Wendell. Henry has a home *and* he travels." She tilted her head and thought for a moment. "Maybe the best definition of a wonderful life."

"It doesn't it mean I can't miss an old friend. I can be sad and happy at the same time," Bear said, sighing.

Katie cleared her throat. "And who is Bear's new friend?"

Betty backed away from the group, chanting under her breath. "*Don't growl, don't growl, don't growl.*"

"Don't try so hard," Bear said, his voice weak. "Just take a step in and breathe. The rest will take care of itself."

Mary turned from watching the landscape. "Betty is our girl that herds the goats at the house."

Katie looked at Theodore, a smile on her face. "No doubt you're a huge fan. Based on that one talent alone."

Scooping Betty up in his arms, Theodore said, "What's not to love? A cute dog who's a companion to Bear. *And* wrangles goats." He motioned inside the house. "Do you two mind if I run in and see Percy? I missed the last trip to Kansas City and—"

"Percy's dying to see you. You can keep him occupied since my dad hasn't spoken to either of us once he had Violet in his arms."

Before the words were out of Katie's mouth, Theodore zipped into the house, Betty on his heels, before she stopped, rejoining Bear at Mary's side. "You still need help, Bear. I'll sit quietly with you."

Bear panted, nodding his thanks.

"You good?" Katie asked, motioning to the chairs on the large porch. "You look dead on your feet."

Mary dropped into the closest chair as Katie sat opposite of her with the dogs at their feet. "Everything is wonderful. Clay is as professional as you told me. Merivelle has been booming with visitors. Your dad has been running around town like a man half his age. I wouldn't know what to do without him."

"That makes me happy. It's remarkable how much he's done to change himself in such a short time."

Bear looked up, placing a paw on Katie's knee and nodding.

"Did Bear just agree with me?"

Mary laughed. "He has uncanny communication skills."

"I forget that with dogs. They want to please you so much. They look into your eyes and you can almost have entire conversations with them. Violet's cat doesn't seem to care what we think. Hobo acts like it's our privilege that we're living in the house with him."

For a moment, the sun in the western sky flashed before quickly dropping into the line on the horizon. Both women sat in silence for several minutes, the sounds in the evening becoming so clear, even the swaying of the prairie grass was audible.

Katie nodded toward the western sky. "*Gloaming.*"

"*Word of the Day,*" Mary replied, stroking Bear's head as she stared out from the porch. "The poetic definition for twilight, the last remaining minutes of the day when the sun dips below the horizon, and everything appears dusky." The last few words, Mary uttered in a hushed tone as she leaned into Bear.

"There's nothing like a Kansas sky at the end of the day," Katie said.

Mary and Bear sighed together. "Even if it is beautiful and sad at the same time."

"I wish humans knew the views in the sky connect them to the dogs they miss," Betty said. "And one day, when their dogs see their faces on the Bridge, it'll seem like no time has passed at all. And everything they ever wished for awaits them past the Golden Meadow."

Bear put a gentle paw on the Aussie as he gazed at her while she continued. "It sure sounds nice when you say it like that, Betty."

"Until then, I can't believe how wonderful it is when you're sitting with the people and dogs you love here on Earth. Just talking in the twilight," Betty said. "I would have never guessed that before I came to Merivelle."

The dogs sat in silence for a few moments, listening to the women's conversation.

"Do you miss this part of the country?" Mary asked. "I know you live in the same state, but it seems vastly different in many ways."

Katie looked from the sky and the dogs before nodding to the house. "You know, when I'm back visiting, whether it's in town or out here at my dad's home, this feels like a version of heaven. A place where I can be with everyone I've ever loved. The map of my heart's history."

Chapter Thirty-Four

The moon was bright in the sky, bathing the downtown in an ethereal glow. Traffic was still brisk, with Clay's music floating from inside vehicles driving down Main Street. Sounds of people already camping in Steven's Park, anticipating a free concert the next day, drifted from afar. Outside the city limits, the last passenger train for the evening blew its horn in the distance. For generations, the half past ten o'clock train horn on summer nights was a signal to Merivelle children to be home and in bed. Though many snuck out again and headed out to the river for a night of bonfires and mischief.

Two long blasts, followed by one short blast, ending with another, signaled the train's imminent arrival at the station. Gavin stood up from where he'd been sitting on the bench outside the train depot for the better part of an hour. He walked away from the station until he was standing at the corner of the brick-paved parking lot. Glancing at an approaching vehicle, he took a few steps forward as he waited.

Donkey rolled down the window of his patrol car as the air

conditioning inside blew. "Nothing more inspiring to a budding musician than to listen to the trains come in."

"Something ca-calming about them. Allows my brain to relax."

"My dad used to say that kind people with interesting stories usually arrive by train."

"Wish I had my journal."

"It's an easy phrase to remember," Donkey said, laughing as he put the patrol car in park. "I hear you're a talented songwriter."

"From Cybil?"

"It was Clay. A few days ago on a filming break."

Gavin jumped in surprise.

"He was so immersed in whatever you sent through Mary, he missed when they called his name to set. Told me he gave you the premise for a song and the very next day, you had the whole thing written down in verse form, ready for his perusal."

Gavin blinked. "I-I can't remember be-being at a loss for words because I'm happy."

"I love when good things happen to good people. You've been a real help to Cybil. At home and down at the co-op. And being in the right place when Bear fainted? Mary would give you a kidney if you were ever in a bind."

Gavin put his head down. "When I first came to Mer—"

"No need to explain. I have a good gut where people are concerned."

A car drove over the railroad tracks, waving at Donkey as they passed.

"Cybil taught here for years, putting up with all of our nonsense. You'd understand then, when you show up to town as her nephew, even though she has no siblings, that I might still have an on-duty officer drive by and make sure all is well this past week."

Gavin glanced at the red warning lights that came to life at the intersection, signaling the train's imminent approach. "Th-that's what—"

"The upstairs lights went out at a reasonable hour, with no sign of you leaving out a back door or window."

"How d-did you know that wasn't Cy-bil?"

"She sleeps on her couch down in the living room. Scared she'll slip on the wooden stairs. Leaves a lamp on at night when she falls asleep reading. Usually Shakespeare."

Gavin blinked, clearly impressed.

"You also brought Cybil to her bank, maintaining a respectful silence as she conducted her business. Even rejecting being an account co-signer when a new employee fumbled and offered it to you."

"I wouldn't ev-ever take money from Cybil. She's done enough le-letting me stay in her home."

"You didn't call her Aunt Cybil."

"The magazine article. I liked how it explained living in Merivelle—" Gavin stopped, furrowing his brow as he spoke with deliberate thought, breathing deep before continuing. "I decided maybe Cybil would be more truthful."

"You wouldn't be the first kid to call Cybil or Honey by the title. It's an easy reference to fall into with ease. Their house was somewhere we all went when we felt our own parents misunderstood us. One of them would make a snack—something exotic like a *Croque Monsieur*," he said, smiling at the memory. "Then the other would basically say whatever our parents had tried to get through our thick skulls. We'd arrive home with gifts of garden flowers or food from their kitchen." Donkey's expression turned from jovial recollection to quiet and respectful remembrance. "You would have loved Honey and her music."

The train blew its whistle as the rail crossing arms slowly

lowered, red warning lights blinking. Gavin watched the train come into view, swaying with slow speed on the curving tracks. One last blast sounded before coming to rest in the station. Waiting people at the depot got out of their cars in expectation of disembarking passengers. Both Gavin and Donkey looked up as a vehicle that Pavi was riding in pulled up beside the pair.

"Donkey," Pavi said, before glancing around at the kids in the truck near his own age. "I mean—Sheriff."

"Everything good?"

"There's a lot of people not from Merivelle getting rowdy in the park."

Donkey put his car in gear, nodding to Gavin. "I'm here if you need anything," he said before driving from the station. "Good luck with that song of yours."

Someone from the back seat of the truck pushed Pavi forward. "Not cool. You snitched. Doesn't matter if we know them or not."

"Why did you think I said I needed to talk to the sheriff?" Pavi asked, opening the truck door and jumping out. The vehicle drove off with music blaring.

Gavin looked at Pavi. "I think your mom would be happy with you."

"Yeah, I did something *Reyna the Great* would do."

"What's that?"

"Be boring on a Saturday night."

The parking lot continued to empty as passengers shuffled into waiting cars.

"*Reyna*. Does her name mean anything?"

Pavi rolled his eyes. "*Queen*. And believe me, she knows it."

"Is she unkind to you?"

"No. Never."

"Get you in trouble with your mom?"

"Nah, nothing like that." Pavi shook his head. "She's like a second mom to me. But I wouldn't ever tell her that."

"She sounds wonderful. And very helpful."

"You'll have to meet her one day. It's hard to keep up with my *hermana*. I don't even know what path to take. And Reyna's a walking compass. I doubt she's ever been without direction her entire life."

"I bet you make a good pair of siblings. Balance one another out and all." Gavin paused as he watched the last of the cars drive out of the parking lot. "You know, I used to beg my mom for a sister. Told her it was my only wish."

"You have one wish and you'd use it up on a *sister* to boss you around?"

Gavin laughed for a moment before turning serious. "I was alone growing up. My mom worked a lot. Not a lot of friends—"

"Hey, why aren't you struggling to talk?" Pavi's eyes widened before he winced. "Talking about Reyna and I said the first thing on my mind. As Cybil always says, Reyna does not mince words." He paused. "But you *aren't* stuttering."

"I'm not, am I?"

Pavi shrugged, a smile on his face. "Well, there you go. The mere mention of my saint-like sister healed you."

An old truck pulled into the empty depot's parking lot. Gavin watched it as he ran his fingers through his hair.

"Are you waiting for someone?"

Gavin opened his mouth to speak, but no sound came out.

"Should we get out of here?"

The lights to the vehicle turned off and the driver's door opened. A man near Gavin's height got out of the truck and stretched his legs, looking around the area in a cool and detached manner.

Under the parking lot lights, Pavi looked at Gavin. "Are you related?"

"He's my-my—"

"Your dad?" Pavi asked, stepping aside, an excited look on his face. "Go to him now!"

"I've only been with him when my mom was alive. This is the first time—"

"Say no more. Let's *Reyna* this situation. She takes charge of everything."

Crossing the parking lot, the young men arrived at the man who appeared to be in town for an insignificant errand. "I'm Pavi Posada. A friend of your son, Gavin."

"*Mucho gusto*, Pavi."

"You speak Spanish?"

"A little. Picked it up on jobs over the years. *En general, mi español is muy malo. Lo siento mucho*, Pavi."

"*Eso es bastante bueno.* That's pretty good." With an encouraging nod, Pavi urged Gavin to step forward.

Though he clearly saw the interchange, Gavin's dad looked elsewhere. "Nice to see the old train station restored." He let out a low whistle. "I wonder where the money came to refurbish that project?"

"Nobody knows, for sure," Pavi said. "But we all think it's a man who lives here that's trying to really change things for Merivelle."

The man raised his eyebrows, opening his mouth to speak.

"D-dad—"

"You can see your friend and I are talking. Stop interrupting when you have nothing of value to contribute. What were you saying, Pavi?"

The words hung in the sultry summer air, heavy with the silence that followed. In the distance, someone threw trash in a commercial metal garbage bin, the sound of it final and heavy as the lid dropped closed.

Pavi cleared his throat. "Gavin's come to town and helped

everyone. Even Clay Overstreet thinks he's great. I overheard him talking to my mom."

"Did he now?"

"We all think Gavin's going to be a successful songwriter. You should be proud of him. Everyone in town is. And we've just met him."

Turning to only address Pavi, Gavin's dad said, "His mom wanted to be a writer. Both of them always writing in their secret notebooks they carried around."

Pavi took a step nearly on top of Gavin, standing so close they looked almost like conjoined twins. "You should see your son in action. He's kind to every person he meets. Everyone in Merivelle loves him."

"Gavin's always been a bit of a mongrel. Ridiculous puppy eyes while stuttering and everyone melts." He nodded to Pavi. "I bet when you walk into a room, you light it up. I had a stepdaughter of sorts with the same charisma."

"Mr. Ring?"

"That's not my name."

Pavi looked at Gavin.

"I have my m-mom's last name. He never married her. She wanted to, but you—"

"I, what?" The man took a step toward Gavin, staring at him without blinking.

Shaking his head, Pavi asked, "Where are you staying? Maybe we can help you get there."

"No need. I know Merivelle. I'm here for the free concert. And something I couldn't quite get out of Gavin."

"Clay's has a su-surprise for me."

The man hit the palm of his hand against his forehead and sighed. "This is going to be a long twenty-four hours."

"Cybil said that you c-could stay with her."

"Maybe we should check the Windsor," Pavi said. "They might have a few rooms from people who left early."

"Is Cybil the lady with money all over her house? What a character! I can stay there." He looked at Gavin and smiled at him for the first time since he arrived. "You know, since she's been so good to you, son."

Chapter Thirty-Five

"He doesn't want to come to Merivelle," Katie said, the morning after she'd arrived in Merivelle, watching her dad make breakfast.

"Did you explain to him that his family has been waiting the better part of a decade? No correspondence of any kind. But they still have hope that he's going to show up."

Holding Violet on her hip, Katie handed a piece of fruit to the little girl, who took it with great delight. "I thought it might be a huge misunderstanding. That as soon as he heard he was wanted and searched for, he'd be on the way."

Pouring pancake batter onto a griddle—one large circle, followed by two smaller triangles on top—Riven motioned to Violet with the spatula. "It's a cat," he whispered with a smile on his face as the pancake bubbled.

Katie placed Violet in the high chair Riven had ordered for his home the very day he learned his daughter was pregnant. "I tried to tell him how much we loved Lupe. The integral part she plays at the co-op. How artistic and athletic Pavi is. But he told me not to call again. Not even to use their names."

"Was it a language issue?" Riven asked, flipping the pancake.

"He was very fluent when he told me to mind my own business."

Riven stared at the batter as it rose. "It's embarrassing to a man when he feels he's made a mess of things with his kid." He paused for a moment. "You think everyone is judging you, not to mention the crushing sense of failure you have at what's supposed to be the most important thing in life."

"*Fruh-ta-ta?*"

Riven turned to Katie in question.

"A *frittata*. Percy's breakfast influence. Can you imagine?"

"Violet's an exceptional two-and-a-half year old. I say to let my granddaughter use her words. It's fun to watch her brain put things together. In any language."

Though she shook her head, Katie was smiling. She looked down at Violet, her fingers playing with the tiny curls at her neckline. "It's a pancake. You know what those are."

"*Crêpe?*"

"Sort of. A crêpe is a thin pancake. Or is a pancake a thick crêpe?" Katie looked at her dad. "I have no idea sometimes. I just try my best not to confuse or mess her up."

Violet reached out with one of her hands, opening and closing her fingers to her palm.

"I can make her a frittata. Or a crêpe," Riven said, putting the pancake on a plate before reaching for the eggs on the counter.

"Violet, Grandchaps has made you something very yummy. What do we say?"

"Thank you," Violet said, smiling sweetly.

With a sentimental look on his face, Riven looked as if he might melt into the floor. "If Violet wants anything in the whole world, then I want to—"

"Nope. Uh-huh. I will not begin jumping to fulfill every whim of an almost three-year-old child."

"It's only breakfast, honey."

"No, please. I can't bear to spoil her. She's so wonderful, just as she is. Innocent and sweet. Maybe tomorrow you make her one of Percy's silly egg creations. But for now, Violet and I are both so thankful for what we have. At this very moment."

"You know best then." Riven began decorating the cat pancake, placing a pair of blueberries for eyes and two large strawberry halves for ears. He then arranged three banana slices for the cat's muzzle.

"What are the thin apple slices for?" Katie asked, leaning over the counter.

"Cat whiskers, of course."

"You're pretty good," Katie giggled.

Riven held up a can of whipped cream.

"A tiny amount. Or else she'll be bouncing off the walls."

Creating a fur-like mane under the pancake with the whipped topping, Riven then sat the plate in front of his granddaughter.

"Yum!" she said, picking the pancake up with her fingers, scattering fruit onto her high chair tray, smearing whipped cream all over her wrists and hands.

Violet occupied with her breakfast, Riven looked at Katie. "Mind if I ask you a few questions?"

"After a creation like that—anything you want."

Riven started to tidy the counter.

"Here, let me help," Katie said, jumping up.

"Please sit there and talk to me. Bit of a dream to have you and Violet here all to myself." Percy had joined Theodore down at The Hen's Nest after one last band practice before the concert and had not yet returned.

Shrieking with delight, Violet slapped one of her dimpled hands on the tray, red juice dribbling down her chin.

"She loves strawberries," Katie said, wiping her daughter's chin with a napkin before bopping her on the nose in a gentle manner. She turned her attention back to Riven. "What was it you wanted to ask?"

"I sometimes have questions about you growing up. But I don't want to mess this up," he said, motioning between the happy toddler and Katie.

"Try to remember what Franklin always said about good motives."

"Funny enough, Mary and I were talking about that very thing this week." He picked up broken eggs shells, still dripping with liquid, and put them in the trashcan.

"I fully trust your motives. Fire away. I take great pride in coming from a line of tough people."

Riven washed his hands under the faucet, drying them on a dish towel. "Your mom, Julia—" He shook his head. "Let me start from a different direction."

Katie bent down to pick up a blueberry Violet had swept to the floor.

"Trying to find Pavi's dad has me thinking. Do you ever wonder what happened to the man that you thought was your dad?"

"I do. Actually, quite a bit since Violet." Katie's words were slow and thoughtful. "My mom has no idea where he might be. Apparently, he's disappeared into thin air."

Riven gripped the towel in his hand. "Do you miss him?"

"I wouldn't say I *miss him*." She paused, stroking Violet's arm before she spoke again. "Our relationship has cleared up so much confusion for me, Chaps. I think the whole time growing up, I must have had a sense you were nearby. The yearning I felt to be seen by a dad was always for you. I just didn't know it."

The breeze blew through the open windows of the house. Tumbleweeds rolled across the open backyard. The smell of breakfast hung in the air, filling the nearby rooms. Watching the path of the tumbleweeds until they could no longer be seen through the windows, Riven nodded to his daughter. "I appreciate that more than you know, Katie."

"Sometimes I wonder what happened to him." She held up a strawberry for Violet. "I haven't known how to bring him up. My intention isn't to hurt you by being curious about Lance."

Stacking dishes in the sink, Riven ran water over them for a few moments before shutting the faucet off. He took a deep breath. "I need to take responsibility that had Lance not been living in the house with you and your mom—"

"The house you paid for."

"It doesn't matter. I took great delight in bringing him down. That last day—I was so intent on revenge that I had him arrested at your birthday party without thinking of how it would impact you. If I'm honest, I was angrier about the time he got to spend with you more than the money he stole when he worked for me."

Katie let out an audible sigh, her shoulders relaxing. "Then he did steal from you?"

"Quite a bit. I realized it later than my pride wanted to admit. When I finally found out, I pressed charges swiftly. Asked no questions. And gave no mercy. He might have had some noble reason, but I didn't want to hear it."

Katie played with the berries on Violet's tray, mindlessly tracing them in the whipped cream. "You didn't get a proper goodbye from your own dad, did you?"

Glancing toward the front entry of his home, Riven said, "He was gone one day forever. I thought about it all the time. How old he would be when I hit certain milestones—like what he might think of this house? Then one day I realized, after calculating how old he'd be, it was no longer an option to meet him in this lifetime."

Katie reached for Violet's hand as the toddler listened with great interest.

"I wouldn't wish that feeling on my worst enemy. We need to find Pavi's dad, and if your heart needs the same, we can scour the country trying to find your—" Riven paused a moment before continuing. "We can find whoever Lance might be to you and Violet."

Sweeping up crumbs from the high chair, Katie walked around the counter and brushed them into the sink. She leaned into Riven, speaking to him from the side. "If I had one wish on the subject, I would like the option to perhaps talk to him. He was attentive and spoiled me rotten. And then disappeared. How do you do that to someone you've taken under your wing?"

Riven listened with great care.

"I would never abandon Violet. I learned that from you, Dad. You never left Merivelle when most men might have hit the road. And that lesson will always keep me close to my daughter." Katie was tearful as she looked Riven in the eyes. "I never take for granted the time I have with her. All thanks to you."

"I have no words."

Katie pulled a paper towel from the holder and tore it in half, passing one piece to her dad. She blew her nose and sighed heavily, smiling at Violet playing in the mess of her breakfast fragments.

"There is no pushing from me for this offer I'm about to—"

"Dad, you've done enough for me. No more."

"Here me out. Because I might not have the nerve to offer

this so strongly again. And it's important to me we have this discussion. At least once in my lifetime."

With a curious look on her face, Katie paused.

"Lance, the man you thought was your dad."

The room became so silent, the sounds from outdoors tuned in sharply. The breeze whistled as bird wings fluttered in a bird feeder outside an open window. Though not blowing its horn, a moving train was audible several miles away. Violet stopped playing with her breakfast, observing both adults' nearly still countenances.

"You must have some part of you that still wants to—"

Crossing her arms, Katie took a deep, silent breath.

Starting again, Riven continued. "I want to find Lance for you. So that you have no gaps in your own history. You need to be clear on any remaining details."

Tears formed in Katie's eyes.

"You certainly don't need and didn't ask for my permission. But I want to help you with your wish."

Creasing her eyebrows, Katie asked, "What wish?"

"A few moments ago, you said you wished to ask Lance questions. You deserve answers from all the adults who made the choices you had to live with."

Violet fiddled with her food again, happily patting the tray of her highchair. Katie uncrossed her arms, playfully tapping her fingernails on the whipped-creamed surface. "Sometimes when you're a kid, you idolize people and situations. Especially when there's a *gap*—to use your word.

"I've given it some real thought. To cope as a girl, I may have made Lance into more than who he actually was." She chewed on the inside of her lip as she looked around. "For a good deal of my life, I chose to remember fishing trips, ridiculous gifts out of nowhere, spoiling me rotten for whatever reason. But the more secure I get with Percy and the life we're trying to build for Violet and whoever comes after her—"

At the mention of the possibility of more grandchildren, Riven's face lit in joy.

"I always wished for a brother or a sister."

"I never thought past Violet," Riven whispered.

She smiled before continuing. "Anyway, I think what I never allowed myself to see was that those gestures usually came as apologies for destructive behavior with my mom. The morning after late nights out when they both stumbled in." The color drained from her face as she continued. "And the fighting —those were some brawls that I've never seen since. I would have traded every ridiculous present for one week's worth of sleep on school nights.

"So, I'm not sure I want to see Lance again. Does he have his good points unraveled from the behavior I saw as a kid? Would I understand more as an adult woman? Maybe. But those stories aren't mine to work out anymore."

Reeling from his daughter's words, Riven took a breath. "If you ever change your mind—"

"Something tells me that if life ever crosses my path with Lance again, I'll know quickly in my gut if I need more answers. Or if I bypassed a lot of pain in my heart with what I've built here." She motioned, outlining the triangle of herself, Riven and Violet.

"If you're sure?"

"I have a feeling I'm already way down the road from the curiosity of Lance." She reached over and hugged her dad, growling in a funny way that made Violet laugh. "Now enough with sappiness." She pulled back. "Unless you have something more?"

Riven cleared his throat. "A proper goodbye gives closure. A person has to know the ending of the story before they can put the book on the shelf. So they can get on with living. We've got to do that for Pavi."

"I don't know. His dad sounded pretty angry."

"Reyna didn't get that opportunity. We need to keep trying."

At the front of the house, the doorbell rang as Percy opened the door, politely yelling down the hallway. "Hello? Are all my favorite people home?"

"Da-da!" Violet slapped both her hands on the tray, splattering food everywhere as she craned her neck to see the man connected to the greeting. "*Fruh-ta-ta.*"

Both noting the toddler's enthusiasm, Riven and Katie's eyes met. "Let's get through the weekend with Clay and then we'll tell Lupe what we've been up to. Maybe she'll know what to do," Katie said, her eyes lighting up as Percy entered the room.

Chapter Thirty-Six

Twilight arrived the night of Clay's concert for Merivelle. Though still early in the season, summer heat hung in the air so that even when the sun set, the uncomfortable temperature of the day was still present. The hot wind whipped down Main Street, scattering debris. Cybil looked out her picture windows before shutting her front door after several canvas frames fell to the floor. She jumped when the doorbell rang a few minutes later. Mary was waiting on the porch with the two dogs in tow.

"Come in before you blow away!" Cybil said, stepping back from the door.

Betty scampered right over the threshold. "We don't have that kind of wind on the Rainbow Bridge. I still can't get used to it."

"This is western Kansas," Bear said, moving as slowly as Betty was spry. "Those gusts happen all the time." He stopped for a moment and shook his entire body before entering Cybil's house.

"I'm here to get you to the concert," Mary said, laughing as she swatted at the air. "If we can see our way back out from this cloud of white fur." She patted Bear affectionately on the backside.

Betty looked around the entry. "I love the light in Cybil's house. But there's none tonight. Have you noticed that?"

"The sun has nearly gone down. Those lights come through all the glass in the house."

"One of those things you don't know how you know, but you know?"

"I listen closely whenever Mary speaks," Bear said. "Your human will teach you a lot if you listen."

Betty nodded solemnly, audibly closing her mouth.

"Where's Theodore? It wouldn't be like him to miss a big social event like this," Cybil said, easing onto the couch.

"My darling Theodore is already there. Rehearsing with the band."

"Wait, what do you mean?"

"Percy is playing drums—"

"Yes, he's very good, from what Katie told me."

"He didn't say anything, but you can imagine Theodore's fear of missing out. Even though he can't carry a tune to save his life."

Cybil put her face in her hands, laughing as she nodded.

"The other day when they were filming at the train depot, Clay was a sweetheart and offered Theodore his choice of playing a cowbell or a triangle," Mary said, giggling.

"Honey used to offer those same instrument choices to students with similar musical abilities," Cybil said, clearly delighted.

Groaning, Betty said, "I swear. If Theodore plays either of those instruments again, you can *Josephine, Josephine, Josephine* me straight back to Butterfly Academy."

"He surely understands the way we both howled like

coyotes," Bear said, shaking his head. "The sound went straight to the middle of my brain when he was practicing."

Both women continued to laugh—Cybil until she was red in the face. She settled down after a few moments and took a deep breath to steady herself. "I've made you late already, Mary. You should be at the concert. Enjoying the crowning event of everyone's hard work. Not babysitting an old lady."

"Clay's people saved us seats right up front. We can get there whenever it's easiest for you. Maybe when the crowd gets settled a bit." Mary went over and picked up a smaller canvas still face down on the floor, sitting it upright again. "I know I've accidentally neglected you, Cybil. Starting tomorrow, you can catch me up on all things *Ms. Barnes*, summer jam-making and anything else in the entire world you want to chat about. I've missed you so much."

Bear sat at the entrance, his nose sniffing the room as he looked around in curiosity.

"Someone else is here, huh, Bear?"

The Great Pyrenees took a step toward the kitchen.

"That smell," Bear said, putting his nose in the air.

The hair on the back of Betty's neck raised. "Like metal. You know, when you lick something sharp."

"Why would you lick something sharp, Betty?"

"I'm a puppy. I still do silly things."

"Wonder who the smell is from," Bear said, turning his head in question. "I don't like the feeling it gives me."

"Do you have company?" Mary asked. "The dogs look so curious. Borderline frightened."

Cybil motioned over her shoulder. "Gavin and his dad are here. Talking in the garden."

"Another visitor? You should have told me, Cybil. I don't want you overloaded because I'm busy."

"I may forget names and faces. Or need some time to make

194

connections, but helping kids and parents makes me feel like I'm still contributing to my community."

"You already contribute. *Ms. Barnes* is its own helping phenomenon." Mary shook her head emphatically. "Gavin's dad needs to pack his bags. We're going to move him to the Windsor. Or out to my house. Right now. "

Bear walked over to Mary and leaned in, nearly turning his whole head backwards to get her attention.

"She's really worried, isn't she?" Betty asked, scooting on her stomach to where Bear stood.

"Mostly, it's guilt for not being around. She feels that a lot lately." The Great Pyrenees focused on his owner, as they held each other's gaze for a few moments. He nudged her with his snout as he huffed in soft bursts, something that had always made her giggle when they were at home at Sagebrush Farms.

Mary's breathing resumed, and the red blotches on her neck lightened in intensity. "I'm sorry, Cybil. I feel guilty I haven't been around to help. The last thing you need is me firing off a list of questions and orders when I've been absent."

Betty jumped up on to Cybil's lap, wiggling to get her attention.

"You have enough on your plate. Gavin's been heaven sent the last week. I'm the one that strongly encouraged him to bring his dad to town. He needs people around him when he's brave enough to confront what scares him to death."

"Sounds like quite a story there."

"I'll fill you in later," Cybil said, stroking Betty's back.

Betty breathed in, closing her eyes for a few seconds' inhalation "I always smell honeysuckle when Cybil talks. I don't know why, but I feel right at home with her."

"She was a teacher. Mary says they're angels in disguise. Like us dogs."

"Dogs and teachers walking around earth like secret

angels," Betty said, panting in a happy manner. "I love that, Bear. That must be why Cybil gets along so well with everyone."

"She also likes to give people the benefit of the doubt."

"What does that mean?"

"That even when you aren't sure, you see the highest possibility of someone's actions."

"I'll have to work on that one, Bear. I still seem to growl or bite when something confuses me. But I'm trying."

"You're doing better all the time." Bear put a gentle paw on Betty's shoulder. "All you have to do is listen. More time here in Merivelle and you'll be a natural."

Walking through the side patio doors, Gavin's face lit up. He made a beeline to Bear, stroking the dog's head in a gentle manner.

"Did you feel Gavin's heart rate go up?" Betty asked.

"Be as calm as possible. He's really struggling right now."

"My-my dad..." Gavin swallowed hard, straining his neck muscles. Both women waited for him to speak.

"Is this a lick Gavin in the face opportunity?" Betty jumped off Cybil's lap and onto the floor.

"It's a lean in and *listen* moment. Gavin needs to hear his own words."

Betty laid down beside Bear, resting her head on her paws as she looked up at Gavin.

Mary's phone rang as her shoulders dropped. "I'm so sorry. I want to hear what you have to say, but this might be about your song, Gavin." She stepped out onto the front porch to answer the call.

"Well, you've got me and the dogs," Cybil said, smiling. "What can we help you with tonight?"

"He-he doesn't want to come to-tonight."

Cybil rose from where she sat. "Is he ill?"

"He didn't say. I thought we could wo-work through some things. T-talk about my mom. But he won't listen." Gavin looked to the patio. "I thought I-I would have more confidence speaking to him."

Taking a few steps, Cybil said, "Your self-assurance should come from here." She put her hand over the young man's heart. "What innate talent you have bringing words from your heart onto a page for a renowned musician to sing. Perhaps one day for people all over the world."

Looking up, Gavin met Cybil's gaze.

"Your words will reach people you've never met. Perhaps at the very moment when they feel most alone. It's quite extraordinary, Gavin. You have every reason to be proud tonight."

Bear looked down at Betty, a knowing look on his face. "See? That's a teacher for you. No one else will probably ever know this conversation. But it will help him for years to come. I can feel it."

"I don't think I want to have him hear my words. I feel em-embarrassed and want to run when I think about it."

"Running is what your dad always did. The strongest thing you can do to show your strength is to stand where you are when your gifts are being celebrated by those around you."

"I thought if he saw me do well, it would be a new start. I don't know if I can even go to the con-concert now."

"Charge forward among your new friends in Merivelle. No matter what happens, you've already succeeded," Cybil said, reaching for Gavin's hand.

Mary came through the front door with an excited look on her face, almost dancing in place. She waited for Cybil to finish speaking.

"Also, remember people have their own reasons for the decisions they make. Maybe crowds bother your dad."

"Yes, crowds. They can definitely be tricky, Cybil." From the garden side of the kitchen, a man came through the open doors. He chuckled, extending his hand to Mary. "I overheard your voice. Crowds can be daunting when you've lived alone as long as I have. I'll just stay here and listen to the concert on the porch."

"He's going to stay at Cybil's while she goes with us to the concert?" Bear asked, the hair on the back of his neck raising as he growled.

"I thought we were supposed to be giving people the best motives?" Betty asked, standing behind him.

"Listen with your heart, not to your fear, when you give people the benefit of the doubt. But once your instinct kicks in —never question it."

"You never told me that part."

"How do you feel when Gavin's dad walked in?"

"Odd. Like the room went upside down. And I get that weird metal taste in mouth." Betty thought for a moment. "I kind of want to run. But maybe bite something before I do." She bared her teeth, eyeing the man's ankles. "Does Cybil know the instinct thing?"

Thinking for a moment, Bear took a step toward the old woman. "I think when humans get old, they get especially lonely. Sometimes, when they feel the people they love the most have forgotten them, they exchange their instinct for someone to be around. So they don't feel alone."

"That's the saddest thing I've ever heard." Betty's eyes were wide.

"*You* need to keep learning the benefit of the doubt," Bear said as he went up and nudged the old woman's hand affectionately. "And sometimes Cybil still needs to remember her instincts, even when she's lonesome."

Mary gestured with her phone in hand. "That was Clay's

people. They don't want us to tell anyone because they want it to be as authentic as possible."

"What, dear?" Cybil asked.

"They want to shoot one last video. But they don't want to announce it ahead of time. The wrong people might push to the stage, trying to get on camera. After a successful week, we're so close to being finished. The last thing we need is a big, dramatic scene causing mayhem at the concert."

"No, you wouldn't want that, would you?" Gavin's dad looked around the room, studying the books on the wall.

Betty got up, shaking her whole body. "Did you just hear a coyote? I'm freaking out. What is going on?"

"That's your instinct at work," Bear said. "I felt it too."

"Mary, I don't know if it's my idea of fun to stand in a crowd near the front of sound equipment." Cybil picked up a magazine from her entry table and fanned herself. "Just talking about the heat and I'm overwhelmed."

"I'm so disappointed, but I know you're right, Cybil. I shouldn't have brought Bear here tonight, but he was insistent."

"You climbed right into Mary's vehicle and wouldn't budge," Betty replied. "I didn't know dogs could do that. I thought we were always supposed to obey."

"Only in emergencies. I was acting on my instinct—the feeling I shouldn't miss tonight."

"Yeah, but Bear. You also take your sweet time when Mary tries to call you to the house. You wouldn't get high marks for that at Butterfly Academy."

Mary smiled at the two dogs with their noses close to one another. "Trying to haul a hundred-and-twenty pound dog out of a vehicle is its own challenge. I give in when Bear wants to go. Especially since he's getting older. I never want him to feel left alone."

"Why don't you leave the dogs here with me for the

evening?" Cybil said, running her hands through Bear's mane. "Us old folks can stay behind and listen from the front porch." She nodded to the counter and then to Gavin's dad. "I whipped up a batch of muffins, especially for you. We can have a nice cup of coffee before you join the concert. I promise, once you get started, you won't want to stop. They're Gavin's special recipe."

"They were on the counter. I already had a couple."

"Even better," Cybil said, smiling cordially. "Help yourself to as many as you want. There's milk in the fridge, if you prefer."

"We'll keep an eye on this coyote," Bear said, plopping onto the ground with a deep, multi-octave groan. "He can't even keep his paws off her food."

"Maybe I'll take Betty though," Mary said. "So you don't have too many animals."

A text dinged on Mary's phone. She read it as she started walking to the door. "We need to leave now. Gavin's dad—I'm sorry to have missed talking to you." She paused, considering him for a moment. "Have we met before?"

Bear sat up, shifting his attention between his owner and the man.

"She's using her instinct, isn't she?" Betty asked. "Look at the goosebumps on her arm."

Mary's phone rang again.

"And now she's not using it," Betty said, shaking her head. "These humans and their phones."

Chapter Thirty-Seven

"You're sure you can't stay past the concert tonight?"

"Percy needs to fly out of Kansas City tomorrow evening," Katie said, waving to someone behind where she and Mary sat, waiting for the concert to begin. "I wish I would have thought to have him pack a bag to leave from Merivelle. Then Violet and I could have stayed here while he was gone."

Steven's Park was even more crowded than the week before, though traffic had been blocked off around the park. Where Merivellians had spread out leisurely with picnic blankets at the Midsummer concert, Clay Overstreet fans were standing shoulder-to-shoulder. Only in the front rows of park benches was there any sort of personal space.

Mary scooped Betty from the ground and onto her lap so that someone could scooch past where she and Katie were sitting a few rows from the stage. "I haven't had a spare moment to spend with this sweet dog. She follows Bear around like she's his own fan club."

"I'm surprised she doesn't already have a collar with a

name tag bearing the name *Mary Bailey* and your phone number."

Betty looked between the two women, her stubby tail wagging at the conversation.

Mary folded her hands, fingers interlocked, almost as if she were praying. "I don't know if I've properly thanked you and Percy."

"For what?"

"This is one of the most tremendous opportunities to happen to Merivelle—all thanks to you both."

"We just got the ball rolling. Any regrets? It was an enormous undertaking."

"None with Clay. The true meaning of a professional."

"But?"

"I've accidentally lost track with everyone in my orbit. Even Lupe. We went home to change and she and Pavi were nowhere to be found. Her phone goes straight to voicemail. I haven't had time to try and track her down."

"Maybe she's exhausted from all the catering. She left word there's food for the crew to take on the road tonight."

"You saw her?"

"She texted me. Very briefly."

Mary wrinkled her forehead in question.

"I don't think anyone wants to bother you. You look like a walking zombie."

"Well, I hope Lupe and Pavi are here somewhere," Mary said, searching the area. She took a deep breath, fanning herself with her hand. "I'm glad I left Bear at Cybil's."

"Who is Gavin that's staying with her? Everyone gets distracted when I ask."

Mary shielded her eyes from the debris in a gust of wind as Katie bowed her head for a moment. When they looked up, both their husbands were making their way down the center aisle of the seating, Riven holding Violet as he followed.

"They look like they're running for office," Katie said, rolling her eyes in a good-natured manner.

Betty jumped off her lap and stood at the entrance to the aisle, panting in anticipation.

"Who's the young man with them?"

"*That's* Gavin," Mary said, unconsciously reaching for Bear, who was not there. She looked down at the emptiness of her hand.

The gesture was not lost on Katie. "How's Bear doing after his vet visit?"

"Good. For now. But it won't be a long time in the future when—" Mary shook her head, clearing her throat. "I'll save that for another time. I feel lop-sided enough without him tonight. Let's talk about something else."

Katie stared at the group of men walking. "Gavin—how long is he going to be with Cybil?"

"No idea."

"You aren't worried?"

"She told me she has it handled. I'll sort it out tomorrow, if there's a problem."

Katie waved to Violet and her dad. Leaving the younger men stopped in conversation, Riven made his way up the last few rows to his daughter. Violet patted his face as he walked.

"Aren't we too close for her ears once the concert starts?" Riven asked. "I can stand at the back with her. The crowd is already loud."

Reaching into a diaper bag, Katie pulled out a pair of noise-reduction earmuffs with cat ears. "These will help her." She placed them on Violet's head before kissing her.

Mary laughed, leaning over to Violet. "The sweetest cat I've ever seen!"

"Everyone—scrunch together so I can get a picture."

Betty jumped up and put her head next to Violet's, panting in happiness.

The trio of Mary, Riven, and Violet posed as Katie looked at the photo on her phone. She laughed as she flashed her phone screen to them. "One pint-sized kitty with her auntie and Grandchaps. And a silly puppy."

Betty licked Violet right in the face, smiling at the little girl as she wagged her tail.

"Can you text me that pic?"

"Better yet, Chaps, I'll print it out for you." She nodded behind the group. "The rest of our crew is here."

Finally, making their way down the aisle, Theodore was ecstatic. "The gang's all back!"

Mary kissed him. "Where have you been?"

"In Clay's trailer, it's parked and ready to leave the minute the concert is over."

"Theodore's a big hit with everyone," Percy said. "Keep an eye, Mary. He might run away on one of the tour buses tonight. He and his cowbell and triangle."

"On any other occasion, you'd be right," Theodore said, laughing. "But tomorrow, my big wish is to spend all day with Mary."

"Gavin's going to watch from the stage," Percy said, turning to the side to include the young man in the conversation.

In silence, Katie studied the young man, her face still.

"And for whatever reason, Clay wants Riven in the front rows of the audience," Percy said. "So I told him you'd want to watch with your dad, Katie."

The din of the crowd became even louder when the park lights came on with the fading light. A few moments later, the band walked on stage to the cheers of the crowd. Katie reached for Violet, her expression serious.

"That's an air of mystery, wasn't it?" Theodore asked. "Everyone else invited backstage, but Riven needs to sit out front and wait."

"Motives, Theodore. Motives. I don't understand, but I'm going to trust," Riven said. "Benefit of the doubt and all."

Betty stood on her back legs, panting happily at the old man's words.

"What's wrong?" Katie whispered to Mary. "You look like you've seen a ghost."

"You must be Katie, who ev-everyone talks about," Gavin said, his hand outstretched.

Mary looked at her cousin and Gavin. A jolt of energy went through her.

"In case everyone's been too busy to tell you, Gavin's a songwriter," Percy explained to Katie. "He wants to watch at the back of the crowd, but we assured him—center stage is where he belongs."

Waiting for Clay to arrive, the band began playing one of his old songs as the crowd cheered at the top of their lungs in anticipation.

Looking as if he might be sick, Gavin nodded weakly as he staggered forward.

"It's a concert stage, not the guillotine," Percy said, his voice kind. "We'll be there to help you."

"You got this! Either of us will be there to help you," Theodore said. He cupped his hands to his mouth so Mary could hear him over the high-decibel level. "Watch for my cowbell! And maybe a surprise triangle!"

Percy kissed his wife on the cheek before the trio of men moved forward, climbing up a set of stairs on the side of the stage.

Katie searched her cousin's expression. "Everything good?"

"I'm worried about Bear."

"Now?" Katie asked. "The concert is starting." She pointed behind the seats. "You'll never get out of here. Call Cybil, she'll give you an update."

"I'll be right back! Keep your dad in these seats. It's important for him not to move, okay?"

Chapter Thirty-Eight

Mary made her way through the crowd with Betty at her side. The concert had already begun and familiar Clay Overstreet songs rang out into the night. The further out from the band-shell, the more celebratory the crowd. A few people stopped her on the sidewalk, trying to include her in dancing as they listened to the music. Once she'd made it through the turnstile of people shouting their thanks for bringing Clay to town, she nearly ran the rest of the way to Cybil's house.

Out of breath, Mary climbed the few stairs up to where Cybil sat alone on her porch, rocking in a chair. "Where is he?"

"Who, dear?"

"Gavin's dad."

"Oh, he's already gone. He left from the side gate. I was talking to the Posadas on the front porch. Lupe left you a letter. Don't let me forget to give it to you. She seemed pretty emotional."

"When did he leave?"

"Pavi? He left with Lupe."

"No, not the Posadas. Gavin's dad."

"A short time after you. Bear followed him—"

"*Bear did what?*"

"As you said, a dog Bear's size is nearly impossible to change their mind."

Mary took a deep breath. "Bear will be fine. Everyone knows who he is. But Gavin's dad—we need to find him. He didn't say where he was going?"

"He didn't seem overly interested in the concert."

Betty stood at the front door, her nose at the bottom of the screen door.

Mary took a step forward, putting her hand on Cybil's. "Mind if I check the house?"

Swaying in place as the music played blocks away in the park, Cybil waved her on. "Make yourself at home!"

Once inside, Mary held a hand over her mouth as she looked around. Books were thrown to the floor with paint canvases scattered about the room. Paperwork hung out of half-opened drawers. Betty ran through the house, barking as she ran up and down the stairs before coming to rest by Mary.

"Oh, my god," Mary said, under her breath as she glanced out to Cybil sitting on the porch. "It is him."

Chapter Thirty-Nine

"I need to check on Mary. She's been gone too long—the concert's nearly over. I'm worried something might be wrong with Bear," Riven said, craning his neck as he looked to the back of the concert crowd. "Can you take Violet?"

Katie looked at her dad, holding her daughter. "Yes, of course. Are you feeling okay? You're pretty pale." She held her hands out to Violet, who pulled back and put her arms around Riven's neck. "Besides, Clay wanted you to stay put. For a surprise. Remember?"

"I'll be back." He kissed the top of Violet's head, passing her to her mom.

"Remember what you told me at Easter a few years ago? *'Let yourself be celebrated.'*"

Someone approached Katie from the aisle, motioning their intent to sit further down the row. With his daughter's attention occupied for a moment, Riven moved around her, weaving in and out of people dancing in the aisle, making minimal progress against the swell of people pushing forward.

The next moment, Bear made his way through the crowd with ease. Joyful people danced and shouted his name. Paying no attention to the phones videoing his movements, the dog worked his way toward Riven, standing in front of him protectively.

In the wake of Bear's arrival, Gavin's dad came down the aisle, his focus on Riven. The crowd that had parted generously for the dog looked in puzzlement at the angry man. Returning their attention to the concert as Clay finished a song, they pushed toward the stage, closing off any space for further movement.

The man stood face-to-face with Riven, eyes blazing as Bear growled in warning.

"It is you." Riven spoke in a normal decibel, though it was drowned out by sound. "I kept pushing it out of my mind that Gavin had an uncanny resemblance to you. Merely a coincidence."

Clenching his fists, the man said, "I couldn't have dreamt of a better moment. Right here in front of the entire town."

Katie craned her neck as she held Violet. "*Lance*," she said, before looking to and from his son on the stage. "Of course," she murmured. "They almost look like twins."

Violet began to cry, her fluffy-down hairline wet from the heat of the night.

"No, no drama for you. All is well, Violet." The distinct scent of flowers blew into the area, calming the child almost instantly. "There we go," Katie said, stroking her daughter's face. "A little air for you." Her eyes searched to where her father stood with Lance. She took several deep and calming breaths.

"Now a giant dog protecting you instead of the law?"

Bear barked, shifting his weight forward as he bared his teeth, growling in warning.

Riven's hands went to the top of Bear's head. "Calm, Bear. No need to fight this coyote."

A man in a cowboy hat looked at the two men. "Everything square here?"

Riven nodded. "We're getting sorted. No problems."

The lighting of the concert dimmed as Clay spoke from the stage. "I want to thank Merivelle for the hospitality. Let's hear it for this special town!" He nodded to the cheering crowd, their thunderous applause booming out into the night.

Lance spat on the ground, his eyes fixed on Riven. "You ruined my life!"

Appearing from the back of the audience, Mary pushed her way forward. Bear's ears went up, barking to alert her of his whereabouts. The audience was so mesmerized by Clay talking on the stage, they merely bobbled as she passed through.

"Spending time in Merivelle, I learned the stories of a lot of good people. The salt-of-the-earth kind that makes up the thousands of small towns just like it from all over our country," Clay said, nodding toward the crowd as he began strumming on his guitar.

The crowd became even more silent, as if someone had turned down the volume of the entire event. Couples danced in place with their arms around one another. The soft lighting of the stage bequeathed a cinematic glow to everyone in attendance.

"And in that tapestry of stories, a new talent emerged." He turned to the shadows of the stage. "Come on out here, Gavin Ring. Before I perform this song that you wrote overnight."

Gavin stood at the edge of the light on the stage, bowing his head in a modest way.

"I hear Gavin's dad made it tonight." Clay looked out into the crowd, eyes searching the front rows. "Can you give a shout-out so your son knows that you're here? Means a lot to someone who opens their heart and shares their words with the world. Especially the first time they're celebrated."

The crowd waited in silence, waiting for someone to step forward. Lance stood with his back to the stage, eyes glued to Riven, his face shadowed by the light behind him.

Gavin shifted uncomfortably on stage, taking a few steps in the opposite direction before stopping, pointedly anchoring himself in place as he took a deep breath to steady his nerves.

"A moment from you would mean the world to your son. First steps can change everything," Riven said.

Clay pulled the microphone close to his mouth. "Wherever you are, Gavin's dad. I hope you're as proud of your son as the rest of Merivelle. Everyone else—remember this summer night in western Kansas that you were here for the debut of Gavin's song." He plucked a simple melody with his guitar. "I can promise you it will be the first of many you'll hear in your lifetime."

Riven looked nervously to Katie, who motioned to Violet and then in his direction, signaling her desire to be with him but also her protectiveness for her daughter.

Turning his focus to follow Riven's gaze, Lance's face softened, registering genuine surprise that Katie was a mother.

Seeing the change in Lance's expression, Riven held Bear's collar. "We're old men. No need to fight and ruin the night for our kids. We both done enough to them in our lifetimes."

The band played a few simple chords as Clay continued to speak. "We put a few notes to Gavin's words. A surprise for Riven—one of my good friend's dad."

At the singer's words, Lance pushed Riven with his shoulder, nearly toppling him. Bear bolstered his fall, pushing him upright.

"A filthy, flea-bitten animal helping you. Makes sense. You were always more of a mutt."

212

Bear growled in a low tone as Mary continued to push through the crowd, with Betty at her side.

"Did we lose Riven?" Clay said, chuckling.

The crowd began chanting Riven's name. Someone tapped the man in the cowboy hat who had tried to intercede earlier. "That's him," they shouted over the crowd who had grown loud again.

The spotlight followed the cheer of the crowd where Lance and Riven stood facing one another, separated by Bear.

"And look there! Bear Bailey—Merivelle's dog."

At the word "*dog*", the crowd went wild. Phones videoed Bear standing protectively in front of Riven. The Great Pyrenees panted as he stood his ground, legs shaking in the heat.

Sincerely surprised, Clay smiled as he held a hand over his eyes, trying to see into the audience. "Even better—I thought Bear was still heat-stroked and going to miss out on his song tonight."

Hearing his name, Bear looked at the stage. He panted heavily before returning his attention back to Riven.

Clay spoke to each section of the crowd as if he were having an intimate conversation with each person in it. "What would our homes be without our loyal dogs? Gavin was clever to weave Bear into his song."

A wave of sentimental emotion filled the area as the singer spoke.

"Without Bear, I don't know if there would have been a concert tonight. Maybe we wouldn't even be here in Merivelle this week, making new friends. But that's the miracle of a good dog." Clay touched the tip of his hat as he strummed on his guitar before singing. "Give a listen to Gavin's song—'The Old Dog'."

The audience cheered before settling in as they listened to Clay's voice.

Rises with the sun, rests under the stars.
Carries old stories and a couple of scars.
A heart full of memories, no room for hate.
Makin' his peace with the slow hands of fate.

After Clay finished singing the first verse, the crowd cheered. Bear used his snout to flip Riven's hand on top of his head.

"Let's give your son his moment," Riven said, stepping out of the spotlight. "Then you can have a swing at me once this concert is done."

Stepping forward, Lance pushed Riven, unintentionally moving him back into the light. "Don't give *me* parenting advice."

He leans in and listens; he listens with love.
This old dog he was sent from above.
Runs with a limp, guards with pride,
Waits at the door, with his heart open wide.
Won't say much, but it's always enough.
He leans in and listens; he listens with love.

A few people in the crowd repeated the last lines of the chorus, slight echoes after Clay had sung—"*He leans in and listens; he listens with love.*" Gavin looked up, a look of bewilderment on his face as Clay continued with the next verse.

A few good friends, knows his folks by scent.
Gives more grace than most ever spent.
Thinking 'bout old dogs, miracles made right,
The future, the prayers, as the morning turns light.

Hearing the words of the song, Bear whined, turning his head as he listened to the music. He remembered his good friend, Franklin, speaking similar words on his back porch years before. It happened when he was just a young dog, but Bear thought of that morning frequently as he roamed the ground at Sagebrush Farms, watching a new day begin with each sunrise.

Doesn't mind the silence; never fears the rain.
Walks a little slower through the joy and the pain.
One day, he'll be where the good ones know.
Where the bridge meets the sky and the kind hearts go.

The melody of the song accompanied only by Clay's guitar, the charged energy of the crowd with the sound of the words hit Bear deeply. Still standing guard at Riven's feet, he put his nose in the air and howled mournfully. Everyone around him turned, their faces soft. Touched by Bear's reaction, the crowd attempted to join in the final chorus—singing the easier to remember lyrics.

He leans in and listens; he listens with love.
This old dog—he was sent from above.
Walks through the fire, carries the load.
Stands for the lost at the end of the road.
Won't say much, but it's always enough.
He leans in and listens; he listens with love.

Gavin watched, mesmerized, as the audience joined in singing the words he had written. Seeing his emotion, Clay nodded to him, a gentle smile on his face; an expression reflecting his familiarity with the thrill the younger man was experiencing for the first time.

For a moment, Lance glanced at the stage, before returning his attention to his old rival. "I'm going to beat you to a pulp the minute his song is over."

"That's your takeaway from this moment?" Riven pointed to the jubilant crowd. "Your son's night is a triumph."

"You falling on your face in front of the whole town is all I care about. Even better that it's being filmed."

Betty arrived at Bear's side, barking in rapid succession. "Mary's trying to find you."

"I can't leave these two. Gavin's dad is about to lose it," Bear said.

Nodding to the stage, Riven spoke again. "This is a life-changing opportunity for Gavin."

"Don't speak to me about opportunities," Lance said, stepping into Riven, putting both men in the spotlight.

Having made her way through the crowd, Mary pulled Lance by the arm, out of the spotlight, her face furious.

Glaring, Lance yanked his arm from her grip. "Another Margaret. The spitting image of your mother. Mind your own business!"

From the stage, Clay waved the spotlight forward as he sang the chorus one more time. In response, the crowd moved Riven and Bear toward his singing. Bear pulled back, trying to get to Mary through the crowd.

"Bear—go! With Riven. Help him up the stairs," she said, motioning toward the stage.

Sniffing the air, Bear turned in confusion.

"That smell from Riven's chest again," Betty said. "He needs you. I'll help Mary."

Bear nodded and followed Riven as both were guided forward through the singing crowd. The stage crew helped Riven and Bear up the steps of the stage. The bright lights blinding both as they blinked and squinted, trying to get their bearings.

Mary turned to Lance, her expression furious. "This is not how I remember you. I always thought you were innocent. You were always so kind to Katie when we were growing up."

"And look where it got me. Riven Chapowits and *your* dog are being celebrated by a song my son wrote."

As the song ended, Clay waved Gavin to the center stage with one hand. He whispered into the young man's ear and pointed out, stepping back so Gavin could stand in the spotlight as the band and audience cheered him. Next, Clay welcomed Riven and Bear as the crowd cheered for several minutes.

Staring out into the audience, Bear's somber expression was the mirror of when he was guarding boundaries at Sagebrush Farms. The bright lights were disorienting, the heat of the stage almost unbearable as he staggered.

"You okay?" Riven asked, stroking his fur.

"And one last cheer for Merivelle's wonderful dog—Bear Bailey!" Clay bowed to the Great Pyrenees as people applauded, taking video and photos with their phones. "Thank you for a great night! We'll see you next time!" The lights went out as Clay exited, waving to the fans on the far side of the audience. From high on the stage, no longer blinded by the lights, Bear searched the crowd for Mary, growling when he located her.

"What did you take from Cybil's house?" Mary shouted.

"Butt out!" Lance grabbed Mary's wrist as Betty nipped at his heels. He looked down and kicked the Aussie as Mary stumbled with his effort. She landed on the side of a bench, hitting her shoulder, crying out in pain.

From the stage, the ferocious barking of Bear Bailey

brought all after-concert cheer to a halt. Clay turned from his exit. Riven tried to reach for Bear's collar, falling forward, bloodying his bottom lip instantly. The Great Pyrenees launched himself off the high stage and into the crowd, landing on the ground with a sickening thud before all went quiet.

Chapter Forty

"It's beginning to be a pattern that we're here," Mary said, as she clutched several crumpled tissues in her hand, pacing in the front waiting room of the vet's office. She tried to make light of the situation, but the effort only brought forth more tears.

Theodore rose from a chair to comfort her.

"I'm fine," she said, putting a hand up.

A few moments later, Dr. Luke walked out into the waiting room.

Tears welled up in Mary's eyes as she shredded the tissues in her hand. Katie gently reached for her cousin's hands, exchanging the used tissues for fresh ones. Taking a deep breath, Mary waited for Dr. Luke to speak.

Theodore stood beside his wife. Behind her, Riven, Katie and Percy formed a semi-circle. Gavin stood at the door, careful to be on the outer edges of the group.

"As you and everyone attending the concert tonight know, Bear is an old dog," Dr. Luke said.

Theodore put his arms around Mary.

"Even a young dog jumping from the height of the stage

could have caused extensive damage. Bear's age and weight, combined with the fall, injured him seriously. I won't be able to help him here in Merivelle." Dr. Luke cleared his throat. "I wish I could offer you more than two options. Especially where Bear's concerned."

"Do you mean we need to decide if we put Bear—" Mary stopped. "I can't even bring myself to say the word out loud."

"Let's take a breath and just listen," Theodore whispered.

"The x-rays show that Bear's leg and hips have sustained multiple fractures. He needs extensive surgical intervention that I can't perform. All I can do is keep him comfortable until you decide."

Percy lifted Violet from her mom as he looked at Mary. "We'll wait outside to give you some privacy," he said in a kind manner. "Take your time. Clay wanted me to pass on his best wishes. He wants to be updated as soon as we know something about Bear."

Gavin moved to the side of the door to allow Percy to pass, hesitating for a moment, before staying behind as the door closed gently.

"Your decision, Mary, is whether the ordeal of surgery and the rehabilitation afterwards is something you want to undertake. It'll be a Herculean effort to get a big dog like Bear back on his feet."

"Of course! I'd fly to the moon if it would give me one more day with Bear. Whatever it takes is what I want to do."

"Everyone in this room knows that about you. But you also need to think of Bear and how comfortable he might be in the aftermath of his injuries."

Her eyes filling with tears, Mary bowed her head.

"At nine years old, Bear is considered a senior dog," Dr. Luke continued.

"In dog years, he's still only sixty-three. I'm older than

that," Riven said, huffing. "I'd take a hip replacement with a leg cast any day rather than be euthanized." The last word out of his mouth, his expression dropped. "Sorry, Mary," he said quietly. "How thoughtless of me."

Dr. Luke continued. "There's a general thought that bigger stature dogs—Great Pyrenees, St. Bernhards and Great Danes mature at a faster rate. Often, their life spans are much shorter than an average-sized dog. No matter how well they've been cared for."

Mary choked as she looked at Theodore. "Did I know that?" She grabbed for his arm and clutched it tightly. "*How did I not know that?*"

"Every dog is different. And somehow they'll let you know the best decision. Especially the way you and Bear communicate," Dr. Luke said. "Maybe Bear can handle surgery and recovery just fine. A lot of work for you. But as we all know—you'd be up for it."

Wiping her eyes, Mary stood tall. "Let me take him home. We can look after him. I'll know the best thing to do by just spending some time with him."

"Oh, no, Mary," the vet said, shaking his head. "You can't take Bear with you tonight. You'd only cause greater damage. He's heavily sedated to keep him out of extreme pain."

A cloud of anxiety again passed over Mary's face as she shrunk into Theodore's arms.

"You can go back and speak with him. Probably the best medicine in the entire world for Bear," Dr. Luke said. "I'll call Kansas State in Manhattan and see what their schedule looks like for a consultation, if that's what you decide."

"Then let's get Mary back with her dog," Riven said, tears in his eyes. "They'll both make the best decision."

Chapter Forty-One

The sky lit in soft pinks and yellows as Bear opened his eyes and groaned. He tried to get up, but fell back, huffing in exertion.

"Our wonderful friend, Bear Bailey."

He looked around. There was a prismatic sunbeam coming closer with each moment, too bright for him to stare into for any length of time.

As if someone put their finger on a bubble, the scene changed instantly. Bear blinked his eyes, startling at the two angels standing in front of him.

"No fear, Bear," Lea said, stepping toward him with her hand out. "We're only here to help you."

"How do you know my name?"

"You're quite famous here on the Bridge."

Glimmers of light surrounded another angel as she smiled at Bear.

"Josephine?" Bear asked, looking up. The weight of his head was heavy. He lowered down before she answered.

Kneeling, the angel nodded and kissed the top of Bear's head. "I've always wanted to meet you, good boy."

Bear turned his head in question.

"But I've only ever sent messages with other dogs. Your friends Jiff, Henry and Betty."

"I remember your name—*Josephine, Josephine, Josephine.*"

"You like to say it three times," she said, smiling.

He looked up at the angels, a mournful expression on his face. "Am I dead?"

"That's a very Dark Den way to put things, Bear," Josephine said gently. "Don't be scared. Everything will work out in the most perfect way for everyone involved."

Bear squinted, trying to make out the field in front of him. As his vision adjusted, images of dogs playing came into focus. The scent of peanut butter and bacon filled the air. A squirrel came up to him, almost nose to nose, shaking its tail playfully. Lifting a paw in a polite but tired greeting, Bear then looked to Earth and back to the two angels. "Not to be impolite, but you never answered my question—am I *dead?*"

Hearing Bear's last word, the squirrel froze in motion, letting out a squeak before scampering away.

"We don't use that word here on the Rainbow Bridge," Lea said. "You're alive. In a different place." She stroked Bear's head in a gentle manner.

"Why am I hurting? I thought there was no pain here?"

Sitting on the ground for the first time in many, many years, Josephine cradled Bear's head in her lap.

"That feels better." Bear snuggled his chin onto her knee for a moment, letting himself relax.

Running her fingers over Bear's back, Josephine said, "I've always thought that Great Pyrenees' fur feels like angel wings."

Bear looked up in question. "You do?"

"People always assume angel wings are feathers. But from

where we stand up here on the Rainbow Bridge, I believe dogs' fur is very similar."

From the far side of the Golden Meadow, growls and yips floated on the breeze. It was easy to imagine dogs tussling over a bone. "I don't know if I'll see you in a bit, Bear. But I'm off to rain down some more treats. It must be a new dog or two that doesn't realize there's never an end to the goodies here." Lea walked away, disappearing like a mist in a few strides.

Bear yawned in a long and drawn out manner. "How long have I been here?"

"A few moments," Josephine replied.

"It feels longer than *moments*."

Josephine leaned into Bear, a thoughtful look on her face. "Time is different here on the Rainbow Bridge. On Earth, it seems to stretch out until the end of a soul's life, and then it hastens. It's a way someone knows they're ready to cross over."

"*I'm crossing over?*"

Two dogs playing frisbee looked over with concern.

"I would imagine that you aren't, based on the way you reacted to my words," Josephine said.

Bear looked at her in question.

"At the end of their earthly time, souls have a serenity that defies explanation. And you, my furry friend—are not calm."

"Am I doing something wrong?" Bear put a paw on the angel's hand and looked up at her.

"It's simply not your time. Your soul wants to go back to Earth."

"To Mary."

"Yes—to Mary," Josephine answered. "I suspect you merely needed a glimpse of the Rainbow Bridge. Perhaps a visit from old friends to give you some courage."

The next instant, mountains appeared on the far side of the meadow, a train depot in front of the expanse as a locomotive blew its horn in the distance. Two shimmery dog figures appeared against the scene. The sound of a corgi *awwwooooo* and another's dog's throaty bark echoed in the distance.

Bear looked at Josephine. "Jiff and Henry?"

"They're close by. Sending signs to help you."

"But I won't see them today?" Bear asked before turning his head. "I don't know how I know that."

Josephine stood up. "I expect if you stay a moment more, you'll make for a very sad Mary."

At the sound of her name, Bear grimaced, trying to get to his feet.

Josephine stroked his head, instantly calming him. "Rest yourself. You'll be back in Merivelle in a moment."

Bear looked around the meadow as the mountains and train faded with the breeze. "But one day, I'll be back here."

Josephine nodded.

"And it won't be a long time in the future, will it?"

"You're an old dog, Bear. And you've done the best job of helping Mary find a better path for her life. She would have wasted many decades of her time on Earth without you to guide her."

"But she saved me."

"No one saves anyone on Earth. Just two souls helping each other home," Josephine said. At her words, the prism glimmers around her expanded into the sky, scattered in the pattern of stars on a night sky, though the day was still bright.

"One question before I go," Bear said, panting. "Why do you glimmer so much?"

Josephine laughed. "That's a question I'll answer the next time we meet on the Rainbow Bridge."

Chapter Forty-Two

One of Dr. Luke's technicians had been at the concert and immediately offered to come in after-hours to help the vet attend to Bear's injuries. Once Mary knocked softly at the door of the room, the young woman lit a few battery-operated candles and shut off the overhead lights before leaving. "Careful not to move him too much," she whispered as she shut the door quietly.

Mary eased herself down to the floor, careful not to disturb Bear's sleep. She smiled through tears as she heard his audible snores.

The door opened again. The tech pointed to the counter. "I need Bear's chart." She looked down at Mary. "You can still touch Bear."

"Oh, I thought—"

"Don't jostle him or let him get overly excited when he sees you. That's all," the tech said, picking the chart up off the counter as she paused. "I'm sorry, Mary. Especially after the wonderful song that Clay sang to Bear and Riven. You know, it's going viral right now."

Stroking Bear's fur, Mary nodded. "Thank you. That means a lot."

The young girl smiled as she exited the room, closing the door again.

With Mary's touch, Bear opened his eyes and whimpered.

"I'm so sorry, Bear. I shouldn't have let this happen to you." Mary had tears streaming down her face.

Bear put a paw on her outstretched arm.

Seeing the pain in her dog's eyes, Mary wiped her face and tried to smile.

Bear looked up at her and waited.

"What were you thinking, you crazy dog?" She kissed the top of his head. "Jumping off the stage like that?"

Bear closed his eyes and sighed, remembering his attempt to get to Mary when the strange man hurt her at the concert, not fully thinking through his plan to get to her. Immediately after, as he laid on the ground unable to move, Mary's hysterical face at his injuries hurt Bear's heart as much as the sharp pain in his hips and legs.

"I don't know what you need, Bear. But we've always understood one another." She breathed in deeply, taking a moment to collect herself before speaking again. "No matter how much pain it causes me, I want you to let me know if this is the end of our journey together."

Opening his eyes again, Bear nudged her on the knee.

"I think I'll be so furious in the years to come that some stupid, old feud, not even concerning us, took a few years from you. I'm afraid of the angry and bitter person I could be without you, Bear."

Bear scooted close to Mary's side, loving the sound of her voice. Like when she talked to him at length when he was a still a puppy. Only the two of them sitting on the porch at Sagebrush Farms for hours at a time.

"You changed me. You changed all of Merivelle. We're all better people because of *one dog*," Mary said, smiling through tears. "I'm so proud you're my dog. Every time someone says your name, I think, *That's my dog*. And no matter what's happening that day—I feel I can make it through until one of our walks."

At the sound of the word *walk*, Bear wagged his tail.

"Our walks, Bear. It's how we found all our friends together, didn't we? Everyone out in the waiting room. And Cybil waiting at home." Mary's eyes searched the doorway. "You gave real meaning to her life after you ran to her in the cemetery that first afternoon." She paused for a moment. "My parents are buried in Cottonwood Cemetery. I wouldn't have gone in on my own without you, Bear. You were my courage."

The Great Pyrenees moved closer to her, sensing the pain still in her heart when she spoke about her mom and dad.

"Not to mention Pavi and his snakebite." She stopped, looking at Bear for a moment. "Where *are* the Posadas?"

Bear lifted his nose in the air, searching for the scent of Lupe or Pavi. Finding none, he laid his head down.

Mary returned her attention to Bear. "My life is infinitely better with you in it. I have a wonderful life because of my wonderful dog. But you have to let me know what's best for *you*, Bear."

Bear put both paws on her knees and looked up at her, panting.

"I think you're telling me you want to do the surgery?" Mary turned her head in question. "Or are you in pain and need released from it?"

Bear continued to pant, squinting in between breaths.

"I'm so scared to make the wrong decision," Mary said, stroking the mane-like fur around his neck. "I wish there was a sign to know the best thing for you, Bear."

The next moment, music filtered into the room, the speakers above tuning in and out of static and various stations before the same Mendelsohn piece the Merivelle Orchestra had played on the first day of summer could be heard before the station changed again. One of Clay's country songs began playing.

Mary looked at Bear. "Is that a sign? Or what I'm hoping for with my whole heart?"

A thought dropped into each of their minds as they looked at one another in understanding. *"Why can't it be both?"*

Chapter Forty-Three

The next mid-morning, the town was almost eerily silent in contrast to the noise and activity with Clay in town. Before first light, Mary and Theodore loaded Bear up in a vehicle and headed to the other side of the state. Dr. Luke had called in a favor to an old friend who agreed to come home early from a weekend trip to operate on Bear. Percy drove through the night to make his flight, allowing Katie and Violet to sleep along the way. Riven stayed back in Merivelle with Cybil and Gavin. Sleeping in longer than he could ever remember, he eventually found his way to The Hen's Nest, seeking conversation to keep his mind diverted.

"Who's watching the co-op while Mary's gone?" Frannie asked, once the breakfast crowd thinned out.

"Just me," Riven said, mindlessly swirling his coffee with a spoon. He looked around. "Where is everyone?"

"Most of the out-of-towners left last night after the concert. A few might trickle in later this morning," Frannie said, sitting down beside him in the booth. "I think everyone living in Merivelle is going to hibernate for a few days from sheer exhaustion." She put her hand over his to still his movements. "You've been stirring that coffee for ten minutes."

Riven looked at her, his face wrinkled in worry.

She took the spoon from his suspended grasp. "Any word from Mary?"

Glancing at his watch, Riven shook his head. "If anything happens to Bear, I'll never forgive myself."

"No need to work yourself up." Frannie said, leaning into Riven.

"If it wasn't for an old fight, Bear would be home at Sagebrush Farms with Mary this morning—everyone's goals accomplished."

"That *old fight* didn't come from you."

"It did though."

"How do you see that, Riven? Lance shows up out of nowhere and his first thought is to hunt you down at a concert? Punch you before having a go at Margaret's daughter?" Frannie shook her head. "No, he's completely crazy. Has nothing to do with you."

"Gavin is his son. They're practically identical. How did I miss that?" Riven put his head in his hands for a moment before answering his own question. "Though Gavin's personality is much different than his dad."

"You can make a pancake or a crêpe from the same batter with a few tweaks to the same ingredients. Many people choose to become a different version than what they knew growing up. Lance was always a big-talking bully who was charming when it benefitted himself. The time or two I was near Gavin, I would doubt he would ask for a small glass of water in the middle of a desert."

The pair sat together in calm silence as the sun peeked through the morning clouds for the first time that morning.

"If nothing else, I need to be thankful that no lasting harm came to Katie during her childhood. She told me there were many times that Lance had been nice to her."

"Would we say he was *nice* to Katie?" Frannie said, tilting her head knowingly. "Or that he knew it would get under your skin? And what does that even have to do with you now?"

"An old, buried grudge will always seek oxygen," Riven said, taking a deep breath. "I should have known this would resurface one day."

"You and your yoga classes," Frannie said, kissing him on the cheek. "It's been a lonely couple of weeks without our evenings together, old man. Now that you're a celebrity—are you even going to remember this old lady?" She rested a hand on his shoulder.

Looking up at the television in the diner's corner, Riven squinted for a moment. "What is that news story?"

Frannie walked over and reached for a remote at the end of the breakfast counter.

With the volume turned up, the handful of people remaining in the diner glanced at the television. A news banner at the bottom of the screen heralded, *Wild West is a Wild Mess* as one of the news anchors spoke. A phone video flashed on-screen—one of Mary grabbing Lance by the arm as she looked unhinged with anger.

"Country singer Clay Overstreet's extraordinary gesture of gifting a concert to a small Kansas town went awry last night when a fight between locals broke out."

"Lance is no local," Riven said, shaking his head before Frannie shushed him and nodded to the screen.

The woman turned to her on-air partner. "Clay's fans' footage from the concert showed the Great Pyrenees leaping off the stage to come to the aid of his owner fighting below. With all the attention from the videos, Clay's new song has jumped in YouTube views, literally an overnight sensation."

All the silverware clattering on breakfast plates in the diner came to a standstill. Even the kitchen staff peeked over the serving line, straining to see the news story.

In an interview following a video of Bear jumping through the air, a group of young girls spoke enthusiastically. "We love Bear Bailey. He's the ultimate small-town hero. He didn't even bite the man who tried to punch him in the face."

Riven and Frannie's eyes met for a moment.

"Lance punched Bear?"

Riven shook his head. "Another detail that isn't true."

The two anchors looked at one another, shaking their heads as the camera focus returned to their news desk. The man spoke first. "I've met Clay frequently in interviews. He's done so much to help small communities all over the country. It's a real shame this had to put a black eye on the event and small towns everywhere."

"And why wasn't the dog on a leash?" the female anchor asked, shuffling her papers. "What kind of owner lets a dog roam at a big event?"

Riven sat slack-jawed as he looked at Frannie when the segment shifted to the weather forecast.

"It's a slow news day if a national channel is reporting on us, out here in the middle of nowhere. Besides, they always look for ways to portray us as idiots," Frannie said. "I'm surprised they picked the pretty girls instead of someone that looked like they belonged in a *Wanted—Dead or Alive* poster from the last century."

Riven put his head down. "Mary's dream was for everyone to see how wonderful Merivelle is. To encourage people to stop on their way to the mountains or road tripping across the United States."

A man from the counter stood up, reaching into his back

pocket as he examined his receipt. "Weren't you and Lance always fighting over some woman here in town?"

"Pay your bill and be on your way, you gossipy old goat," Frannie said, gesturing toward the door.

Riven's phone rang. He took a deep breath as he answered. "I already saw it." He listened as he nervously tapped his fingers on the table, eyes searching the diner. "Which channel?" He looked up, pausing for a moment. "No, this was a different one."

Frannie walked back to Riven's table, a look of question on her face.

He put his hand over the lower half of his flip phone. "*Katie*," he said.

She nodded, helping the bus boy clear away the dishes from the morning rush at the table next to Riven.

"I'll be at the co-op," he said, before stopping to listen. "Nobody knows where Lupe and Pavi are. It's only me and Cybil."

"I can pitch in and help too," Frannie whispered.

The front door opened, ringing the bell as both Riven and Frannie turned.

Gavin entered, appearing as if he might be sick. His eyes searched the emptiness of the diner as Betty ran through the door before it closed.

"I won't say anything if any other media shows up." Riven nodded to the young man as he listened to his phone call. "I've got it handled here. Try to keep up with Mary on your end. Give Violet a big hug."

Frannie turned a coffee cup over, sitting it on a saucer as she waved the young man forward.

Riven shut his phone and looked up at Gavin. "Don't be scared. You've done nothing wrong."

Swallowing hard, Gavin took a few steps as Betty nipped at his heels.

"The little dog is sweet but she can't be in here or I'll have the local food inspector writing me up," Frannie said. "We better do things by the straight and narrow. Until everything blows over."

Riven stood up. "Let's go outside. Under the umbrellas on the patio. Betty should be cool there."

"You don't have to talk to me."

Pushing the front door open, Riven looked at Gavin in question.

"I don't even know how I ended up here. Betty kind of pecked at my ankles, directing me here."

"Maybe she's missing Bear and wants some company."

Betty ran around in circles, barking. She stopped and looked up at Riven, putting a paw on one of his shins.

"He's going to be fine, little cowgirl. And you have friends here until he's home." Riven sat at one of the tables, motioning Gavin to do the same as Betty took cover under the shade underneath.

"I don't even know him."

Riven raised his eyebrows.

"My dad—Lance. My mom hated him."

"You don't need to prove to me how much you don't like your dad. The man is still your father."

"That's not how he said you'd react if you found out it was me."

Riven squinted as the umbrella twirled slightly in the wind. "How's that?"

"He said you'd go ballistic, destroy everything in town if he ever showed up again."

"I'm too old for that nonsense."

"Another lie then."

Shaking his head, Riven looked Gavin in the eyes. "A few years ago, before I sorted things out with my family, your dad would have been spot on."

"What changed?"

"Living in Merivelle with Mary's dog."

Betty stood up and barked with excitement.

"Bear?"

"Sounds silly. But yes—the dog. I feel sure that without him, I'd still not have a relationship with my daughter. Finding peace with her changed everything for me."

On the opposite from where they sat, the traffic light changed. Tamru crossed the street from his coffee shop. He ran at a rapid pace, making his way to Riven's table. "Have you heard anything about Bear?"

"Nothing yet. But have faith, they'll get him fixed up," Riven said.

Tamru placed a small paper bag on the table that his children had decorated on the outside with crayons and stickers. "Wishbone treats for Bear. For when he comes home."

"I'll mention it to Mary to tell Bear," Riven said, reaching for the bag and sitting it on the table as he patted it gently. "Very kind of you, Tamru. Please tell Saba and the kids thank you."

The tall man with a lithe physique swallowed hard. "Bear was my children's first friend in Merivelle—actually, in the entire United States. They were terrified of dogs before we arrived. Nearly fainted at the size of a Great Pyrenees. But Bear was gentle and so good to them, even before they spoke English," Tamru said, squinting away tears at the memory. "Always leaning in and listening to them, even when they spoke another language."

Riven reached for the man's hand. "Have faith that Bear will be fine."

"Do you think he's going to make it?"

"As soon as I know something, you'll be one of the first to hear."

As the two men watched Tamru jog back to his coffee shop, Gavin thought for a moment. "Do you think there's any way you would have been friends with Tamru without Bear?"

A busboy ran a plate of bacon out for Betty. "From Frannie," he said simply, before running back in.

As he thought, Riven tore the bacon into small pieces and fed it to Betty under the table before speaking. "There's no way I would have seen Tamru or his culture as something to welcome."

"All because of a dog?"

Riven chuckled. "Hard to believe, but the simple traits he exhibits taught me how to interact with people in a different way."

"Like what?"

"He's curious. Loves everyone but coyotes," Riven said, chuckling. "And you get the sense he really listens."

With Riven's words, Betty jumped to the man's lap and faced him, turning her head as she waited for him to speak.

"Is it my imagination or does he also lean in?" Gavin asked, reaching out to pet Betty.

His face igniting with light for the first time that morning, Riven smiled. "That one inch or two more can make you see the people in your world in an entirely new way."

Chapter Forty-Four

After breakfast, Riven and Gavin walked through Steven's Park. The area was as bad as the phone footage from the Clay Overstreet fan on the news had shown. Possibly even worse. A few cars passed, surveying the damage around various points of the large city block.

"This is how my dad l-leaves things."

Riven leaned down to pick up a few pieces of trash to toss in the trash bins scattered throughout the park.

"Always angry." Gavin kicked a can on the ground.

Betty ran forward, picking the can up in her mouth and trotting it back to Gavin as she presented it to him.

He took it from her and held it a few paces before placing it in a trash bin. "I'm sorry that I stutter when I'm trying to talk."

"Didn't even notice, to be honest. Take your time."

Gavin nodded as he spoke slowly. "My dad could also be charming. Just when I thought I hated him, he'd become a different man."

Riven put his hands in his pockets, listening to the younger man with great care.

"My dad loves fishing. He was di-different with a pole in his hand."

"Do you like to fish?"

"I hate it. Only tried to love it because he did," Gavin answered. "Holding a rod and waiting on a fish had a real calming effect on him. He'd really listen." His face relaxed momentarily. "Almost like how a proper dad is su-supposed to be."

"Those moments bridge a lot of gaps, don't they?"

Gavin nodded, picking up the trash Betty continued to bring him as they walked. "My stutter drove him crazy. Blamed my mom before she died. Said she babied me too much. He once made me use a pacifier in junior high. Said if I talked like a baby, then he'd treat me like one. He tried everything to get rid of it."

Riven turned away for a moment, his hands clenched. He took a deep breath to steady himself before reaching out to pat the young man's back.

The two men walked in silence, Betty nipping at their ankles playfully as they moved across the park and toward Cybil's house. In unison, they crossed the street, stepping onto the curb before continuing. Someone rolled down the window of their car as they passed by. "Is Bear alive?"

"Yes!" Riven said, careful to control his aggravation at the bluntness of the question. "Getting the best care. He'll be back home in no time."

The driver bumped the brakes for a moment. Holding their phone out the window with the volume up, they said excitedly, "You and Bear's song is viral. Almost half a million hits overnight!"

"I have no idea what he just said," Riven said, looking at Gavin in confusion.

Taking a few steps forward, the younger man looked thunderstruck as he gazed at the phone.

"What does that mean?"

"That an insane amount of people love Clay's song," the driver replied, before moving on when another vehicle pulled up behind, tapping on their horn.

"Why do you suddenly look so happy?"

An expression of wonder crossed Gavin's face. "They like your song, Riven," he said, his voice slightly louder than a whisper.

Betty barked enthusiastically, twirling around in place.

Riven stopped. "*You* wrote that song."

"All thanks to you. You were the one who had Clay talk to me."

Coming to the edge of Cybil's front sidewalk, Riven chuckled. "I didn't make anyone do anything. You earned that all on your own, Gavin. And in between listening to it and trying not to get my butt kicked by your dad, I completely agree—it was a touching song."

Biting his lip to keep from laughing, Gavin reached down to pick up Betty.

"I want to show my gratitude for including me in your song," Riven said, holding his hand out to Gavin. "You should be mighty proud. You have a real way with words."

Gavin bowed his head. "Thank you, sir." He looked up at Riven. "I don't want to start any trouble, but I have a question."

Riven nodded.

"Everyone sure likes Katie around here. Is there any chance she and I could talk in the future? She seems like a real kind-hearted woman."

"She is, Gavin. And I promise you this—you won't find a better friend than Katie. When the two of you are ready, I'm sure you'll have a lot to discuss."

Betty went to Cybil's front door and sat down, tail wiggling as she pawed the door frame.

"When's the last time you've seen Cybil?" Riven said, climbing the steps, nearly toppling in his hurry.

"Last night, before the concert. I never went home. I didn't want to disturb her."

Chapter Forty-Five

"Where has everyone been?" Cybil stood at her front door, music playing at a high volume from the record player inside.

Gavin took a step forward. "I tried calling. Your phone goes straight to voicemail. And I didn't know your landline number. I didn't want to bother you by coming home too late last night."

Betty leaned into Cybil's shins as she peered through the screen door.

"I've misplaced my phone. Who knows where it is?"

Scattered papers still littered the inside of Cybil's home. Riven was aghast. "Were your windows opened last night? What happened?"

"I don't remember," she said, dropping into a chair. "And I'm overwhelmed with the cleaning up. So many papers. So many memories."

A large plastic garbage bag was at Cybil's feet. Only a few pieces of paper were inside.

"When was the last time that you saw my dad?"

Cybil looked at Gavin, shaking her head. "I don't recall."

Gavin's expression was of deep remorse. "I should have

known better. He's torn your house apart, searching for money."

Patting the young man's hand, Cybil shook her head. "That would have been here for the taking had you not gathered it all up and taken it to the bank with me."

"Was there any money left behind?" Riven asked.

Cybil shook her head. "None—thanks to Gavin."

"But I'm the one who brought my dad here. Bear's the worst casualty of this whole thing"

"Where's Bear? And Mary? What happened?"

Betty jumped up on Cybil's lap, leaning in to steady the old woman.

"Mary's fine. Bear's hurt, but they're fixing him up right now," Riven said, rolling up his sleeves.

"Good heavens! What?"

"We'll know more later. For now—Gavin and I are going to get your house put in order."

Chapter Forty-Six

"I'm back again?"

Josephine smiled at Bear. "We're not on the Rainbow Bridge this time."

Bear jolted for a moment. "Where are we?"

"In your dreams, Bear. You seemed like you might need a friend to help you relax. You're fighting the anesthesia before your surgery."

"Then I'm not dead?"

"Bear—stop saying that word. Don't put it into your overly active imagination. Focus on where you want to be."

He sighed. "I want to be home in Merivelle. With Mary. With my head on her lap as she reads or talks on the phone. I love listening to her voice. Seeing her face is my idea of heaven."

"That's a wonderful place for your mind to go," Josephine said, nodding. "Anything else?" She ran her fingers through Bear's fur, calming the dog even further.

"I want to let Riven know that everything is going to be all right. I have a feeling that he's anxious."

"You're both very fond of each other. It's much different from when Jiff and I were looking down at Merivelle. You've been a wonderful dog, Bear."

Lifting his head, Bear asked. "Does that happen a lot?"

"Does what happen a lot?"

"Coyotes and dogs ending up as friends?" Bear yawned, struggling to hold his eyes open.

"It's rare on Earth when souls in opposition come to a level of peace. The very definition of a miracle. When something that seems impossible happens anyway."

Bear grew drowsier with each passing second. "I do it all to make Mary happy." He took a few more breaths and closed his eyes, smiling. "When am I going to see you again?"

Josephine stroked the dog's head. "A bit more earthly time. But not now, Bear Bailey."

Chapter Forty-Seven

"Bear's out of surgery. We should be home tomorrow."

Riven's face relaxed hearing Mary's words over the phone. He and Gavin had spent the better part of the day helping put Cybil's house back in order. Once both men insisted on sorting the paperwork still left on the floor, Cybil asked Gavin to help her upstairs. "Nothing allows me to sleep more than to hear someone else moving about the house," she'd told them as she gripped the banister, holding onto Gavin's arm. "A wish come true."

"How are things in Merivelle?" Mary asked. "I hated I had to leave. Especially with the mess from yesterday."

"Fine. Nothing for you to worry about other than the Bear's recovery."

"Where is Lance?"

"Disappeared. Almost into thin air." Riven looked to the living room wall of shelves as Gavin dusted the last few books and put them back on the wall. "I don't think you should even consider things like that right now. Plenty of time later."

"It'll keep my mind calm if I know exactly what's going on.

Theodore changed the waiting room television, so I didn't see a news story."

"Let me think of a better sort of distraction for you," Riven said, inspecting the room still strewn with paperwork. He focused on the little dog moving about the room as if she, too, had a job. "Cybil is convinced that Betty can read."

"Sounds like a funny story."

"She's been bringing papers to Cybil in the most coincidental way."

Betty twirled around Riven's feet.

"Who am I to make fun when I'm sure that Bear and I have conversations with one another every day of my life?"

Leaving Riven's side, Betty carefully picked up an envelope in her mouth before crossing the room. She presented it to him as if they'd rehearsed the trick a hundred times before.

Riven took the envelope. "You aren't going to believe this," he said, adjusting his glasses. "But Betty brought me something with your name on it."

"In Cybil's house?"

"Yes, in a myriad of paperwork. Must be a sign."

"What does it say?"

"It's addressed to you, but it's a sealed envelope."

"Please open it. I could use something to entertain me right now."

Riven paused, thinking for a moment. "I'm being silly. It clearly says, *Mary Bailey*," he said, his phone in one hand while using the thumb of the other to open the letter. He paused for a few moments. "You're never going to guess who it's from."

"My dad?" Mary asked, her voice hopeful. "Would he have given a letter for safekeeping with Cybil?" She shook her head before correcting herself. "That's a ridiculous wish. I think I'm remembering what I told Theodore this week."

"What's that, Mary?"

"I told him I wanted to hear one more story about my dad. I'd do anything to hear his name again. Especially today."

Riven stopped, clutching the envelope and letter. "That's your wish, Mary? To hear something about Parker?"

Studying the words on the piece of paper, Betty turned her head.

"I haven't heard my dad's name forever outside of me using it. You know, I almost wanted to name Bear—Parker. Isn't that silly? I thought it would be wonderful to hear his name every day at Sagebrush Farms again."

Gavin approached Riven and motioned he was going upstairs to check on Cybil for a moment. Riven nodded, walking over to the front windows. "*Parker Webb*. There was a guy who truly listened. Second only to your Bear."

The sound on Mary's end of the call became still as she waited, holding her breath for a few moments.

"You probably don't hear a lot about him because he was a man of few words. He saved those for Margaret."

Betty came over to Riven's side, sitting down as she looked up to him, a smile on her face reflecting her love of stories.

"Parker loved your mom. He always tried to be one jump ahead of what she wanted. Attended to the farm and finances so she could focus on you, I think."

Mary listened, the stillest breathing on her end of the phone.

"I didn't understand the strength of the quiet love between Parker and Margaret. The youthful part of me thought it had to be dramatic and full of ups and downs to fully express what you felt in your heart. Like many things, I got that wrong," he said, shaking his head. "In my anger at your mom's sister, I wasn't easy to be around for either of your parents. And for that, I'm truly sorry, Mary."

"You were young. If you only knew all the things I would go back and change in Chicago."

"That's very magnanimous of you. But still wrong on my part." He crossed the room to sit in a chair, laying down the opened envelope on the side table. "Your dad knew how to do anything. He had an encyclopedic knowledge base for any problem. One day, I was stuck outside of Merivelle with a flat tire. And it was raining cats and dogs."

Betty jumped on his lap, turning her head as he continued talking.

"Parker drove up as I was trying to fix my tire. I didn't know what I was doing. No one had taught me something as simple as how to change a tire. In frustration, I flung the jack out into the field, cursing the situation. So much anger that I couldn't even fix my own broken-down car—all that I could afford."

Outside Cybil's house, a car honked in a friendly manner at a walking pedestrian. Riven and Betty looked out the window, the dog's tail wagging as she then pawed Riven to continue.

"Without a word, your dad got out of his farm truck, grabbed his own tools, tipped his cowboy hat and changed my tire."

Betty gave a small woof of approval.

"I remember that day because it was also so cold. Your dad didn't have a coat. Rain was pouring down from the brim of his cowboy hat. He went right to work, finished the task at hand and left me with a parting words that I never forgot."

"Do you remember what he said?" Mary asked quietly.

"*It's one rainy day, Riven. It always gets better.*"

"Anything else?" Mary's voice was child-like in hope.

"*A little light and reflection after rain and you get a rainbow.*"

Betty sniffed the air as she leaned into the old man, listening to his chest.

"I remembered '*it always gets better*' every time I felt like giving up over the years. How the rain stops and you catch enough of a break to make you believe in things again."

"That story is exactly what I need to hear today." Mary said, sighing.

Riven looked down as Betty sniffed at his chest. He tried to take a deep breath before continuing. "You should also know that you were the apple of your dad's eye, Mary Bailey. He carried you on his shoulders from the moment you were old enough. Paraded you all around town. Parker is the model I always kept in my mind when I imagined getting to be with Katie when she was young. I still think of him with Violet. Parker Webb taught me how extraordinary it is to have a daughter wrap you around her pinky finger."

"Thank you, Riven," Mary said, her voice barely above a whisper. "You've answered my wish. And more."

"My pleasure. Give that big dog of yours a hug from me and his sweet friend, Betty." Hanging up the phone, Riven glanced at the letter on the table, his face scrunched in pain. He looked at Betty, who had a paw on his chest. "Tighter than normal today," he said, trying to catch his breath. "Feels pretty heavy. It usually helps every—"

Betty jumped from Riven's lap before he collapsed to the ground, racing up the stairs, barking in warning as she searched for Gavin.

Chapter Forty-Eight

A week later, Riven arrived home from the hospital. Saved by Betty's speedy action, Gavin had raced downstairs to find Riven unconscious on the living room floor. Cybil called an ambulance as Gavin performed CPR until the paramedics arrived. The local doctor at Merivelle's small hospital told Riven what a lucky man he was not to have been home alone outside the city limits.

Katie hadn't left her dad's side since he arrived in Kansas City on a Medi-flight the previous week. Getting him the best care possible, she'd left Violet's care primarily to Percy while she spent day and night at his bedside, her face being the first and last thing he saw as he drifted in and out of sleep after by-pass surgery. Given the all-clear by doctors to return home with a new regimen of medicine, Percy, Katie and Violet drove him home, his friends in Merivelle lining up outside his front door to welcome him back.

Theodore practically ran to the car, the first to open the door to help Riven out.

"Are you crying, Theodore?" Katie asked, shaking her head but smiling.

"You bet I am. Got teary all week while we were here recuperating with Bear. Otherwise, I would have been by your bedside, Riven."

Mary followed a few steps behind. "A hundred-and-twenty pound dog who needs moved for the bathroom is more than I can do alone. Or you know we would have been there, Uncle Chaps."

Riven paused getting out of the car.

"I hope you don't mind. A term of affection once in a while?" Mary extended her hand to help him to his feet.

Embracing her, Riven smiled. "I'll be delighted to hear you use it whenever you want."

Violet shrieked from the backseat of the car, holding her hand out to her Grandchaps, opening and closing her hand rapidly.

"Hang on, Violet. I'll get you out so you can follow him," Percy said, looking over the roof of the car. "She held his hand nearly the whole ride."

Holding the car door for support, Riven beamed at his granddaughter.

Katie ducked under his arm and fished for the cane on the floorboard of the vehicle. She stood up and placed it in front of him.

"I don't need that."

"You most certainly do." She looked to Mary and Theodore, a serious expression on her face. "Do not let him move about without this."

"Is he even supposed to be walking?" Theodore asked. "Should Percy and I each grab an arm and a leg and carry him in?"

Mary covered her mouth to conceal her laughing. "As

much as I'd love to watch that scene, let's see how Riven does on his own with the cane." She looked at Katie. "Walking is probably a good idea?"

"As long as he takes the weight off his sternum." Katie's voice was of the pre-Violet era. "I'm not kidding. I will flip if you put yourself in any danger."

Percy arrived from the other side of the car, holding Violet. "Honey, he's out of danger. A few pointers and I think he'll be fine."

Exiting the house in a subdued manner, Gavin approached the group, his footsteps crunching the gravel of the driveway.

Katie's face lit with joy, nearly dropping the cane before placing it under Riven's hand. She held her arms out and took the few steps to Gavin, hugging him as she cried. Shy at first, he looked over her shoulder at Theodore, who nodded in an encouraging manner.

"My family's own knight in shining armor. What would we have done if you weren't there to save my dad, Gavin? We can never repay you."

Gavin smiled, his expression one of a person still uneasy with recognition.

"You better get used to it," Theodore said, nudging the younger man with his elbow. "The way you've helped in Merivelle, you're going to give Bear a run for his money."

"Where is Bear?" Riven asked expectantly. "I know he can't walk to us, but I thought maybe I might see him soon?"

"He's inside the house with Cybil and Frannie," Mary replied.

"Frannie?" Katie asked, nudging her dad's arm and nodding to the doorway to get him moving as they spoke.

"She's cooking up a storm in your giant kitchen," Mary said, following them. "I don't know what army she's expecting, but you'll have plenty of food for weeks."

"You're living the life, old man. Frannie cooking The Hen's Nest menu in your own home." Theodore rubbed his stomach. "Dreams do come true."

Mary nudged him. "I think you'll find her cooking much different here at Riven's while he's recuperating. Bacon is a thing of the past for Riven and the dogs."

Riven stood in front of Gavin, a solemn look on his face as he grabbed the younger man's hand, balancing his weight with his cane.

"You look good, Mr. Chapowits. Color in your face."

"I owe you a lot—"

"I did what anyone would do in the same situation."

"Give mouth-to-mouth resuscitation to his dad's long-time enemy?" Riven asked. "I think that's above and beyond in anyone's book."

"Oh, god, keep me from saying something," Theodore whispered to Mary, who had already gripped his arm in warning.

"I can hear you, Theodore," Riven said, rolling his eyes.

Cybil appeared at the front door, a smile on her face. "There's a big white dog in this house about ready to spring from his convalescence bed. Betty and I are having the hardest time keeping him calm after he heard Riven's voice. Can we bring this welcome home celebration inside?"

Chapter Forty-Nine

Riven asked that someone bring Bear's bed closer to the dining area where everyone was gathered after Frannie fed them an early dinner. Gavin insisted on cleaning up the kitchen with Theodore and Percy helping as Frannie took her seat by Riven's side, the quiet easiness of decades between them.

"The thing that really gets me is that Lance got away scot-free," Theodore said, drying plates with a towel. "All that mayhem and he rides into the sunset."

"I agree," Frannie said. "To top off all of Lance's emotional abuse over the years, Mary's dog needed surgery. Theodore, didn't you tell us down at the Hen's Nest that phone videos show Mary grabbing Lance by the arm first? So if she presses charges, she'll have the same brought against her?"

Betty shook her head. "Theodore sure loves to chatter down at that diner, doesn't he?"

"Theodore's just trying to make sense of things in his mind," Bear answered. "I don't think he's ever seen Mary so angry *or* sad." He put a paw on her leg, nudging her hand with his snout.

"He slithered away, like he's always done," Mary said, her fingers tracing between Bear's eyes. Momentarily contrite, her face sought Gavin's. "I don't say that to hurt you. He is your dad."

Taking the plate from Theodore's hand, Gavin shrugged. "You're right though—some justice would be nice. In memory of my mom, if nothing else."

Cybil cleared her throat.

"Why do you look like the cat that ate the canary?" Katie asked.

"The cat that baked the muffins, to be more precise," Cybil said mischievously.

Looking up from rinsing the last items in the sink, Percy said, "This is going to be good."

"Didn't you think it was odd—at the end of over a week, with everyone pulling out all the stops that I refrained from going to the concert? Gavin's glimmering lyrics sung by a country music superstar and I said I was going to stay home with a fast-talking con man?"

"You'd already listened to some lyrics," Gavin said. "I understood you were tired that night."

"But I wasn't. Music makes me feel as if Honey is right around the corner. You'd have to haul my dead body from a live-music venue on any other occasion."

The room was quiet as Riven and Frannie looked at one another, holding each other's hands under a pillow.

"I sat with Lance in my kitchen feeding him an amped-up version of Gavin's fiber muffin recipe, making small talk before I excused myself to listen to the concert on the front porch."

Katie was already grinning. "When you say *amped-up—*"

"I mean, there's no way that man got outside Merivelle's city limits without a bomb going off in his drawers."

"Cybil," Mary said, covering her mouth with her hand as she laughed. "Do you mean to tell me you laced his muffins?"

"With a well-deserved laxative and anything else I could find to send him running for the nearest bathroom," Cybil said. "If that man thinks he's going to leave Merivelle without the stench of his deeds following him, the interior of his truck in this summer heat should remind him for years to come. A certain poetic justice to it all. I crossed my fingers that his backside exploded at the concert. But not all wishes can come true."

Percy and Theodore looked at one another.

"What?" Katie asked.

"Your husband loves portmanteaus," Theodore began. "And Cybil came up with a brilliant solution. I believe her term was *poetic justice—*"

"You idiots," Riven said, shaking his head. "Don't go there. I know exactly what you're thinking."

Mary, Gavin and Frannie looked at one another, all three perplexed.

"Poo-etic justice!" Percy and Theodore said in unison.

The entire room groaned as they threw crumpled napkins leftover from dinner at the pair.

Percy drummed the counter, miming hitting a cymbal. "It was there. Had to be said."

Theodore shrugged at his friend, clearly loving his moment with Percy. "Not all will appreciate the treasure of a well-placed portmanteau. But remember how they brought you and Katie together?"

Lost in stories, the group laughed, reminiscing about the previous few years' events as Violet fell asleep in between her parents. Theodore nodded to Mary, a sincere look of excitement at Frannie and Riven's closeness. Gavin and Cybil spoke together as she filled him in on events that preceded his arrival in Merivelle.

"It's nice to listen to everyone's memories," Bear said, talking to Betty at his side. Lifting his head, Bear watched the humans. The hum of several conversations going at once in harmony with the outdoor sounds of nature. "It almost sounds like music."

"What does, Bear?"

"Everyone's voices as they speak. Individually, but together too."

"Stories—my favorite," Betty answered, closing her eyes. "I could listen to this sound forever."

"Nothing lasts forever," Bear said, laying his head back on the bed.

"Henry told you that when he was here, remember that, Bear? It's the nicest thing about stories—you can remember them all the time in different situations and they still make sense."

Bear gazed at the little dog. "I forget you're still a puppy, Betty. You're a clever dog."

Betty put her head down demurely. "Thank you, Bear. You're the one who taught me so much. Lean in and listen. It helps in almost any situation, doesn't it?"

Bear nodded, closing his eyes. His breathing was heavy.

"Are you in pain, Bear?"

"Mary's trying so hard to help me. No need to worry her."

Betty got to her feet. "I can let her know—"

"Let Mary enjoy today. She's been so busy. It's nice that everyone's together."

"What about the Posadas?"

Bear opened his eyes as he sniffed the air. "I can't pick up any smell from them. I dream about them at night, but I don't know where they may have gone."

"There was a letter. At Cybil's. I think everyone forgot about it."

"What letter?"

"Riven had it in his hand when he was talking to Mary about her dad. Before his heart attack," Betty said, whimpering. "I don't like remembering that story."

"Who was the letter from?"

"Lupe. She tried to explain to Mary that it would be better if she and Pavi stayed away from Merivelle for a while. She has a few things to line out."

"Anything else?"

"She wrote a letter because she knew that if she told Mary in person, she would jump in to help and Lupe needs to do something important on her own—once and for all. That's all I remember. It was hard reading it on the table. Riven collapsed right after I read it."

"The Posadas belong here in Merivelle," Bear said. "They can't leave now."

"Maybe when you saved Pavi from the snake, that was all you were supposed to do in his story."

"You don't understand about the Posadas. They were our first friends in Merivelle. We have to find them. No matter where they are." Bear rose, trying to get to his feet before he whimpered and lowered back down again. "Even if it's the last part of my story."

"You can't be every character in everyone's book. And you're an old dog now." The moment the words came out of Betty's mouth, her eyes widened in regret.

"You're not wrong," Bear said, sighing. "But still—we need to find the Posadas. They're *our* family. And families are happiest together."

Betty looked at the group around the pair of dogs. Percy and Katie watching Violet on Riven's lap as Frannie sat next to him, leaning into his joy with his granddaughter. Gavin and

Cybil chatted happily as Theodore's arms were around Mary—her face soft with happiness at her dog's presence.

"I think for the first time, I'm ready to find a family of my own, Bear. I didn't realize how wonderful humans could be until I spent time in Merivelle with you."

Bear turned his head and sniffed.

"What is it?"

"I expected you to disappear out of thin air. And I'd never see you again. Like Jiff and Henry. It's the saddest thing about friendship, if there's no clear ending."

"That's why I want to say a proper goodbye to you, Bear. So you don't always wonder what happened to your friends."

Theodore's phone rang as he looked down at the screen. "It's Reyna," he announced to the group. The room was silent except for happy toddler sounds from Violet. Theodore answered the call as both dogs leaned toward the sound of his voice.

"Have you heard anything?" Theodore asked. He listened for a moment, shaking his head. "Us either."

Mary and Katie exchanged worried glances.

Theodore's eyebrows went up in surprise. "When?"

Grabbing onto his cane, Riven pulled himself forward, a concerned look on his face.

"We'll find them. Don't worry," Theodore answered. "Yes, of course. Come home. We'll all wait together and figure out a plan." Speaking for a few moments as the rest of the group whispered among themselves, Theodore gave a few quick instructions to Reyna. Hanging up, he looked around the room.

"What?" Mary said. "I couldn't tell if it was good news or bad news."

"Tell us," Riven answered. "My heart can't take a lot of drama."

"Of course," Theodore said, nodding. "Reyna called to say her mom's permanent resident card arrived in the mail."

"That's good, right?" Katie asked.

"More than good—it's nearly the end of Lupe's road to citizenship. On any other day, we would be jumping for joy and throwing a big party."

"But?" Percy asked.

"She needs to take a civics and English test. I don't know where she's at with something like that."

"I've been helping her on and off for years. Piece of cake," Cybil said.

"After her results, *if* she passes—"

"She'll pass," Cybil replied. "Mark my words—that brilliant woman will pass with flying colors on her first try, Theodore."

"—then she'll need to take the Oath of Allegiance at a naturalization ceremony."

Mary put her hands on her cheeks. "She's that close?"

"And nowhere to be found," Riven said, looking at Gavin. "You and Pavi were fast friends. He didn't tell you anything?"

Gavin shook his head. "I wish I'd listened closer."

"No need to worry. Just trying to sweep up any details we might have missed in the busyness of Clay's visit to town," Riven said, smiling in a kind manner.

Frannie looked to Theodore. "How long does she have to schedule her test?"

"Reyna was receiving all her mom's paperwork in Chicago. For reasons that made sense between the pair of them," Theodore explained. "Reyna made the appointment immediately, not knowing that her mom disappeared into thin air."

"When's the appointment?" Mary asked.

"The beginning of November."

Everyone was quiet. The sun was in its final descent of

261

twilight. A wind gust blew through the windows that Frannie had opened earlier in the day.

"I hate to be the person who asks the pragmatic question," Riven said, eyes drowsy from his medication. "But what happens if Lupe misses her appointment?"

Theodore's face was solemn, no trace of humor on it. "Her case is closed. She starts nearly at the beginning again."

"I don't understand how it's taking Lupe so long, but Tamru and his wife sailed through the process," Cybil said. "She's been in the country longer than both of them."

"Of course, I can't say everything about Lupe's case."

"Pretend you're at The Hen's Nest. Fill us in," Katie chided.

Frannie shook her head. "You definitely have two different personas. One at the diner hearing stories and the other tight-lipped and legal bound." She smiled. "You know, I'm only teasing you."

"No offense taken," Theodore said. "But still—hypothetically and not at all related to this case, although it might be a factor if one knew all the details—"

"He's trying to say that this is all about Lupe's case without compromising his legal obligations," Bear said, yawning.

"You don't know how you know that, but you do, huh, Bear?"

Bear put his paw out to Betty. "You're absolutely right, friend."

The little Aussie wiggled in delight, scooching over to Bear as she looked up at him.

"If Lupe had a sponsor—"

"A sponsor?" Riven asked.

"Someone with good moral character that showed by their own example that Lupe would be an ideal candidate for citizenship,"

Mary answered. "Lupe told me that when we were first getting acquainted. It was why she wanted to be isolated in the country instead of getting into trouble with the wrong people somehow."

Theodore nodded. "Exactly. If she had a sponsor that got into trouble, then it has the possibility of undermining Lupe's chances at citizenship. She'd have to start again."

"Do we know who her sponsor was?" Frannie asked. "Maybe one of the kid's dads?"

"Reyna's dad has passed. Lupe started her paperwork with Pavi's dad. I'm sure of it," Mary said. "But she doesn't like to talk about him. No matter how much I ask."

Katie glanced at her dad. He shrugged his shoulders.

"What do you two know?" Cybil asked.

"I took a vow. I can't say."

"You've proved yourself. Everyone trusts your motive. Go ahead."

Riven shook his head. "It's not how I wanted people to find out."

Taking a deep breath, Katie looked around the room. "We —my dad and I—have been searching for Pavi's dad."

Mary's face lit with joy. "When? How?"

"After Reyna found out her own dad had passed, it occurred to us to look for Pavi's dad before it was too late."

Betty's ears went up as she tilted her head. "Hey, Bear! I thought of something."

Shushing her, Bear kept his eyes on the humans' conversation. "Not now, Betty."

"I've gotta tell you before I leave—so you'll know."

"I'm trying to hear about the Posadas."

"But, Bear!"

"Sit!"

On command, Betty stopped, begrudgingly closing her

mouth, though her whole body wiggled apart from the stillness of her head.

Riven cleared his throat. "In the middle of Clay Overstreet Week, Katie contacted Pavi's dad."

"Who wanted nothing to do with my phone call? Bit my head off to leave him alone," Katie said. "There was no charming the man."

"Poor Pavi—does he know?" Cybil asked.

"We kept it to ourselves. The busy week kept us from proceeding any further."

"Bear—it's almost twilight. I need to tell you something."

"One minute, Betty. They're almost done. I don't want to miss anything about the Posadas."

Mary took a deep breath. "So, Lupe and Pavi are missing. Reyna's on her way here with her mom's paperwork, done with her last internship and we have a clock ticking to the first part of November. Now what do we do?"

Everyone looked at each other as the sky turned a deep purple, seen through the windows surrounding the room.

Betty whined, pawing at Bear incessantly as he watched the people in the room from his bed. Mary went to the door of the room and opened it to a side patio, nodding at Betty to the outdoors.

"She thinks I need to do my business, Bear. But I need to talk to you—I don't want you to think that you lost another friend without knowing."

"In a minute. I promise, Betty."

The room grew darker each minute as the sun descended.

"We have to help Reyna. It's too much for a young girl to figure out all on her own," Katie said.

"What a bunch we are to be helping someone as bright and clever as Reyna," Cybil said, almost laughing. "I remember half of everything said these days."

264

"I'm here to pitch in," Gavin said. "And you remember more than you think."

"My heart has seen better days. But whatever resources we need, I'm here," Riven said, leaning back as he took a deep breath.

Frannie and Katie looked to one another and nodded. "You have both of us," Katie said, patting the older woman's hand beside her. "I can do legwork in Kansas City."

"I can keep everyone fed. And whatever else pops up," Frannie added.

"Bear—I'm running out of time," Betty said, nipping at his heels gently.

Mary fought back tears before shaking her head and smiling. "My dog needs a lot of help for the time he has left. But I know Bear would want to me focus on our friends."

"I'll help you, honey," Theodore said, squeezing Mary's hand. "We can balance the search for the Posadas and still take care of Bear."

"See there? Everyone's going to pitch in. It's all going to work out," Bear said, turning to search for Betty.

"It's twilight, Bear. On the fourth of July I don't think I ever told you. Josephine said I couldn't stay on Earth any longer."

On the horizon toward the direction of Merivelle, fireworks lit up the evening sky. Gentle popping could be heard in the distance as light streams flew up into the sky before raining down again in bursts of color. Bear whimpered as he tried to pull himself up to watch with the others.

"Rest now, Bear. I only wanted you to know I hadn't abandoned you here at the end of the story. Maybe one day we'll see each other again and then we could—" Betty stopped midsentence before she faded away, leaving a glimmering trail with her exit.

Chapter Fifty

"I'm here at nighttime. When all the dogs are asleep," Betty said, looking around the Golden Meadow.

"You arrived at sunset. All the dogs from Earth arriving on the Rainbow Bridge cross over at sunrise," Josephine said.

The sound of crickets and locust filled the air. Betty listened for a moment, staring up at Josephine in wonder. "The summer orchestra of small things."

Josephine smiled and put her fingers in the air, tapping the space around her as spots of light appeared at her fingertips. She blew the dots into the expanse as fireflies came to life, their bodies blinking in the distance. From somewhere in the distance, music played.

"Betty's back from Merivelle?" Lea asked, appeared out of nowhere, a sleeping dog in her arms.

"I want to go back," Betty said tearfully. "I was right in the middle of telling Bear goodbye. And I don't think the humans remember Lupe left Mary a letter."

"Perhaps one day you'll see Bear again," Josephine said, reaching down to pet Betty.

"You don't understand. I'm at Butterfly Academy and when Bear crosses, he'll be on the Bridge. We'll probably miss each other entirely. His ending on Earth is when my beginning starts."

"Maybe we focus on what you enjoyed with your time on Earth," Lea said.

A firefly flew around Betty's nose, making her giggle through her tears. "It was happier than I thought it could be."

"There was a lot that happened while you were there—not all were things you thought you could handle. Remember?" Josephine asked.

Betty looked out into the Golden Meadow, the expanse of stars seeming to go on forever. "But when you're there, with your friends, it's the most amazing time. Even when your story hits a few bumps in the road."

Josephine smiled as the breeze blew her robes. "And if a soul is wise, they look for all the signs that Heaven is trying to send to help things along for them."

"Bear's very good at knowing a lot of things," Betty said, wagging her tail. "He listens. Forgives humans when they didn't know any better. And he always told me to believe the best in people's motives."

"There is no end to Bear's gifts," Lea said, gazing down.

Looking between both angels, Betty said, "But I wonder if Bear skipped Butterfly Academy—he won't sit. And he takes his own sweet time when someone calls him."

"Great Pyrenees have a mind of their own. All souls have shadow qualities with their light," Josephine replied, laughing.

Betty stood in the meadow's darkness, mesmerized by all the sights and sounds. "Everything here is so beautiful. It's hard to imagine ever wanting to leave it."

A shooting star fell above where Betty was standing, her back to it as the two angels looked knowingly at one another.

267

"Something in me wants to go back and try again. With my own human—like Bear is to Mary."

"It's your wish, Betty. It will match with the heart of a human. Both your souls have to want the same thing," Josephine said. "You're in control of your own destiny. Like all souls."

"Do I go back to Butterfly Academy first?"

"That's unnecessary. Unless you want to go?"

"I don't want to hurt the nice man's feelings who came to see me. You know, the one who wanted me for his daughter?"

"We remember him. One of the kindest souls to have crossed here," Lea answered.

"I think I know who he may be—"

"Don't say it, Betty. Keep it in your heart. It helps if you take it with you on the next step in your story."

"Don't switch me up like you did with Jiff. He was a Labrador waiting here on the Rainbow Bridge and then a corgi on Earth."

"We were trying to teach our friend, Jiff," Josephine replied. "Your journey is entirely different."

"Remember how you said Jiff needed to learn that something small can make all the difference? I already know that." Betty wiggled her fluffy bottom. "I love this booty—I mean, body."

"Duly noted," Josephine said, smiling. "We won't send your soul into a large canine body."

Betty scrunched her eyes closed. "I'm so excited—not the least bit of scared." She opened one eye. "Well, half-way scared," she said, before opening the other. "But much more excited." She paused. "Can you make sure Gheeta knows you graduated me early over here? She sure was a good teacher to me."

"I think it's safe to say that Gheeta already knew your path before you realized it," Josephine answered. "We'll get word to her you graduated to Earth with special honors."

"And now, let's get my story started," Betty said, peering at the clouds at her feet. "Let me drop!"

"Spend one more night with us," Lea said, gently laying down the cocker spaniel in her arms into a bed of wildflowers. "And we'll get you ready to meet your human at the perfect time. They could use a wonderful moment in their life right now."

Betty's ever-moving bottom wiggled again. "Can you tell me any details? Where am I going to meet them? Do I have brothers and sisters? Or only me? Do I live in the city? Or am I a cowgirl country dog?" she asked, her voice twangy with the last words. She took a deep breath to continue on with more questions.

Josephine put her fingers over Betty's eyes, causing her to yawn drowsily. "Insisting on knowing all the details takes out all the fun of your next adventure, Betty."

"Let's call it my next story. Remember how much I love stories? That's a word that fits a dog my size."

"Very well, Betty. Get a good night's sleep and you'll be ready for your next *story* on Earth." Josephine's glimmers filled the night sky, intermingling with the stars and fireflies, giving the area an ethereal backdrop.

As Betty's eyelids grew heavy with sleep, a man appeared in the Golden Meadow, smiling in a kind manner as he approached. "*Que sueñes con los angelitos.*"

Josephine nodded. "*Sleep with the angels.* One of my favorite earthly sayings."

"A Spanish blessing from parents for their sleeping children."

"Thank you for giving us time to get your puppy ready,"

Lea said. "She only needed some help from a Great Pyrenees friend to give her courage."

The man looked to Earth, eyes searching the expanse as he thought for a moment. "*Gracias, ángeles.* The sweet puppy will be perfect for my daughter."

The next moment, the angel Gheeta from Butterfly Academy appeared. "Do you remember how Betty couldn't decide whether she wanted to go to Earth?"

"Thing of the past," Lea said, pointing at the sleeping Aussie. "She's headed there tomorrow."

Gheeta turned to the female soul who had accompanied her to the Rainbow Bridge. "Well, that's just the thing. While we were waiting for Betty down on Earth, another soul came to Butterfly Academy, absolutely sure that the Aussie would be perfect for *her* son."

Butterflies danced around the woman, the same way glimmers surrounded Josephine. She spoke, her voice serene and calming. "My son's gentle personality would benefit from Betty's spirit and spunk. He needs her to guide him forward and give him direction."

The man gestured to Earth. "Please—my daughter feels that she's all alone. The little dog will bring her companionship as she makes her way home."

Gheeta looked between the two souls and Josephine. "Which person do we pick for Betty to help?"

Josephine held her hands in the air as glimmering light gently rained down to Earth. "Why can't it be both?"

Chapter Fifty-One

Stands for the lost at the end of the road.
Won't say much, but it's always enough.
He leans in and listens; he listens with love.

The radio was playing the end of "The Old Dog". Crickets, frogs, and other sounds of summer intermingled with Clay's voice, accompanied by the sound of his guitar, swelling with the sound of a full orchestra. The song ended before a few seconds of on-air silence. Reyna turned her car radio's volume up, unsure of the pause.

"Well, there you have it from Clay Overstreet, folks. Country music's number one hit for another week," a morning disc jockey announced. "Sorry to do that to you on your early morning drive here at sunrise. But even in its heartbreak, there's also a real beauty to the song too. Isn't there, Betty?"

The morning radio personality's partner tried to speak, but her voice cracked.

"Oh, dear, folks. This never happens. Betty's at a loss for words."

271

The woman tried speaking again. "That song," she half-whispered. "I think everyone knows an old man or an old dog they can picture when they hear the words. It's so, so..." The sound of soft crying came through the microphone.

"You have such a big heart. Do you mind if I share your story with our listeners?"

There was silence for a moment.

"Betty's giving me the thumbs up sign, friends. So without humor and all the love in my heart—Betty lost her own dog last week. Clay's song is touching on its own, but after the last week of nursing her beloved dog, it's a lot to process. We're going to give Betty a quick break with another song. You listeners all over the country, please send her all the love and prayers you have today. To lose a dog is one of life's hardest experiences."

The next song played almost instantly over the man's last words. Reyna Posada wiped her eyes before she spoke aloud to herself, driving somewhere in Missouri on her way home to Merivelle. "I don't even want to think about the real dog of the song. Bear—you'll break all our hearts when you go."

The windshield wipers were on high as a morning summer shower pummeled the area, dark grey clouds rolling with the wind. Several semis had pulled over to the shoulder, emergency lights blinking. Riven had called earlier that very morning, watching the weather for Reyna as she made her way home on her second day of traveling. Her nerves were on edge with the traffic and she'd felt an eyelash away from crying when she'd heard the old man's voice.

"It's one rainy day, Reyna. It always gets better." His voice had inexplicably cracked before he hung up, promising to call her throughout her travel day.

In deep thought, remembering the call, Reyna shook her head to focus on the road ahead. "Maybe I should stop," she said aloud to herself, noting the emptiness of her cupholder. "I don't even know where I am. I've never felt so lost."

A billboard appeared as she squinted to read it through the rain streaming on her windshield.

Your Next Stop Could Literally Change Your Life!

Reyna rolled her eyes at the advertisement for local banking services.

A much larger SUV sped around Reyna's car, showering her with a deluge of water, nearly blinding her view completely. Sitting up taller and widening her eyes as adrenaline flooded her body, she hit her brakes when the same vehicle cut in front of her. In order to keep from slamming into the back of the SUV, she veered sharply right, thankful for the opening of a highway exit. Her heart hammered in her chest as she turned into the nearest gas station off the interstate highway to calm her nerves and wait for the storm to pass.

Inside a quarter hour, Reyna had topped up her gas tank, used the restroom facilities and grabbed snacks and drinks for the road. She was stretching her legs under the canopy when she paused as the sun came out. A rainbow appeared faintly outside of the gas station. People gazed in awe as it became brighter with each passing moment.

"Sure is pretty, isn't it?" a man said, passing by.

Reyna stood wide-eyed at the sight of the rainbow positioned perfectly over her car on the far side of the parking lot. When the man disappeared inside the convenience store, Reyna's attention turned to a woman with an open cardboard box. Someone had scribbled *Free Puppy* on the outside.

Slinging her purse over her shoulder, Reyna approached the woman in full view of the store's front door. "Are you someone our parents warned us about growing up?" she asked, a smile on her face. "My mom always said I would be the kid carried away by a stranger with a puppy."

The woman, not quite senior age, nodded. "This is the locals' gas station. The national chain up the road gets most travelers passing by. I was hoping someone from the area might take our little girl here."

A driver pulled around the gas pumps, rolling their window down to wave to the woman as they passed by. Returning the greeting, she turned her attention back to Reyna.

"She was the runt of our litter. I think her small size worried the farmers who picked her siblings instead." The woman leaned down to stroke the puppy's head. "What she lacks in size, she more than makes up for with intelligence. My grandson swears she can read."

Reyna came up to the box and peered in. A tri-colored mini Aussie puppy popped up, wiggling enthusiastically. "May I?" she asked.

The woman scooped the puppy up from the box, handing her over to the young woman. "One warning, though. This puppy is feisty at first, but then her true, lovable nature shows up quickly."

The moment the puppy was in Reyna's arms, she licked the side of her face, giving Reyna's heart a courage she did not know she was lacking. Tears formed in her eyes as the puppy's tongue mopped away the salty moisture, whimpering as she snuggled into Reyna's neck.

"Look how much she likes you," the woman said. "Her calling card is to growl at new people. She's distrustful, but sweet as pie once you get to know her."

Reyna looked at the dog as their eyes locked in understanding. "Does she have a name?"

"My husband won't let me name puppies. Says it's too hard to let them go. You'll have to pick one out on your own."

Reyna thought of her own morning on the road and the woman on the radio who needed prayers and comfort for her own heartbreak. For the first time in ages, she giggled as her nose scrunched in delight at the smell of puppy breath. "Her name is Betty."

The little dog barked in agreement as the pair began their story together.

The Old Dog

Rises with the sun, rests under the stars.
Carries old stories and a couple of scars.
Heart full of memories, no room for hate,
Makin' his peace with the slow hands of fate.

He leans in and listens; he listens with love.
This old dog he was sent from above.
Runs with a limp, guards with pride,
Waits at the door, with his heart open wide.
Won't say much, but it's always enough.
He leans in and listens; he listens with love.

A few good friends, knows his folks by scent.
Gives more grace than most ever spent.
Thinking 'bout old dogs, miracles made right.
The future, the prayers, as the morning turns light.

Doesn't mind the silence; never fears the rain.
Walks a little slower through the joy and the pain.
One day, he'll be where the good ones know-
Where the bridge meets the sky and the kind hearts go.

He leans in and listens; he listens with love.
This old dog—he was sent from above.
Walks through the fire, carries the load.
Stands for the lost at the end of the road.
Won't say much, but it's always enough.
He leans in and listens; he listens with love.

About the Author

Keri Salas is the author of *It's a Wonderful Dog*, a four-book series about soulful dogs, second chances and small-town magic. She lives in Oklahoma with her husband and four dogs.

Made in United States
Troutdale, OR
07/16/2025

32964020R00169